Igniter

Books by Charles D. Taylor

Show of Force

The Sunset Patriots

First Salvo

Choke Point

Silent Hunter

Shadows of Vengeance (Pen Name: David Charles)

Counterstrike

Warship

Boomer

Deep Sting

Shadow Wars

Sightings

Summit

Igniter

by

Charles D. Taylor

dmc books
Dover, NH

Published by
dmc associates, inc.
PO Box 1095
Dover, NH 03820

James Blomley's photo used with permission
of Chariot Publishing.

ISBN: 1–879848-24-4

Printed in the United States of America

First Printing

Dedication

I'd intended to dedicate this book to the Boston Fire Department, its firefighters both past and present, and especially to those who gave their lives in the line of duty – their pictures line the walls of Memorial Hall on the top floor of City of Boston Fire Department Headquarters.

But after the attack on New York's World Trade Center, I would be remiss if I didn't dedicate this book to all those who have given their lives as firefighters throughout the world. For anyone who picks up this book, stop for a moment and give thanks to these very special people.

Acknowledgments

This book could not have been written without the cooperation of members of The Boston Fire Department (BFD). Each of the individuals I worked with took pride in the BFD, their particular unit, and their contributions as members of a team. It is my fault if I fail to acknowledge someone who assisted me for everyone wanted to help. Martin E. Pierce, Jr., was Commissioner at the time I worked with the Arson Squad, Paul Christian, then Deputy Chief, Division One, is now Chief of Department, Kevin P. MacCurtain was Chief of Operations, and Joseph M. Fleming was Deputy Chief, Fire Prevention.

Without mentioning rank or responsibilities, I received special help from James Loftus, Ed Daley, Al Lynch, Robert Dillon, Jim Fitzgerald, George O'Brien, William Kelley, John Citrino, Robert C. Peterson, and Joseph W. Murphy. The Director of the Boston Fire Academy at that time was Captain Hugh Duffy, who welcomed me to every phase of a firefighter's education. Lt. Gil Quinchea, an instructor at the Academy, fitted me out in full firefighter's gear and led me into the flames that the students are taught to attack; he taught me how to crawl beneath the smoke and gases, how to understand the heat of the fire, and helped me with my breathing unit after tasting the smoke – just as each firefighter must. Dick Kelleher, Dennis Corbett, and Joe Brooks taught me the technical aspects of Boston Fire Alarm.

The Arson Squad, technically known as the Fire Investigation Unit, was run by District Chief William Rice and Captain Kevin O'Toole, and the following people were of great help: Rick Splaine, who ran the Major Case Unit, Bob Staunton, Jack O'Sullivan, Dave Malcolm, Hector Medall, John Sullivan, and ATF Special Agent Tim Wyse. What meant most to me was the privilege of working with Group Two of the Arson Squad at my convenience over a two year period – this included working a normal duty section at Arson Squad Headquarters whether it was busy or quiet, eating and socializing with them, sleeping in the dormitory-like quarters, taking part in pre-trial investigations, racing to fires, searching through burned-out structures for evidence, and even digging for origin and cause while the fire was still being fought. Group Two was patient with a novice and enthusiastic about teaching me how arson investigators work. Moreover, they became good friends I would have trusted with my life had I the privilege of becoming a Boston firefighter – so, my sincere thanks to Joseph Connolly, Billy Mitchell, and Bill Noonan.

My undying gratitude and respect are reserved for Arson Squad Lt. Henry T. Hickey, then head of Group Two, now directing the Major Case Unit. Henry has been a teacher, a mentor, and a friend who taught me what it means to be a firefighter.

Igniter

1

Henry Hyde squatted uncomfortably on the soot-darkened sidewalk. His knees, as usual, were killing him. They were knees that had slogged through Vietnamese jungles, knees that had pounded up too many smoke-filled stairways of too many burning three deckers and scaled too many ladders under two-and-a-half-inch hoses and heavy air tanks. Hyde was also the other side of fifty and sported a beer belly that tumbled comfortably over his belt. But he was damned if he was going to kneel in the soot and the shards of broken glass shining under the street light.

A momentary vision of squatting Viet Cong POWs, hand-rolled cigarettes in the corners of their thin, scared lips, flashed through his mind and he closed his eyes. Another world, another time...better forgotten. Yet he never ceased to wonder how the hell the little bastards ever looked so comfortable in that awkward squat.

"What do you say, Henry?" The on-scene commander was bending down, peering over Hyde's shoulder. "Wasn't Bud in that bottle, was it?"

Hyde squinted against the reflection from the street light on his bifocals. He turned his head slightly and looked up at the friendly black face. "No, Roscoe, it damn well wasn't Bud." He shifted his feet slightly, easing his weight from the sorest knee, and ran an index finger down a crack in the sidewalk. He held the finger to his nose.

"Gasoline. Unleaded 87 octane. Want me to guess the brand?"

"No need to play the game, Henry. No rookies to jerk around tonight."

If there'd been a new guy on his truck, Roscoe would have bet him that Henry Hyde could tell just by sniffing which oil company had made the gasoline used in the Molotov cocktail. If the rookie bit, Roscoe would have won because Henry knew where every gas station was in Boston, he knew their hours, and he claimed that every *triple-A* bought his accelerant at the nearest one. A *triple-A* was Henry's term for "average asshole arsonist." It was a sure bet three out of four times, maybe even four out of five. New guys always bit.

"We have an alarm box on Atlantic Avenue." The scratchy voice of Fire Alarm Headquarters came from the two-way Motorola in Hyde's jacket pocket. "Rowe's Wharf. Harbor Hotel. Nothing from the hotel."

"District Three. That's going to piss off the troops at Division HQ," Hyde said. "Dragging out all those units at this hour for some short circuit."

He pulled on a pair of yellow surgical gloves and, using a brown paper towel, he scraped up some sidewalk dirt soaked with unburned gasoline. He placed the dirt in a shiny aluminum can.

"Aha, evidence," said Roscoe. "You're going to foil the dirty bastard who woke us up."

"When are they ever going to learn how to torch a car properly? Goddamned Molotov's a useless toy." Henry called over to his partner, Leo. "I got a theory already."

"Just a second," Leo Carmichael said over his shoulder. He was sitting on the front steps of a three-decker passing the time with two laughing black men who were enjoying his company. That was Leo's style of interviewing witnesses.

"A broad did this." Hyde smoothed his graying mustache unconsciously. "I'm not shitting you, Roscoe. Look for Christ's sake. The bottle smacked the front window of the car real good, broke, but it bounced off before it could do the job right." He picked up some pieces of the bottle still stuck together with a charred label and dropped them in another can. "So most of the accelerant sloshed off, burned itself out on the sidewalk. A guy would have started it inside the vehicle or else touched it off underneath so it was a total."

Carmichael came over, nodded a greeting to Roscoe and squatted down beside Hyde. He looked as undistinguished as Henry. His long, dark, swept-back hair was graying to match his mustache. Leo was short, slender, dark and looked more North End Italian even though he was South Boston Irish. The .38 on his right hip glinted under the streetlight.

"Looks like an ex-girl friend probably did it. The vehicle belonged to the new screwee." He snorted with disdain. "Another poorly executed crime of passion."

"You yanking me around?" Roscoe shook his head. "Your buddy here said it was done by a broad, too. No shit, you two dudes almost make it worthwhile to show up at every half ass fire."

The familiar voice from Fire Alarm over Hyde's radio was partially drowned out by a car engine.

"That was a second alarm for Rowe's Wharf," Hyde said. "Not a short circuit after all. We got flame and smoke in the high rent district." He rose unsteadily to his feet. "Oh shit, these knees are going to turn me into an old man while I'm still a horny young man."

Every person in the department, starting with the commissioner, knew that Henry Hyde was one tough son of a bitch even if he didn't look the part. He wasn't shy about his reputation – "a fucking legend in my own time!" Every probationary firefighter learned that fact within a week or so after reporting to his first assignment. But the legend would never have a chance to play himself in the movies, not with the belly, not with the sagging jowls, not with the bifocals.

A legend, yes – movie star, definitely not.

He took powerful drugs every other day to counter the effects of a jungle disease he'd acquired in Vietnam, but he claimed that was better than the alternative, a slow, painful death. His once famous drinking, which he blamed on his ex-wife who was the only person who ever got away with calling him an asshole to his face, had become a distant memory.

Hyde lifted one leg at a time and flexed his knees. "They're going to want our asses down there soon, Leo. Multiple alarm. How you doing with witnesses?"

"I was thinking we ought to chase down the former screwee, but I guess that can wait. What've they got downtown?"

Hyde shrugged. "Don't know yet. Rowe's Wharf. High class. A whiff of smoke attracts attention. But they struck a second alarm so – " He paused and put a finger to his lips, turning up the volume on his radio. "That's three. I guess they got more than smoke in the kitchen exhaust down there. Time to saddle up."

Roscoe clapped him on the shoulder. "Take care, you old nighthawk. Don't let the ladies screw off those funny looking ears."

"Don't I wish, Roscoe. Don't I wish."

The Arson Squad was not a visible unit. They often preferred their own civilian clothes rather than fire department uniforms. They also rode primarily at night when their quarry operated.

Arson had no budget of their own from the City of Boston, surviving on what the fire department gave them. Their vehicles were hand-me-downs from the police force, ancient, black Fords that had seen their last law enforcement days years before. But they were transportation and they were all you needed when you operated under Code C, which meant you had to obey traffic laws unless an emergency was declared. When that emergency was announced – or you declared it yourself to get by the assholes in your way – then you could put a portable blue light on the dashboard, hit the siren, and run red lights and break the speed limit.

Leo turned down toward the piers to avoid the Central Artery. "If anything's going on, it'll be easier to come up this way."

Leo always drove and Hyde preferred it that way. Leo knew every street in Boston.

"You're the chauffeur." Henry grunted. "You know, I've been thinking that the broad that torched that car back there was sending a warning to the new screwee. You know how it is. Even though the guy walked, she's sending the message – you keep servicing my main man and your ass'll be the next thing burning."

"That's how I got the name and address of the ex-screwee. Told the new talent the car was just a message, that the next time the fire would be coming up her stairs and there'd be no way out." Leo snickered. "The cop there couldn't get a damn thing from her, but she was ready to tell me her life story once she realized what could happen."

"For a little sucker, you're a smooth son of a bitch. How come you don't get laid more?" Hyde leaned forward to turn the volume up on the radio.

"Because I'm married. How the hell else am I gonna'..."

"That's four alarms," Hyde interrupted. "Let's break some traffic laws." He pulled the blue light out of the glove box, plugged the business end into the cigarette lighter, and placed it on the dashboard. His hand was on the siren when he heard an unfamiliar voice over the radio.

"Get your ass in gear, Hyde." It came by surprise – a detached, eerie flow of words emerging from the void. "I don't see you here yet and I don't want you to miss the fireworks." The speaker pronounced each word separately and succinctly, none of them in the familiar Boston accent that was an integral part of the fire department net.

"Huh?" Hyde frowned at his partner. "Did you hear – what was that crap?"

Leo's expression was a reflection of Hyde's. "I didn't say anything." He pointed at the radio, shaking his finger in frustration. "That voice – it came over channel one."

Henry picked up the mike. "This is K-Six. Say again."

Nothing.

"This is K-Six...this is Hyde. Repeat."

There was silence, followed by a more familiar voice. "This is Fire Alarm, K-Six. We've got a big one on the waterfront. All stations on Rowe's Wharf, switch to channel two."

Hyde put down the mike. "I've got a big one, too," he muttered to himself as he punched the button for channel two. Then he glanced over at Leo. "It's like Alarm didn't hear that."

His partner shrugged. "Maybe we're not getting enough sleep."

There was only a vast darkness ahead as they roared past Pier Four and up Northern Avenue. The lights of Logan Airport to the east shone back across Boston Harbor twinkling off a light chop. "Where's the Rowe's Wharf lights?" Leo muttered. "You know...the Airport Water Shuttle...the *Odyssey*..."

"They aren't. Shit, there's no lights...no power. No, wait. I can see some reflections off some boats... "

A brilliant flash exploded from the upper floors of a building, illuminating the harbor area. It reflected off the high rises around Rowe's Wharf, and the boats alongside the ferry terminal piers.

"What the fuck?" Leo said.

"Would you look at that," Henry said with wonder. "White hot...metal or..."

The sounds over the radio had grown to a chorus of voices and sirens. The on-scene commander had called in two more alarms.

"Pull over here." They were at the corner of Atlantic Avenue. "It'll be faster on foot from here." They removed their firefighter's gear from the trunk as the din of chaos overwhelmed every other sound of the city.

There was light now, and smoke, and they instinctively sorted the various aromas that came to their nostrils as they approached the scene. Giant arc lights powered by portable generators illuminated a chaotic display. The street was jammed with police and emergency vehicles and fire apparatus – ladder trucks with their shiny stairs stretching skyward, pumpers with hoses snaking in every direction, a Tower with hose guns aimed toward the building. But there were no streams of water playing on the structure.

The deputy chief in his white coat held one radio to his ear while he spoke into another. "That's right...every piece of equipment we can spare from every district. If there's anything else big, we'll just have to redeploy from here." He beckoned the two Arson Squad investigators.

"Anybody still in there?" Hyde asked.

"Yeah, Henry, but I don't know how many. We haven't found any on-duty hotel personnel yet. I can't get guys up to the floors. Stairs are blocked. Too much heat."

"Water?"

"The first guys here hooked up and hardly got a dribble, regular hydrants or high pressure. We're running hoses from the marine unit now and we've got some coming from the other side of the expressway."

Hyde grimaced. "Does that mean the sprinkler system didn't function properly?"

The chief never answered. Instead he reacted to others who pointed at a window that had just been smashed out on the sixth floor of the hotel. They saw a woman in a nightgown, her screams lost in the deluge of sound that is part of the urgency of every fire. A ladder swung up and toward her, a fireman racing up the rungs as it extended. But before it could reach her, an angry puff of flame burst from behind, hurling her bodily into the night air, her nightgown and hair burning as she tumbled to the street.

The chief's expression did not change as he turned to Hyde. "That's the third one we've lost that way. It's hotter than a sonuva bitch up there. That building's supposed to be almost fireproof. Had to be an incendiary of some kind to get this going so fast. Even if there was water, it would be like pissing on – " His voice died away as a series of windows on the fifth floor exploded outward. "On napalm," he finished.

A stream of water arced out from the Tower. Then a hose on the street level tensed, then another, and then the remainder of the limp hoses filled with water. Moments later a team was moving through the front entrance.

"Get in there as soon as you can, Henry. See if you can find out where the employees were when this thing started."

Leo Carmichael stood at Hyde's side near the hotel's front entrance while a third hose team moved through ahead of them. Both waited in their firefighter's gear – helmets, bunker coats and pants, rubber boots. The stink of smoke and steam and char combined with the din of firefighting was overwhelming.

"Ever been in this place?" Leo shouted.

"Nope. Never knew anyone with enough money to stay here," Hyde answered. "How about you?"

"When they were building I went along with the inspection team. My uncle was with the department then."

"So, what'd you think of this joint?"

"We wanted to see how the other half lived and we found out – very fuckin' elegantly."

"You just saw how they die. Just like the rest of us."

A firefighter appeared in the doorway and beckoned.

"Know where the front desk is?" Hyde asked.

The fireman jerked his head around and pointed to his right before disappearing behind a cloud of smoke and steam.

"That's our first stop." Hyde paused inside the lobby to gain his bearings. Steam...smoke...ankle-deep water... more steam...more smoke. It swirled before their seal beam lights revealing soot covered walls and ceilings. The decorative columns were fire-stained.

"There must have been some pressure in the sprinkler system on this level," Hyde said. "Furniture's just scorched."

Carmichael led the way toward the front desk. The gold letters displaying the word RECEPTION could still be distinguished in the beam of their lights. Leo peered over the counter. "No one here." His light picked out a closed door to his left.

Hyde swung his own beam around until it fell on a doorknob. He removed a glove, felt the door for heat, then touched the knob. He turned it, stepping to one side at the same instant he kicked the door open. Thick smoke oozed out at the top but there were no flames.

Henry dropped to his knees in the dirty water and crawled a few feet, swinging his light from side to side. What smoke remained had risen to the high ceiling. The carpeting in front of him was unburned. He turned to Leo who was on his knees beside him. "Fire must've run out of oxygen."

They proceeded cautiously until they were certain there was no fire, then separated, splitting the room in half. There were two desks and Leo called out from behind one. "Over here."

Hyde crawled to the body lying behind the desk.

Leo's hand felt for a neck pulse. "Nope, gonzo," he commented.

Henry removed his gloves. "Nose," he said, tilting back the corpse's head.

Leo flashed his light up the man's nostrils. "Clean."

Hyde squeezed on either side of the man's jaw with one hand, using his free index finger to lift the tongue.

"Clean again."

"Let's get him outside before some well-meaning idiot screws up our evidence," Hyde said. "Give me your light. Your back's younger than mine."

Water was pouring down the sides of the building when they emerged from the front entrance. Hyde led the way to the deputy chief's white car where the rescue company eased the limp corpse, now in a body bag, into the back seat.

The deputy chief had followed them over. "What do I want with him, Henry?"

"Evidence. No soot in his nose or mouth. Poor bastard was dead before there was any fire."

Raymond Fairchild worked his way to the front of the crowd until he was near the yellow police tape. The gasp from the crowd when Carmichael appeared with the corpse over his shoulder added to the whole spectacle.

Fairchild saw a look in Hyde's eyes – was that anger as Hyde contemplated the faces in the crowd? Fairchild hoped so. Angry men were so much easier to manipulate. And Henry Hyde was going to be his tool.

As Hyde's studied survey of the spectators swept in his direction, Fairchild's gaze joined those around him staring upward at the flames gushing from an upper window. It was an exquisite, almost erotic, sensation to know people were dying inside. The first time that special feeling – that deep chill in his loins – occurred was when he tortured a neighbor's dog to death. He was twelve years old at the time and the creature's pitiful cries excited him.

Since that initial experience, he gradually learned to control those feelings. Concentration and discipline were important to avoid being caught. You had to be smarter than everyone else to get away with acts society considered wrong. Now it seemed that each act, each event that he created, had to be bigger and more elaborate than the last in order to achieve equal satisfaction.

Fairchild avoided public notoriety whenever possible. He preferred being a power behind the throne rather than being a public figure. It didn't matter *jack shit* to him that people looked down on his money or his power as long as he had both. Tonight, he remained invisible among the vast throng that would gather for any spectacular fire. It wouldn't take too many more days before the public would be impressed with the guy who could bring Boston to its knees, and then it would be even better to know something they could only wish they knew.

This is just the beginning, Hyde.

Fairchild noticed a photographer snapping pictures of the crowd. It was time to leave – and time to call Jean-Paul and offer his congratulations. Tomorrow he would deposit a bonus in Jean-Paul's account for a job well done.

2

Hyde was painstakingly tracing the failure of the hotel's automatic systems when the beam of Leo Carmichael's flashlight fell on the security officer's corpse. Unlike the body in the lobby office, this one had not escaped the fire.

Most of the security officer's clothes had been burned off, the body charred to a meaty black. Its limbs were drawn into the pugilist attitude that occurred as the muscles contracted from the heat. But the oxygen supply had been depleted so quickly in the tight room that the flames died before the corpse could be destroyed.

Leo removed surgeon's gloves from his outer pocket and pulled them on carefully. Even a grilled corpse could be contaminated, and that could ruin a carefully prepared case in court. He pried open the victim's mouth, holding it open with his fist, and peered down the throat with his flashlight until he could confirm what he'd anticipated – no soot in the larynx. This one had also been dead before the office had been torched.

The fire investigators were following the firefighters as they secured additional spaces in the hotel. When Hyde studied the structural damage on the fourth floor, he knew a metal accelerant had been used. "Magnesium," he told Leo. "I'll bet on it. When we were coming up Northern Ave, those explosions of white heat we saw were probably caused by burning magnesium. Let's see if we can find a trace of it for the lab."

Even though fire retardant construction had been emphasized when the building was designed, literally nothing with an ignition or melting point could survive six thousand degrees of heat. When magnesium burned, it turned from solid to liquid to gas – and mostly disappeared into the air, leaving only a trace of white powder.

"Thank God they couldn't haul in any more of the stuff than they did," Leo said.

Whoever had engineered this fire had followed a well-crafted master plan. Hyde had found where the transformer coordinating the hotel's power had been disconnected and where the backup generators had been sabotaged. The result was perfect: no alarms from the heat detectors or the sprinkler system, no normal or emergency lighting, emergency exit signs were dark, fire doors failed to close, the elevators jammed – enough of a delay. Plus something he had yet to figure out had been done to confuse the computers at Fire Alarm Headquarters. Basically, nothing had been left to chance.

Henry and Leo met with the senior department officers in the lobby as the sun was rising over Boston Harbor. It was agreed that what they'd determined up to that point wasn't ready to be released to the media. Hotel security had been neutralized before any fires were ignited. Fire suppression systems had been negated. Timing devices had probably been used in areas where fires originated, although the intense heat had destroyed most of the evidence. Incendiary trailers had been used to spread fire down corridors. Dozens of tins of suspected accelerant residue were sent to the lab for analysis. It would take days, perhaps weeks, for the entire squad of investigators to detail exactly what had happened.

Henry Hyde learned long ago to leave the bell on his apartment phone set on maximum. After a night without sleep, it was the only way he could hear it. But he still hated the sound, this morning as much as any other.

The answering machine clicked on after four loud, insistent rings. His message was anything but fancy: "Leave the time, the date, your name, and your phone number." Beep. There was no personal identification, no background music, no humorous catch phrases, and no promises.

He glanced at the digital clock as he waited for the response after his message. Ten o'clock.

If it were his ex, she'd leave a couple of choice obscenities, mostly as a balance to those he left on her machine. His teenage daughter could be scolding – "I know you're there, Daddy" – or coy – "If you were there, Daddy, I'd bring over your favorite dinner." His older daughter usually left a detailed message concerning the progress of her first pregnancy which Henry forgot in moments because he'd yet to adjust to the idea of being some kid's grandfather.

The machine beeped and there was an ominous silence. The calling party was still on the line but not responding.

Henry's favorite messages were the dirty ones from the girls at the Arson Squad desk: "I want you so bad, Henry, I've been rubbing myself you-know-where all day." There'd be a pause with some giggling in the background. "And by the way, Henry, Albert says there's an important message from one of your rats. And Assistant DA Donovan says he's going to throw out one of your cases if you don't call him back in the next hour. Ta ta, honey."

A sharp voice issued from the answering machine. "Hyde, I do know you're there. I always know where you are." After a few seconds' pause, "Just like I knew you were in K-Six last night." The words were succinct, yet cold and distant, mocking. "And I was at Rowe's Wharf when you arrived...and when you brought that body out...and...I guess that's enough to prove I was watching you."

Christ!

Hyde lifted the receiver and snapped off the machine. "Who is this?"

"Top of the mornin' to you, Lieutenant." An Irish lilt this time.

It wasn't the commissioner and it wasn't the deputy chief. He knew their voices, plus neither would start out that way. "Why don't you just go take a flying fuck," he growled.

"Come now, Lieutenant Hyde." Back to the polished, clipped, no nonsense speech. "That's not a polite way to treat me. After all – "

"I'm not a polite person. I'm a mean son of a bitch, and right now I'm meaner than you can imagine because I didn't get any sleep last night."

"Well neither did I. That was one spectacular fire we were involved with. I watched until it was under control – I should say more or less under control since it was pretty difficult for the Boston Fire Department to get a handle on it." He intoned each word separately, as if attempting to explain something complex to a child.

"Who the fuck is this?"

"I simply wanted you to know that last night's fire was just the beginning, Hyde. There will be others, equally disastrous, until you get me what I want."

Hyde's head fell back on his pillow. He massaged tired eyes with the other hand. "Hey, I don't know who the fuck you are, I've never heard from you before, and – "

"I beg to differ, Hyde. You heard me last night, on your radio while you and Carmichael were driving to my fire." No accent now – none at all. Not someone from the department. "Now once you allow your thick head to digest *that,* you'll know I'm not kidding you. Playing or perhaps toying with you a bit, though, if you can take a joke now and then."

That voice over the radio, taunting.

"Okay, I remember. You said you wanted something from me." Hyde rose on his elbow. Wackos want you to talk with them, Henry, so don't be a dipshit. "What is it you want?"

But the phone went dead.

The grey, metal desks were dented and scratched. Blackened cigarette burns edged pocked formica surfaces. The decay was compounded by hand-me-down file cabinets, worn, lumpy chairs, and a copying machine that might have been a reject from the Xerox museum. The cramped office resembled a decrepit movie set from the thirties, but the Arson Squad made the best of whatever they were given. They were the City of Boston's orphan.

Henry Hyde inserted five bullets into his .38 and stared intently at the snub-nosed revolver before he returned it to the holster on his right hip. He glanced down into the street below the window, shaking his head slowly from side to side.

"You look like you want to use that on some bad guy, Henry. Got a mad on?"

Hyde turned back and eyed Albert Horgan without smiling. "Yeah, I got a mad on, Al. And, no, I wouldn't shoot at a bad guy with this thing unless I had the goddamn barrel in his mouth. Wouldn't be able to hit the son of a bitch any other way with this pea shooter."

He and Al Horgan, the senior Arson Squad investigator who ran the Major Case Unit, were the only investigators in the office. The rest were down at the Rowe's Wharf fire scene.

"Go ahead! You carry the same piece of crap. Take it out of your holster. I'll stand right here. Try to shoot me. I promise I won't move."

Horgan grasped both hands together in front of him and pointed his index fingers at Hyde's middle. "If I held it like this and aimed at your gut, it'd be hard to miss something that large." Then he leaned forward and rested his thick arms on his desk. "You do have a mad on, Henry. That why you're here, not downtown?"

Hyde frowned. "I guess so...yeah, I suppose so." He plopped himself down in the chair beside Horgan's desk. "Anybody can figure out the basic causes of that fire. They don't need me. There were pros involved. I just decided to go through my files, think things out while it was still quiet around here. You know how it's going to be when the guys start coming in."

Al Horgan was a broad-shouldered, husky man. He had wide-set blue eyes, reddish hair, a flushed Irish complexion, a nose that had been broken a number of times, and a broad smile that could disappear in an instant when he was crossed. "Controlled insanity. Then again, maybe not so controlled with the media climbing in the windows."

The phone had been ringing constantly all day. After an hour of fending off media inquiries, Horgan had put a message on the squad's answering machine that there would be a news conference at four in the afternoon at Headquarters.

"O'Brien will handle them in his inimitable manner."

District Fire Chief William O'Brien was the chief of the Arson Squad. He had ordered that no one in the squad was to field any phone call from outside. Anyone who needed them knew of the squad's unlisted number. If a call didn't come in on that line it was double trouble, especially with fourteen deaths recorded at the hotel.

"I'll be out of here before they show." Hyde smoothed his mustache absently. "Those were real pros last night," he repeated.

"I understand you were the brain who figured out what happened to the city water."

"Not too difficult after hearing the problem. Some writer, a guy from up on the North Shore doing research for a novel, once asked me if there was a way to keep water from flowing through a water main without anyone figuring out the cause. I said you had to freeze it, plug the main. He asked how, considering it was under the street. I said why not carbon dioxide – dry ice. Critically low temperature. Freezes everything it comes in contact with quickly, including city water mains." Henry shrugged. "And when heated water from the fire sloshes down the manholes into the sewers, the evidence evaporates into thin air."

"You're approaching genius level, Henry."

"Except someone beat me to it – last night. I never saw that happen before. That's why I came in here. Found the writer's name, called him, figured in about ten seconds he wasn't involved." Hyde stroked his mustache ruefully. "No, the genius isn't me. It's some son of a bitch who's too fucking smart for his own good, playing with a lot more shit last night than dry ice. The sadistic bastard wanted to kill."

Henry wasn't about to mention that phone call to anyone yet. Either the caller had it in for him for some reason and it was a personal matter, or he was the victim of a crank. Either way, it would be embarrassing to hang out your dirty laundry only to find out some nutcase was making a fool out of you. Hyde's ego wasn't ready for that.

"Your stress level's peaking. Do me a favor. You need to relax."

"That's exactly what I'm gonna do. Different approach. I'm going to take the new kid with me when everybody comes back here."

"Robbie Scott?"

"Naughty, naughty." Hyde scolded. "Not all blacks are called Robbie or Willy or Junior. His name's Robert. He's Bobbie to his friends."

"I stand corrected. Bob. Bobbie. Whatever. And I like the kid, too. Lots of potential. Now tell me – why him?"

Hyde nodded. "Why not?"

Horgan shrugged. "For one he doesn't know shit. He's only two weeks out of that ladder company. He hasn't been to the range to qualify to carry. He wouldn't know how to arrest a stray – "

"Yeah, I know. I like that. But he's gonna qualify tomorrow."

"Shit, I heard him explaining to someone the other day that all of a sudden he's telling all his old buddies not to rip out all the ceilings at a fire scene. He was laughing because he said it wasn't so long ago he loved to pull everything apart."

Hyde grinned. "Step in the right direction. He knows to preserve the evidence already."

"The guy's from Dorchester. We both know there's not supposed to be prejudice in the department anymore. But, shit, the only blacks ever got into that hotel other than the help are goddamn dignitaries, mostly foreigners probably. He wouldn't know what to look for." Horgan frowned. "I don't care how bright he's supposed to be, it'll take the kid a year before he's really capable of knowing what to look for in a fire like that."

"You took the words right out of my mouth. A fresh approach from a babe in the woods. I'll teach him everything I know, but I'm banking on Mr. Scott being such a novice he sees what I've become too jaded to see in my advanced years."

"Okay, okay, you've made your point. If it works, if the chief says you're a genius, I'll say it was my idea."

"Fine, I'll never say a word. Now how about doing me a favor?" Hyde's expression was as serious as it had ever been. "I'm saying please on this one. Don't take this case over. I know it's already a major case unit assignment. But I need to – "

"Relax, Henry." Horgan winked. "We're working together. No one gets cut out, no one's a hero. After all, you're the fucking legend – not me."

Hyde parked the black, almost antique Crown Vic in a no parking zone on the Cambridge Street side of City Hall Plaza. A fire helmet was on the rear window ledge and he stuck the blue bubble light on the dashboard. The cops would leave it alone. He hoped the meter maids would too.

"Come on, Bobbie, let's get this over with," Hyde said.

They walked down the stairs to the plaza and across toward Boston's seat of government.

City Hall hadn't been a place Bobbie Scott expected he'd ever visit officially when he was a teenager. Now he felt on top of the world strolling across City Hall Plaza on business with a Boston fire inspector's badge in his wallet. And he was partnered with a man who important people recognized and respected.

Boston City Hall was all angles, not pretty, not efficient, and not as functional as the "New Boston" designers had planned. But it would continue to serve its purpose in the next century.

"Hey, Henry!"

He searched the faces near the entrance to City Hall until he saw the woman waving in his direction. Her smile appeared to grow as he approached.

"I was afraid you were going to go right by me."

Hyde grinned happily. Nomi Cram always seemed to make his day. "Nomi, how goes it?" Hesitating only for a second, he put an arm around her shoulders and gave her an awkward squeeze. "What brings you over here today?"

Nomi Cram did look good to him, even if her hair was blowing. She didn't look like the average, well-coiffed television reporter, but her features were striking enough to keep her on screen almost every day. She rested her cheek on his shoulder momentarily, then stepped back. "You're looking as good as ever, Lieutenant Hyde. You here for the mayor's press conference, too?"

"The chief asked me just to keep an eye on anything behind the scenes."

Nomi's eyes turned to Scott to appraise the tall, well-built young man. "So who's your handsome friend that you don't dare introduce?"

Scott was good-looking. He had a broad face featuring large brown, laughing eyes and a mustache that enhanced a steady, bright white smile.

"You haven't met Bob Scott yet?"

"Nope, but I'd like to."

"Tip your baseball cap, Bobbie, and say hello to my favorite lady, Nomi Cram."

She shook Scott's hand. "New guy, huh?"

"I'm fresh caught, ma'am," Scott answered. "I was told that working with Henry would give me a chance to meet famous people. Pleased to make your acquaintance."

"You're riding with the best, a legend right up there with Wyatt Earp and Doc Holiday." She turned back to Hyde. "How about if I get you on camera for a moment today, Henry? You know, get the facts from the expert's mouth. Nicki thought she had the choice spot for tonight's news over at Headquarters, but I'll bet a dinner at Grill 23 you could one-up her for me."

Hyde shook his head. "Actually, I've already been told that one of the dumbest things I could do was say anything around the mayor, so – "

Nomi interrupted. "Right. You'd think I'd know better."

"Sorry," Hyde said. "Just comes from associating with the wrong people."

Nomi looked at Scott. "You heard about how our buddy here made an enemy for life with our dear mayor?"

Scott shrugged innocently. "Like I said, I'm so new I haven't caught up on all the stories yet."

Nomi tapped Hyde's chest with her index finger. "Nobody screws with this guy, Bobbie. Children's Hospital has a program for kids who are first offenders. You must've run into them...kids playing with matches who start a fire and get caught. You know, the ones who aren't bad yet. Your Arson Squad puts them in this program at Children's rather than getting them involved with cops and the courts."

"Yeah," Scott said, "one of my cousins had a kid who ended up there. I think he's straight now."

"Well, it seems Henry was in the wrong place at the wrong time and came down on Mayor Jordan's son. The kid and one of his friends tried to torch a vacant building. Henry caught the mayor's kid, I picked up the story and put it out on the eleven o'clock news, and...bingo... we're both on Mayor Jordan's shit list for life."

"I don't mind," Hyde said. "I can't stand the asshole anyway. His shit list's a compliment."

"Jordan has to put up with me," Nomi said. "But he hates Henry, especially since he couldn't get him fired."

Scott glanced at Hyde. "He tried to get you canned?"

"He did. When he couldn't get the commissioner to go along with him, he tried every angle he could, called in every rotten debt he was owed," Nomi said.

"And nothing?"

"I got friends in high places." Hyde grinned. "Right, Nomi?"

"Right."

"Be nice to her, Bobbie. I'm very attached to this lovely lady. So, Nomi, why don't you go in ahead of us. The last thing you need is for Jordan to see the two of us together."

"Nice to meet you," she told Bobbie. "Let's see more of each other, Henry."

"Where the hell's Nicki Adams?" Boston's second term mayor peered down at the assembled media from the anteroom of his City Hall office one floor above. "And Stadius? I don't see him out there with the Channel Five group. Where the hell's Stadius?"

Jordan's public relations aide, Dennis Campbell, scanned the faces below. "Let's see now...the *Herald* and the *Globe* have their big players..."

"Screw the *Herald* and screw the *Globe*. By the time they're on the streets the city will have everything from television anyway. Where are the heavy hitters? I want the lovely Nicki Adams and her erotic perfume at my side, and I want her beaming up at me with those baby blues, mike in hand. And Prunella's not here either. For Chrissake, I want that afro of hers right here looking good, too."

"Press conference, sir. They had a four o'clock press conference with the Arson Squad. Maybe Nicki and the others went to see if there was anything interesting there before they came here."

Jordan indicated the media gathering below. "Second team down there. And you know why? Their renowned compatriots haven't a prayer of getting to City Hall from Fire Department Headquarters through rush hour traffic, especially with the mess around the goddamn Central Artery."

"We can delay until they get here."

The mayor's famed temper was rising. "The second team has the mayor today. The first team has the Arson Squad. Nicki Adams will finish up with something like…" He mimicked holding a mike to his face. "…and that's how the Arson Squad sees the Rowe's Wharf situation the first day after the tragic fire. And now to Howdy Doody at City Hall to see if Mayor Charles Jordan concurs."

"Sir – "

"And that broad who just came in down there, Nomi Cram – " The mayor gestured below. "The one with the mousy hair and rimless glasses will be the one to ask if I concur with the Arson Squad. And I suppose that smarmy know-it-all will be preening for the cameras?"

"Hyde?"

Jordan looked down below just as Henry Hyde entered the area. "And there he is." The mayor gritted his teeth audibly. "Some day I'm going to give that sunuvabitch the same chance he gave me when he sent my kid to that place."

Hyde sauntered over to the media group and began introducing a black man with a BFD baseball cap who hung closely at his side.

"Who's Danny Glover down there with Hyde?" Jordan growled.

"Never saw him before. Obviously with the fire department."

"Okay, you set this trap. Let's go down and watch you bail me out."

"Turn on the news, sweetheart. I'll be there in a moment." Raymond Fairchild had barely lifted his finger from the intercom before he depressed it again. "Get Channel Five for me."

Fairchild's office, a loft in an ancient stone structure on a wharf overlooking Boston Harbor, was as elegant in its decor as the man was in his attire. He stretched his arms out over his broad desk so that the huge gold cufflinks, his favorites, were fully displayed as he rose to his feet and let his arms fall to his sides. He flicked imaginary threads off his silk tie and unconsciously felt the knot to make sure it was tight. Fairchild never loosened his tie or collar, even when he was alone, nor did he remove his suit coat, even in the summer. Expensive clothes radiated power and he knew he wore them well.

There were times when Raymond Fairchild wished he could show off his hideaway, maybe pose in his elegant clothes for one of those Sunday newspapers, or even *Boston Magazine* – one of those features on a successful Boston businessman in his office, the type of digs that most other men could only dream about. But none of those local shit-sheets would feature anyone who made money in the manner he did. *Screw them all!* They'd never have what he already possessed.

Fairchild crossed over to the full bathroom at the rear of his office, which was even larger than the one his wife had designed for them at home off their bedroom. With a square marble shower, a jacuzzi that would service four comfortably, a sauna, and a dressing room, it had entrances from both his office and the suite behind.

After relieving himself and rinsing his hands, Fairchild again checked his tie, this time straightening it ever so slightly as he studied himself in the floor-to-ceiling mirror. Dark, tailored, pinstripe suit, light blue form-fitting shirt with white collar, crimson tie, thick dark hair graying elegantly at the edges. *Still got that cocky, tough-guy look from your hockey days.* He winked at his image.

Dorothy Murray looked up with a fetching smile when Fairchild entered the suite. Dotty had picked out the furniture and colors to please Raymond, and he was pleased as much with her efforts as with the way she fit the place so well. There was a relaxation area at one end with three plush sofas surrounding a large rosewood coffee table. A gas fire twinkled in the fireplace beyond the table. A large screen television was set into the wall to the right of the fireplace. At the opposite end was a formal dining area with a full kitchen in a separate room behind it. The bedroom was beyond that.

Dorothy covered the space between them as if she had floated through the air. Her smile was broad and enticing as she circled her arms around Fairchild's neck. She kissed him longingly as if he was just returning from a trip. "I was about to buzz you and explain that you weren't allowed to work past cocktail hour."

"Not tonight." He rested his hands on her rump. "I don't like to think of you without me," he said, lightly cupping her tight cheeks, "wrapped around you."

"Sounds delicious. Now?" Dorothy Murray was dressed as expensively as Fairchild. It was a special touch he insisted on. A deep purple designer dress cut just below the knees accommodated her figure perfectly. Her shoulder-length hair was naturally blond and wavy and set off high, patrician cheekbones and a sculptured face that women envied. She wore large pearl earrings to match the pearl necklace that complemented her low cut dress.

Money bought women. What had been the germ of an idea in high school – to have as many women as humanly possible – had become a goal by the time Raymond Fairchild graduated college. A man who amasses money has the right to select any woman he wants whenever he wants. It was a bother as a teenager to have to talk your way under their skirts, an even greater bother to have to get them drunk in college. When you had money, no woman screamed "date rape". You simply got what you wanted because you deserved it.

Fairchild nuzzled her neck, nipping at an ear. "It's not easy to say no to a woman who smells as exotic as you do, but I'll make a reservation for a few hours from now." He pulled back and nodded toward the television where the evening news was about to start. "How about a drink?"

"Crown Royal?" she asked, giving him another peck before she dropped her arms.

"Ummm." He nodded. "Lots of ice."

"Make yourself comfortable."

Fairchild settled himself in one of the sofas. He planned on a comfortable evening. Then he'd watch the eleven o'clock news at home with his wife.

Two women were nice, good for body and soul. At one time, Dorothy had seemed a necessary luxury. Now, she'd become a necessity, like a second car.

But recently he'd been thinking – could he handle three women? After all, he owned three cars. Of course, that would require another apartment. But what the hell, he was going to own the city of Boston shortly anyway. Along with the asshole mayor who would deliver it.

3

While Mayor Charles Jordan was speaking, Nomi Cram slipped over to Henry Hyde. "These artificial lights aren't kind, Henry. You look beat to hell."

"I am, Nomi." He grinned good-naturedly. "Not much sleep. Us old guys don't bounce back like we used to. What I need is to spend more time with foxy young girls like you, get my vigor back."

Nomi wrinkled her nose. "Maybe Christmas will come early this year."

Hyde grinned. "Ever hear of Christmas every day?"

He enjoyed an easy relationship with most of the women in the Boston media pool, young and old. He was always good for an off-color joke or two when coverage was boring and he wasn't averse to leaving a tip on an answering machine when one of them was desperate for a story.

"I'd put on my Santa Claus outfit," she said, "if I didn't have to wait in line outside your door with all the other girls." She slipped an arm through his. "What can you do for me that would make me a broadcast hero?"

Henry shrugged. "How about if we got married for the night?"

Nomi grinned.

"Then, in between, you can tell me why you insist on being called Nomi Cram when you could adopt one of those sexy television names."

"First of all, since in-betweens are supposed to be for sweet nothings, you get to find out now. First, people never forget a name like Nomi Cram. And secondly, I'm not sexy enough to compete with Nikki's looks."

"Us old guys know better. I see a gorgeous girl behind those specs."

"And I see a gorgeous guy sweet-talking me. Maybe there ought to be an in-between sometime soon." Her smile said that she saw something special in Henry Hyde, but as she was about to speak, she lifted a finger and cocked her head to the side as she listened to the producer's voice through her earpiece, then moved back near the mayor.

"Thank you, Mayor Charles Jordan." The camera panned in on Nomi Cram's face. "I've just been talking to one of Boston's leading arson investigators, Henry Hyde, who may be able to provide us with some interesting insights."

She moved toward Hyde even though Henry remained in place shaking his head to show that he didn't want to get involved during the mayor's press conference.

"Lieutenant Hyde, the mayor has just indicated you have some excellent leads in your investigation. Can you share some information about these with us?"

Hyde blinked in the bright light. Bobbie Scott, squinting in the glare, stared at the unfamiliar camera. "To be honest, Nomi, we haven't got much of anything except a good idea that the fire didn't start by itself."

"What about the chances of an early arrest, Lieutenant?"

Henry shrugged. "Who would I arrest?" He looked sideways at Scott. "Wouldn't you agree this is going to be a long range investigation, Investigator Scott?"

Scott gulped. "Oh very long range," he said rapidly.

"You see, Nomi, there were some extremely sophisticated methods employed at Rowe's Wharf. I believe magnesium may have been involved. Magnesium is a highly volatile metal that can create temperatures up to six thousand degrees when it burns." Hyde smoothed each side of his mustache thoughtfully, then he shrugged and offered Nomi a half smile. "But we have to understand how the fires started, how the magnesium got there, how the magnesium was ignited before we can begin to look for clues."

Hyde glanced over toward the mayor. "There's a lot more than magnesium involved, so that's just one element of the investigation. There's really nothing more I can say at this time."

Shortly after ten o'clock that evening, a freshly showered Fairchild used his office phone to request a taxi in front of the building in five minutes. Then he dialed a second number from memory, listening to the phone ring three times on the other end before a groggy voice mumbled, "Ummm...yeah... hello."

"I'll bet you're catching up on your beauty rest, Hyde." He paused for just a second to let his voice register before he added, "You certainly do need that rest if you always look like you did on the six o'clock news."

"I'm already tired of this shit." Hyde's tone was sharp and angry. "Who the fuck are you? Some faggot getting his rocks off because I'm in bed? Want me to send you a nude photo?"

"Your sense of humor's going to do you in, Hyde. This is just to remind you that we're going to work together. You're going to make me rich if you don't want your city to burn down."

"Why don't you take a flying – "

"I've also decided that your schedule at home is erratic. No wonder your wife left you."

"Shove it, asshole."

"Since I know your work schedule, I'm going to start calling you at the Arson Squad. And why don't you clean up your language."

Dorothy Murray was stretched out on the king size bed watching television when Fairchild came back into the bedroom. She was still nude. "Back home to the little lady now, Raymond?" she asked without looking away from the screen.

He sat on the edge of the bed and, when she didn't look up, bent down and, catching a nipple between his teeth, shook his head gently. "Unfortunately so," he answered as she squealed and pushed his head away. He blew in her ear, kissed her forehead, her nose, and then very lightly brushed her lips. "Until the final deal is done, I still reside with my wife in our home like every respectable citizen should." He turned her chin until she had to look at him. "But I promise you from the bottom of my heart that I love you more than life itself and when it's all over I will divorce my wife and marry you instantly." There had never been a woman born who wouldn't flop when she heard those words.

She pulled away, stretching suggestively on the satin sheets. "Show me once more how much..." but she stopped as she recognized the look on his face.

Fairchild rose to his feet just as quickly. He knew better than to climb into bed with his wife when he carried the aroma of another woman on any part of his body. "Offers like that are made to cherish until the next time, Dottie. I love you more than you can ever imagine."

Handling three women simultaneously would be a challenge, he thought as he rode the elevator down to street level, but if anyone could do it, Raymond Fairchild could.

•

Carolina Fairchild looked up from her novel and smiled automatically as her husband entered the bedroom. Would it be love and kisses tonight? Or would it be rough, demanding sex? In the past year something she'd been unable to place in perspective seemed to be altering her husband's personality. She never knew which Raymond Fairchild would walk into the bedroom.

Before she could put down her book, he was perched on the edge of the bed, both hands already under her shoulders lifting her slightly as he bent down and delivered a long kiss. "Miss me tonight?" he asked, gently easing her back down on the pillows.

It was the man she used to know.

She nodded. "If you greet me like that every time you work late, I guess it's okay." She licked her index finger and rubbed some of her lipstick from his chin. "What was it tonight? Business dinner?"

"Nope. Late night at the office all by myself." He brushed hair back from her forehead. "Big deal coming, but I'm going to make your life easy by not wasting your time explaining it to you so you don't have to explain it to someone else."

"Explain what? And to whom?"

"I don't know." He shrugged and raised his eyebrows dramatically. "Maybe the press. They could call and ask questions about me and you could be honest and say your husband never brings work home from the office and you didn't know. How's that for being a superb husband?"

Carolina nodded. She really didn't know much about what Raymond did except that he made a great deal of money as a middle man in business transactions with people she often didn't care for the few times she met them. Since she lived much better than the girls she'd grown up with, she determined early on that she was going to keep her nose out of it as long as she continued to have whatever she wanted. "I suppose the next thing my superb husband is going to tell me is that he's too tired to perform his husbandly duties for his horny wife?" She flipped the sheet back. She was naked and still very appealing even after two children.

"Not on your life, Mrs. Fairchild," he responded softly. "You didn't marry the finest stud in Boston just to be disappointed, my love. Shall I drop my clothes right here on the floor, or will you give me time to hang them up?"

"Since I was the one who picked out that suit for you, I guess I can control myself while you put it on a hanger – but not a second after that."

As he crawled into bed, Fairchild looked down at his wife and said tenderly, "If there's ever only one thing in my life I did right, it's marry you. God how I love you, Carolina."

What would three be like in one night, he wondered, as he took the nipple of his wife's right breast in his mouth and shook his head gently.

The phone was ringing as Bob Scott entered the room. "Hey, Bobbie, catch that will you. I'm up to my wrists here." Leo Carmichael raised his arms to display the Shake 'n Bake covering his hands.

Scott picked up the phone on the third ring. "Arson Squad, Investigator Scott speaking." He pressed the mute button on the TV remote to cut off the sound. "One moment please." He put his hand over the phone. "Leo, where's Henry? Some guy wants to speak with him."

"He was here a second ago. Said something about taking a dump, I think. Check the head." He placed another piece of chicken in a baking dish. "You eat more than one boneless breast, Bobbie?" he asked as Scott headed out the door.

"I like to eat, period. You got extra, I'll chow. Hey, Henry," he called out from the hallway outside the men's room, "you on the pot?"

There was a muffled response.

"I don't know. Guy didn't give his name. Wasn't sure whether you were in the can or not. Sit easy, man," he called over his shoulder, "I'll get a number." He picked up the phone. "Henry's on another line. Said to take a message and...right, I'll pass it on."

"Who was that?" Leo asked. "One of his women pleading for his body?"

"Guy didn't say. Just said he'd call back." Scott pressed the remote button and *Jeopardy's* sound came back on the television.

When Henry Hyde entered the room, the first words out of his mouth, "Not Shake 'n fuckin' Bake again!" were followed by, "Jesus Christ, Bobbie, you should know by now not to bother a man when he's on the crapper. You ruined my concentration."

"Yeah," Leo said, "he's concentrating on the centerfold."

"So who was so important you had to bother me?"

"Sorry, Henry," Scott answered. "Guy wouldn't say. Just said he'd call back in ten minutes."

Hyde eyed the television set for a moment. "How the hell you supposed to make a buck with categories that tough?" he asked. The Double Jeopardy categories disappeared from the television screen as the phone rang. "Arson Squad, Hyde speaking."

"Did you enjoy your beauty rest?"

Henry's face flushed visibly at the sound of that voice. "You fucker," he shouted into the phone. "Start talking."

Leo whirled from the counter in a cloud of Shake 'n Bake and Bobbie Scott, a look of wonder on his face, hit the mute on the TV remote.

"How does it feel to have your nuts in the grinder, Hyde?" The voice was insistent, mocking, a presence that now provided a weird fascination to Henry Hyde.

"You're trying to tell me that you're certain you have my attention. So go ahead."

"Are you watching *Jeopardy?*"

"I was. Turned off the sound when the phone rang because I figured we might be getting called out soon."

"Oh, you'll be working tonight. Without a doubt, you'll enjoy yourself this evening. But what I'm more interested in is your appreciation of my creativity."

"Meaning?"

"Don't act dumb. I know you better than your mother. You are one smart son of a bitch. Not up to my level, of course, but I respect your abilities. A man like you gets pissed when he runs into someone like me. Do you want a hint of what to expect tonight?"

"I'm game if you are."

"Try this on for size. What Boston grande dame appeared at Fenway Park wearing a *Go Red Sox* bandanna? How's that for a hint?"

Hyde's eyes narrowed. "What is it you want?" he shouted. "Talk to me." He turned and banged the phone back in its cradle. "Son of a bitch hung up."

"What...?" But Leo decided it was wiser to wait until Henry was ready to speak.

Hyde gestured toward Leo. "Go ahead, get back to the chicken. I'm as hungry tonight as Bobbie always is." He nodded at Scott. "Turn up the sound. I want to see if I can answer any of those fucking questions. Ichthyology," he muttered. "How you supposed to answer if you don't know what the category means?"

After a few *Jeopardy* questions, Hyde spoke without looking away from the television. "A real fucking psycho. Says we're going to be busy tonight." As an ad flashed on the screen, he looked up and found the other two watching him curiously. "Don't burn the fucking chicken," he said to Leo. And then with a sideways glance, "And you make sure he doesn't burn the fucking chicken, Bobbie."

Isabella Stewart Gardner had been one of Boston's great women, a turn-of-the-century belle dame. Well educated, she was a social doyenne, setting the standards for Boston's elite in the late 1800s, and a patron of the arts who left her city an unmatched cultural heritage.

The *Gardner* had been her home, a magnificent mansion aptly named "Fenway Court" where she hosted the cream of Boston society in a setting overflowing with European art treasures. When she died in 1921, the people of Boston inherited a museum. Her home was a treasure trove of famous paintings, tapestries, statuary, and priceless antiques. Her center courtyard, soaring four floors to a ceiling of tinted glass, remained green throughout the year. Isabella Stewart Gardner's taste and sense of beauty would influence Boston for centuries.

Angry gouts of white flame were licking from the windows of the Gardner's second and third floors on the front and east side when Leo Carmichael pulled the car in behind Ladder 26. Hyde watched in fascination as District Chief Charlie Kincaid leaned a huge framed painting against the side of his white car.

"Henry!" Kincaid straightened up, eyes flashing angrily from his soot-covered face at Hyde's approach. "What the fuck?" He blinked and repeated himself.

Hyde pulled on his black bunker coat that had been slung over his shoulder and took the helmet that Bobbie Scott handed him. "What Charlie?"

Kincaid half turned and pointed. "Look at the color, Henry. When the guys from Engine Thirty Seven laid a stream on it, it seemed to explode. It's chemical. Eats water."

"Like the hotel," Leo said.

"Looks like it." Henry stepped closer to the chief. "Those the only hot spots?"

"Top floor, too. That's office space and the director's apartment. No chemicals. Just a distraction to piss someone off. But those hot spots – multiple origins." Kincaid took a deep breath. "We were able to control the top floor pretty quick, sort of like whoever the bastard was who set it off wanted to send a message."

Hyde pointed at some paintings that had been brought outside. "Those things worth something?"

"A bundle. The director says you're looking at millions right there. Strange thing. Someone called in the fire to Fire Alarm about the time it was starting. Gave us a chance to get a lot of stuff out without too much water or smoke damage to the rest of the place." He looked Hyde squarely in the eye. "I don't know why one section of the building was tagged for the chemical shit and not the whole place, Henry." Kincaid gestured over his shoulder. "This is just like Roxbury in the seventies, except this time it's not the slums being cleared. Someone's burning the best Boston's got."

"I don't want to interfere with your guys, but I gotta get in there while it's still hot."

Kincaid spoke into the mike on his collar. They all heard the response. "Go ahead." He pointed behind Hyde. "Use the door on the far side there. Go back to your right. Stairs against the west wall. Follow the hose lines. And my guys got a corpse for you, too. Third floor rear, and not touched by the fire. Has a problem with a hole in his forehead."

Leo led the way, the beam from his lantern following hoselines. They were working their way through light smoke and steam on the third floor toward the front of the museum when the floor under them began to shake. A groaning sound, like the warning howl of a cornered cat, quickly turned to a single sharp crack that echoed through the building as the rumble of falling debris lit the area with a sudden brilliance. A fireball exploded through a distant doorway and raced down the ceiling toward them.

Their next moves were instinctive, diving face down away from the heat as the oxygen-starved flame licked overhead. A cloud of smoke and dust followed, enveloping them in a choking haze.

Hyde, on his hands and knees, was scrambling back the way they'd just come. "Leo...Bobbie...you with me?" his voice a hoarse bellow.

The voices of both men came from close behind just as Hyde suddenly found himself tumbling head first down the flight of stone steps they'd climbed only moments before.

The eleven o'clock news opened with the eerie glow of the Gardner Museum behind Nomi Cram's brightly lit face. Her features were pinched, horror reflected in her eyes, and her voice cracked as she spoke. "At least four Boston firefighters lost their lives tonight when a section of the Isabella Stewart Gardner Museum gave way beneath them as they worked to control a raging blaze. City hospitals are operating on an emergency status until Commissioner Duggan can account for each man from the four engine companies and three ladder companies who were fighting the fire at the time…"

For Henry Hyde, everything had suddenly become personal – brothers were dead. Murdered.

None of the silent men looked up as Al Horgan came through the doorway into the Arson Squad room. He placed two boxes of doughnuts in the middle of the table.

"Breakfast," he said, surprised at how soft his normally gruff voice sounded.

Leo Carmichael looked up at him, blinked, looked back down into his folded hands. Hyde's cigarette smoke hung in the stale air. No one responded.

"You gotta' eat something." He ripped the tops off each box. "Dig in." He pointed at the array of doughnuts. "Go ahead."

Carmichael was the only one to reach into a box. He extracted a doughnut and placed it on the table beside his coffee mug without looking at either the doughnut or Horgan.

"No wonder," Horgan said, looking over at the coffee maker. The pot was empty. A red light indicated that the burner was still on. "Shit, you'll bust the goddamn pot, start a fire right here…" But his voice trailed off when Hyde raised his head for the first time to stare at him.

"Go fuck yourself, Al."

Horgan went over to the coffee maker and removed the pot. "Better yet, I'll make a fresh pot." He emptied the coffee basket, put a new filter in, filled it with fresh grounds, added water, and set a fresh pot in place.

Horgan looked back at the men around the table. "Better idea, fresh coffee. Fucking myself, Henry, if I did it right here, might be the thing that would drive you guys over the edge."

"Easy does it, Lieutenant. Two of the jakes who went down last night were good friends of Bobbie's." Carmichael's lower lip quivered ever so slightly. "One of 'em pulled Bobbie out of a basement just a couple of months ago...and he wasn't a brother either. Had four kids." He reached across and squeezed Scott's hand.

Horgan moved over behind Scott and set his hands on his shoulders, squeezing gently. "You're tight, Bobbie. Gotta loosen up." He began to knead Scott's muscles with big, rough fingers. "I've been there before. I've lost some good friends, too." He bent from the waist and said in a soft voice that everyone could hear, "The only thing we can do is get the bastards who set that fire – get even. You're in this with us just like you'd been an investigator as long as any of us. Right, Henry?"

"That's right."

Horgan straightened up but his hands still worked over Scott's neck. "You're damn straight that's right. I don't know how much the rest of you know, but Henry's a lot deeper into this than he's been letting on. Isn't that right, Henry?"

"That's right, Al." He pawed through one of the boxes and selected a doughnut.

"All these fires happen on your watch. These other guys completely in on it?"

Hyde took a large bite and chewed thoughtfully for a few seconds. "Pretty much."

"No more secrets?"

"Just one, Al. I don't have the vaguest idea who's behind this. If I did, if I had him, I'd put a fuckin' bullet in each knee and each elbow. In between each shot, I'd help him remember each person who died in those fires." Hyde got up and walked over to the window by the fire escape to look at the sun rising over Boston. "But I'd save my best for the four jakes who died last night."

4

It was a quiet night at Boston Fire Alarm, a respite after the multiple alarm at the Gardner a few nights before.

"Shit." Dave Kennedy checked the numbers on the television screen against his own lottery tickets once more and shook his head in disgust. "Double shit." He leaned his head back and stared at the high ceiling. "And, for the world at large, triple shit."

Leona Blake winked at Vartanian at console number two. "Should I quote you on channel one, Dave?" She made a thing out of fluffing her thick, blond hair. "Sort of...let's see...All stations, Lieutenant Dave Kennedy, Group Two watch commander at Boston Fire Alarm, has just released his opinion on today's lottery numbers – *shit*. That's right, all you nice folks hanging on every word from the nerve center of the Boston Fire Department – *shit*."

Leona pointed at a blinking red light on the board behind Kennedy's command module. "Ahh...action. We'll have to wait a few minutes to reveal Dave's problems to all the department's amateur shrinks."

The familiar hollow beep of an alarm box struck pierced the muted voices of the watch section – twelve two five three four. It once sounded like someone striking the side of a bell, but now it echoed with the hollow electronic sound. The number of the box and the address appeared on the computer screen.

Leona Blake pressed the button that automatically sounded the alarm and activated the lights in the station house assigned to cover that box.

Seconds later, the voice of the duty officer responded to Fire Alarm, "Engine Forty Two, what have you got for us?"

"Alarm box at the corner of Washington and Boylston, near English High," Leona explained. "Just an alarm so far. No phone calls, no anguished citizens yet."

"Forty Two on the way."

Engine 42's progress from that point on would be recorded by the minute on the computer screen and would also later be printed out on a hard copy. Coordination would be turned over from Leona to console three when they arrived at the scene.

Two phones rang almost simultaneously on the enhanced 911 circuit.

"Nine one one," Vartanian answered. "English High? Do you see flames, sir?" After a pause, "Where are you located in relation to the building?" Although he could see the address on his computer screen, he wanted a confirmation before he passed anything on to Engine 42.

Kennedy could hear one of the callers' voices over Vartanian's. "Yes, ma'am. We already have equipment on the way. Can you describe your location in relation to the school?"

Kennedy pressed the speak button on his transmitter. "Engine Forty Two, we have calls from the neighborhood. Fire showing."

"Fire Alarm, this is Forty Two. Roger fire showing. We've just passed the corner of Washington and Green, about one minute to on scene."

Ringing telephones, all of them calls from the English High School neighborhood, were the dominant sound in Fire Alarm. Callers saw flames from a variety of different locations around the gymnasium.

"Fire Alarm, Engine Twenty Eight. That automobile we were sent to investigate on Center Street was abandoned, no plates, no fire. It belonged to the cops all the time. We are close enough and able to divert to English High."

"Roger, Twenty Eight. Ladder Ten and Rescue Two also in transit."

Leo Carmichael struggled out of a restless sleep and picked up the phone receiver on the second ring. "Arson squad, Carmichael." Pause. "Copy English High. Right. On the way." He dropped the phone in the cradle. "Hey, Henry..." Hyde's bedside light was on before Leo finished the sentence. "...English High. Bobbie, Forty Two just struck a second alarm." The Arson Squad automatically responded to every multiple alarm fire.

"Bobbie, isn't that your alma mater? English?" Hyde blinked sleepily as he pulled his sweatshirt over his head. "Don't I remember your smiling face on the front of the *Globe* sports section leading them into the state basketball finals?"

Scott stood up to zip his pants. "Long time ago. Ancient history." He sniffed the air. "Man, Leo, I love that corned beef and cabbage of yours, but I know why you shouldn't cook it often. This room stinks like a skunk's butt."

Carmichael bent over to tie his sneakers. "Naw, it's not the chow. You haven't been around here long enough. That's just standard Henry Hyde. It happens to guys his age, Bobbie. He's rotting from the inside out. He does the same thing with milk and honey."

Hyde lit a cigarette and exhaled. "Fuck you, Leo."

Carmichael winked. "That was a test, Bobbie. Now we know Lieutenant Hyde is fully awake and ready for action. Don't forget your .38, Henry. There may be bad guys about."

"Fuck you, Leo." He turned sideways to display the holstered gun on his hip as he walked out of the room.

"Hey, Carmichael," he shouted from the bathroom, "you driving or do I call a cab?"

"Coming, Lieutenant." Leo was in the hall outside the toilet with the Motorola to his lips. "Roger, K-Six here. We'll take care of K-Seven, Fire Alarm. Hey, Henry, I'll have the car outside and loaded if you make sure Newton's awake. They just struck a third alarm at English and that means there's definitely gonna be some need for photos tonight."

Bobbie Scott had checked their gear in the trunk – helmets, bunker coats, boots, heavy duty lanterns, evidence containers – and was sitting in the back seat when Hyde climbed in up front. The blue bubble light was already rotating on the dash board as Henry snapped on the siren. Leo bulled in front of two taxis racing each other for the corner.

Leo Carmichael knew the streets of Boston. Weaving through traffic, red lights, and stop signs, he got the black car onto Washington Street and slipped in behind a police car racing in the same direction. "Bobbie, this is one of the few times when cops aren't the big pain in the ass they usually are. Use 'em for blocking like this...but never, never tell 'em you're glad they're there."

"That's because they just become bigger pains in the ass," Hyde said, winking back at Bobbie. "Not all of them are bad though. My brother's okay...sometimes."

When they reached the intersection with Green Street, the evening was overwhelmed by flashing lights and screaming sirens. "I didn't know you had a cop in the family, Henry," Scott said.

"Oh yeah," Hyde assured him, "typical Boston Irish family – one cop, one fireman, and one in the slammer. Tradition, Bobbie. And if there's more than one girl in the family, it's a good bet one of them will be a nun."

They were waved past the police road block and Leo pulled over the sidewalk onto the campus grass. Flames licked skyward reflecting pink-orange off rising clouds of smoke and steam. "Lookee there." Leo gestured with his free hand. "Where there's smoke, there's fire, kids. Fully involved."

They donned fire coats, boots, and helmets by the open trunk of the car. "Seems to be just one section of the school," Henry noted.

"That one section just happens to be the gym," Scott said. "Looks like the whole thing's involved."

A white-coated district chief near the command unit called over to Hyde. "Henry, looks like you're going to earn your keep tonight." He walked over to the car. "First guys on the scene reported fire in three separate locations in the gym."

Henry lit a cigarette. "Fires don't usually start that way, now do they, Nick?"

"According to the manual, that's absolutely true. We don't even need you guys to tell us that. But, then again, we're just supposed to put them out. Then we go back to the station and finish a cold meal while you wade through the mess we made."

The chief, still a good friend, had served with Henry on Ladder 2 in East Boston.

"You got it right. The intrepid fire investigators have to crawl through the wet, cold, messy ruins doing cause and origin. Would you consider asking the city to give us a raise, Nick?"

The fire had been weakened enough that flames were now below the roof level. Steam and smoke formed a stinking blanket over the scene. "Not on your life, Henry." He looked over to Carmichael. "How do you work with this guy, Leo? He never gives up conning people."

"That I can live with. What I've been trying to do the last year is teach him how to cook for us occasionally and that, Nick, is a lost cause."

"You must be new with these characters." The chief had just noticed Scott and now he nodded to himself. "But you look familiar – "

"Fort Dudley, Chief," Scott said, "Ladder Four."

The chief smiled. "I remember now. You got a commendation last year for pulling some kid out of a three decker."

"Oh what a breach of etiquette," Hyde said, slapping his forehead dramatically. "I'm so careless. This is District Chief Nick Stokes, Bobbie. Nick, say hello to Bob Scott. I'm teaching him everything I know."

The chief extended his hand. "He's always a wise ass, Bobbie, but you're in great hands. They're going to write books about Henry some day. They just won't be able to quote the language he uses."

The chief pressed the button on the Motorola on his chest and spoke into the transmitter: "I didn't hear your last, Mike." After a pause, he said, "Roger, I'm with them now. We'll meet you over by the east entrance."

He turned to Henry. "Let's go. It's safe to get in through the east side. The deputy chief thinks he's found the origin – or one of them at least."

Bright flood lamps that turned night into day reflected off the soot and debris floating in three inches of liquid scum. Filthy water dripped down from the ceiling where openings had been cut to vent the fire. Smoke and the stench of soaked, charred wood filled the air.

Hyde flashed his light around the space. "Looks like we're in the main part of the gym."

"Basketball court," Scott answered. "I spent four of my best years running up and down here."

"The fire was confined to the gym area," the deputy chief said. "Strangely enough, no other part of the school was touched, even though I suppose someone could have done a lot more damage elsewhere in the building."

"These guys always have their reasons," Hyde muttered. "But I'll never understand why they want to take something from city kids who need it so bad."

He swung his light slowly around the area, pausing occasionally until his beam settled on a single spot at one end of what had been bleachers. He squatted down beside the spot, ran his hand through it, and sniffed his fingers. "This is one point of origin." He pulled on a pair of rubber gloves as he spoke. "Someone didn't seem to give a shit. But why a high school gym?"

He scraped samples from the floor with his pocket knife and placed them in one of the evidence cans Scott had brought with him. "Almost like they wanted to make things easy for us. The lab shouldn't have much trouble confirming an accelerant here."

Carmichael brought the Motorola to his ear at the sound of another alarm and listened to the orders from Fire Alarm. "Busy night," he announced. "Mass General, main building, will be our next stop."

After taking samples from the other sources of origin, Hyde said, "Someone knew what they were doing. They wanted to make sure the place was involved quickly and they weren't overly concerned about hiding it." He smoothed his mustache. "There's someone's name here...I think." He bent down on one knee. "Look at this, Leo. Incendiary used in four different places around each target area. Some sort of chemical, I'll bet...maybe silver nitrate or white phosphorous. How about Thomsen's signature?"

"Willie Thomsen?" Leo squatted down beside Hyde. "I thought he retired after his last stretch." He beckoned to Scott. "Get down here, Bobbie, and look at this. Henry's probably right again."

Scott squatted beside him.

"See how there's four separate hot spots where the igniter started?" Hyde's finger pointed as he spoke. "We haven't seen anything of Willie for a couple of years because he was doing time, plus property's gotten too valuable to torch these days. Willie Thomsen – what's he got against kids?" His blood pressure was rising. "Burning this gym is the kind of shit that puts them back in the streets."

"We assumed he was out of business," Leo added. "But I think that steel trap Henry calls a mind is on to something." He looked up at Hyde. "You got a point, Henry. This smells like Willie's trademark. Get in, set up efficiently so you get the biggest bang for your buck, then get out."

But the arsonist hadn't gotten out.

As Leo was speaking, they overheard a voice over the chief's radio: "Chief, we got a stiff in the locker room."

The body lay near the origin of a less successful fire in the locker room. The condition of the corpse confirmed a concentration of intense heat, but that fire had been terminated by a lack of oxygen in the confined area.

"Let's see what we've got here." Hyde slipped a new pair of plastic gloves over his hands while he studied the corpse. "Leo, get the light down here."

Hyde pried open the blackened victim's mouth with crossed fingers. "Uh huh, uh huh...Bobbie, no time to be squeamish even if you got a weak stomach. Looky here." He pointed an index finger down the victim's throat. "No soot, and it was smoky in here."

Scott peered over Hyde's shoulder. "Gold teeth," he noted bravely. "Haven't seen that many before."

"And you'll never meet Willie Thomsen either. Willie loved those gold teeth." Henry eased around to the other side of the corpse and bent down until his face almost touched the charred floor. Carefully, he twisted Willie Thomsen's head, then asked Leo to shine the light at the base of the skull. There were no burns where the head remained in contact with the floor.

"Bobbie, you're getting a hell of an education tonight. Get your face down here level with mine," Hyde said. "I'm not planning to kiss you. Just take a look at your first murder."

Without moving his hands, and lifting the corpse's head just a bit, he continued, "Shot. You can see the entry wound near my thumb where the skin's puckered. Since the entry point was protected by the floor, the flames didn't touch that, although the blood that escaped did burn up. You know, this M.O. smells too much like those other fires."

Hyde went on to point out a few other facts before he finished. "Now since we have a murder, we have to get the police involved, medical team, all that bullshit, and they get pissed if we mess up the crime scene. So we're just going to leave Willie here. He won't mind."

"Course there is one thing Henry hasn't mentioned yet," Carmichael said.

Scott had risen to his knees and now came slowly to his feet. He looked like he was about to vomit. "What's that?"

"While we are now forever free of one arsonist," Leo said, "there is at least one new one out there scot-free. Maybe more than one. And killing people doesn't seem to be a concern." He winked at Hyde, on his knees, who looked up at Scott and nodded. "Probably wouldn't be upset if we were killed either."

Hyde pushed himself up from a kneeling position and stood with a groan. "Fucking knees." Then he punched Scott playfully in the shoulder and winked back at Carmichael. "Don't sweat it, Bobbie. Fighting fires is a dangerous job. Chasing bad guys is, too. But, none of my guys have been murdered...yet."

Dicky Newton, the group photographer, was leaning against their car. "Guys, just got a call from Fire Alarm about Mass General. That fire was confined to the gift shop and some storage areas and it's been knocked down, but the chief on scene wants us now. Says it wasn't accidental."

"Where you been, Henry, taking a beauty rest?" The deputy chief, a huge black man, was even larger in his white bunker coat, helmet, and boots. "Maybe you wanted us to bring the fire to you?" His booming voice and white-toothed smile were a love letter to everyone in his beloved department.

"If I didn't care for you so much, I'd tell you to go fuck yourself, Wally." Hyde flashed him the finger. "Besides, if you were at all my fires I wouldn't have such a bad attitude."

"Hey, Leo," the chief greeted Carmichael. "See you got one of my brothers with you, gents. Yo, Bobbie, let me know if the old fart gives you a tough time." Then the man's face suddenly became serious and the white teeth disappeared. "Could have had a tragedy here tonight, Henry. No doubt about it being set. What I can't figure out is why a professional would start a fire that he didn't want to spread."

"What makes you say so?"

"Follow me, guys. I'll fill you in on the way."

The chief explained that there were two separate fires. One had been started in the gift shop and one in a storage room next to the store. The strangest part was that the fire alarm had been turned in by hand yet there was no one from the hospital's duty staff who claimed to have activated the alarm.

"Well, this is a new one on me," Hyde said. The doors to both spaces had been forced. It was obvious from the nature of the fires that both had been set. And it seemed that both had been set by someone who not only used sophisticated methods but also made sure that they wouldn't spread. That someone had probably been the one to turn in the alarm. "We got a torch with a heart of gold. I haven't run into one of those recently. Any ideas?"

"That's your job, Henry." The chief flashed a smile that again disappeared as quickly as it appeared. "Fires at Mass General are more than just a problem. The CEO of this place has no sense of humor about anything that affects the operation of his hospital, and even less if any lives are threatened. He's asshole buddies with Mayor Jordan, too. So guess who's going to be all over your ass tomorrow morning."

"Jordan's a nasty little prick. Pisses me off whenever I see his face in the paper." Hyde winked mischievously. "I think I'll tell him that the next time I talk with him."

"That could be in a couple of hours, Henry."

•

It was close to five that morning when Carmichael pulled the car into the Arson Squad garage. "Bobbie and I'll stow the gear, then go around the corner to get some fresh donuts. I'll be up to help with the paperwork in a few minutes, Henry."

Hyde trudged up the stairs slowly. He was tired but it was the type of weariness that keeps you from sleeping. Two fires, one a big loss with a corpse added to it, and one a potential tragedy that for some reason had been alleviated by the instigator. He poured a cup of coffee, took a tentative sip, grimaced, and spit it into the sink.

The phone rang just as he finished preparing a new pot. "Arson, Lieutenant Hyde speaking."

"I'll bet you're not having a good night, Hyde." It was the same clipped, efficient voice. No accent. Not a hell of a lot of expression. "Am I close? Bad start? A couple of days after the Gardner, and two more fires on your watch. One that's going to piss off everybody in the city with kids, especially if another gym is destroyed in the next few days. Bad publicity. Scares people. Puts pressure on the mayor and the commissioner."

"Hey," Hyde growled, "are you getting your rocks off calling me, or – "

"And the other fire. Ooooo...could have been nasty. Just like Rowe's Wharf. Except for one thing, Hyde. There could have been helpless victims at Mass General – the lame, the halt, and the blind. And the fire department would have gotten a lot of blame."

"Why'd you knock off Willy Thomsen?"

"Mr. Thomsen made a serious mistake. He learned who I was." An audible sigh came over the phone. "If you haven't figured it out yet, Hyde, there aren't any bread crumbs leading to my door. I don't leave a trail."

"You will, asshole. I'll find it."

"Well I'm impressed. Imagine someone like you thinking they can find someone like me. Won't happen," the voice concluded sharply. "I'll bet Mayor Jordan's going to be on the phone with Commissioner Duggan early this morning because of Mass General. Then Duggan's going to call your boss, and Chief O'Brien's going to tell you to come up with an answer fast."

Hyde lit a cigarette, resisting the desire to scream at the faceless individual on the other end. Draw him out, Henry. Flakes like to talk.

"Ahh, controlling your famous temper and your dirty, dirty tongue. That's honorable, Hyde, considering your reputation. What are you going to tell Chief O'Brien after he tells you what Mayor Jordan and Commissioner Duggan are saying?"

"I'm going to be a good boy and control my temper and only say nice words," Hyde responded acidly. "What is it you want?"

"I'm not ready to discuss it quite yet because I don't think you understand my powers. You have to fully appreciate what I can accomplish. When I'm ready, Hyde, you'll know it. And when you do, you're going to work with me to make sure I get exactly what I want and that our city doesn't burn to the ground."

Hyde picked a mug out of the sink, rinsed it under the faucet, shook out the water, and poured himself some coffee. After one sip, he made a face and dumped it in the sink.

He could feel their eyes on him, patient. "Okay." He turned around and faced them. "I'm an asshole."

Neither Leo nor Bobbie responded, content to wait.

"Aren't you going to ask me who the love of my life is who keeps calling me?"

"Okay," Leo said. "Who?"

Hyde pulled out a chair and sat down at the table. "Beats the shit out of me," he said with a sigh. "Haven't got a clue ...other than he's fucking up my head."

"How?"

"All these fires. Tells me about them ahead of time." Hyde pointed at Carmichael. "Remember that voice that

— 51 —

came over the radio before we got to the Rowe's Wharf fire – the one shitting on me?"

"Yeah."

"Same guy."

"Why? What's he want?"

"Sounds like money." Hyde closed his eyes and rubbed them with both hands. "But he's killed people. And he doesn't care. I don't know how to find him, but I need your help, both of you."

"You got it," Scott said. "You know that. But..." he shrugged his shoulders in question.

"Leo," Hyde said, "we need to use some of your buddies."

Carmichael rarely mentioned it but his old neighborhood had produced more than its share of the high-end criminal element in Boston. The brighter ones were still in business, underground. And a few of them had been Leo's friends growing up.

"Sure. What?"

"Put something on this phone that'll trace these calls. And we're going to tape everything."

Carmichael nodded. "Yeah. I think I can arrange that. But if any of the guys find out..."

The Arson Squad phone was sometimes used by members on duty calling a girlfriend or a bookie. Their privacy was respected. No one complained. No one said a word. As long as those calls didn't affect their work, it never happened.

"We're not going to tell anyone. Besides the calls only come when I'm on duty. The guy seems to know every move I make. I don't think it's any of our guys, but we'll find out."

Raymond Fairchild listened to the phone ring on the other end – once, twice, three times. He hung up and dialed again.

There was an answer on the first ring.

"Bonjour," a female voice said.

"Let me speak to Jean-Paul."

There was no response.

"What can I do for you this evening?" The voice that came back was deep and rich.

"You can accept my congratulations, Jean-Paul. I'm pleased with your efficiency. You deserve another bonus."

"Merci. I thank you in advance." The man's speech was accented and carried the pleasant sing-song pitch of the islands. "I am ready anytime." Jean-Paul knew other specialists were sometimes used. He wanted more jobs.

"Soon. I'll call you when I'm ready. I just wanted you to know that I'm very pleased and you will be a little bit richer tomorrow."

5

"Raymond, what the fuck is going on?"

Charles Jordan stood by his office window, cordless phone to his ear. It was just after eight in the morning and he was looking down on a City Hall Plaza crowded with people hurrying to work. Yet he saw neither the workers nor the sun that warmed them. However, he had his closest friend – the man who understood Boston as well as anyone in the city – on the phone and he was going to dump his bucket. "Really, what the fuck is going on in this town?"

Raymond Fairchild had anticipated Mayor Jordan's early morning call. "You're no doubt referring to the fires last night, Charles."

Fairchild, in his own office just blocks away looking over the harbor to Logan Airport, was immediately aware that he had control of the conversation. He responded with a practiced voice that was both rich and soothing. His was an inherent charm, a natural precocity that he'd learned to maximize at an early age.

"The cardinal's front man has already been yanking my chain, the old fart's so upset," the mayor continued. "Got me out of the goddamn shower before six thirty. The fucking cardinal!"

Fairchild gave out with a hearty chuckle. "I'm sure His Eminence would prefer you leave off the adjective, Charles."

"When Cardinal McGuire gets pissed," Jordan said, "word travels fast. Hotels and museums don't bother him one way or the other. Basketball courts? Nope. But a hospital? Arson? You know who gets the word next? The media, that's who. And that's because Bigmouth Feeney will leak it to them if I don't make his boss happy super-quick." Monsignor Feeney was chancellor of the Archdiocese of Boston and served as the cardinal's heavy when His Eminence was unhappy.

"My, you really are pissed this morning, Charles. Nasty way to start a sunny day. You're firing slap shots faster than I can knock 'em down. I'll get on the phone with the good cardinal as soon as we're finished here."

Awareness is something that comes upon young people gradually – awareness of self, of family, of home or neighborhood, of peer group. That awareness came to Raymond Fairchild as a young boy. He somehow understood that his ability to charm adults made his control of and leadership over his classmates a simple process. His teachers said he was a born leader. So everything he did from an early age was done according to his own intuitive master plan, a plan that was easily altered at each stage of maturity. But, nevertheless, it was a plan that was uniquely his own. Yet he was wise enough to allow family and authority figures to feel that they were influencing him.

Growing up in a three-decker near Dorchester Heights in South Boston, Fairchild led a pleasant life as a youngster. His father, a lawyer who spent twelve years working his way through college and Portia Law School after World War Two, had never made it in the big-name Boston law firms. He'd worked hard to become the first educated member of his family and resented the patrician requirements to gain access on State Street. He'd opened a storefront office in South Boston and been reasonably successful, but too much of his work was often involuntarily pro bono for Southie residents who paid him with return services rather than cold cash.

His mother remained at home to raise Raymond and his brother and sister, volunteered in their parochial school classrooms, and became an officer in the PTA. There was never a time in elementary school when Raymond wasn't on the high honor roll. And, because he displayed tremendous athletic ability at an early age, his mother and father became hockey parents, often driving him to a city rink for practice long before the sun rose. It was in these early years that he met another hockey player, Charlie Jordan, who lived only a few streets away in South Boston. They became close friends playing on the same junior team, and it was during these early teen years that they learned of each other's ambition to grow beyond their parents' worlds in the rough and tumble Boston political and financial climate.

While Jordan's talents were only good enough to play a lesser brand of high school hockey, Raymond's ability got him into Matignon High School, one of the top hockey powers in the competitive Catholic League, where he became a star. Through scrimmages and interleague games with high schools in the greater Boston area, and even some of the private schools, he established contacts that he would take advantage of in the future. In the process, he learned about and appreciated a world beyond South Boston, a world with more money, more demanding social standards, and sometimes even dress codes where athletes wore coats and ties when their teams travelled. During this growth period, he retained his friendship with Charles Jordan and shared his knowledge of the larger world beyond their tightly knit community.

Raymond, a tough, little bulldog of a hockey player, established himself as an all-scholastic wing in a league known for some of the finest hockey potential outside of the Canadian Junior A teams. In the process of expanding his athletic prowess, he understood, again intuitively, that Bostonians would revere local hockey heroes long after they'd hung up their skates.

Fairchild surprised family and friends when he turned down a scholarship at Boston College, the school chosen for him by his parents, his coach, and the sports media. Instead, he selected Babson, a Division Three college with a powerhouse hockey team. From his own vantage point, his decision was simple and logical. BC was loaded with national talent and he would be one of many. At Babson, he would be a big fish in a small bowl and his name would be in the sports headlines for four years. He broke the division scoring record and Babson was division national champ his final three years.

"You wouldn't sound so goddamn smarmy if you had to answer my phone this morning," Jordan said more quietly.

"I've been compiling a list of names I might call while you've been bitching at me. I'll have the referees on our side and the crowd in the stands calmed down before noon today."

"Sounds good to me," a mollified Jordan agreed. "And will you be kind enough to call me when you've got something?"

"You know I wouldn't let a friend down. I don't want anything messing up your resume when we go for the big one."

Fairchild had already told Jordan that he would someday occupy the corner office under Beacon Hill's golden dome. Mayor Jordan always enjoyed the reference to Governor Jordan.

"Just remember, there won't be a big one if the shouting gets much louder."

"Not to worry, Charles."

Charm, personality, good looks, manners – Raymond Fairchild took full advantage of his advantages. He possessed an unquenchable desire to have the world revolve around him. He understood that money talked, regardless of the means used to acquire it. He relished control over others, especially those who pandered their influence to his wallet. Commercial real estate in a rapidly growing metropolitan area provided a reputable image and a reasonable flow of income. But he created a number of alternative sources, small businesses on the periphery of respectability which allowed a much greater profit.

He reveled in the sheer pleasure of coercing others into following him and accepting his decisions without question. If he failed to charm someone with his overwhelming personality, he did everything in his power to destroy them and then forgot them. It never occurred to him that other people's ideas or reasons for doing something could possibly be better than his own. The world and its pleasures should revolve around him.

"Trust me, my friend."

"You look beat to shit, Henry," said District Chief William O'Brien. "As a matter of fact, you actually look like a piece of shit!"

Unlike his plainclothes investigators, the chief, a gray-haired man with a gentle, Irish face, always dressed in a freshly pressed uniform with a white shirt. His rank was displayed on his collar with polished insignia. He was not a man who needed to reign over the fire investigators in his Arson Squad. He managed certain individuals or shifted responsibilities when pressure became excessive on one man or one duty section, and he kept an eye on their health if he thought they were pushing too hard.

All but a few men in his squad had attended local high schools – Eastie, Charlestown, Roxbury, Southie, Burke, Madison Park, Roslindale, Hyde Park, even a couple from the Catholic schools. They grew up in the era when you graduated directly into the front lines of Vietnam. The survivors had been welcomed back by the fire department and the police department with lifetime jobs that started at forty eight hours a week plus overtime. Those few who qualified for Chief O'Brien's Arson Squad more often than not had served at least twenty years in various engine and ladder companies of the Boston Fire Department. Over those years, if they hadn't encountered almost every individual in the department battling fires side by side, then they'd met during union affairs in Florian Hall.

Chief O'Brien's hands-off policy on his men was management on a higher plane. He was there to support his pros when they needed help.

Henry Hyde lit a cigarette. "Tired, yeah," he finally answered exhaling a deep puff of smoke. "Beat to shit, yeah. A piece of shit, not quite yet. Pissed off, definitely."

"Al Horgan was sitting where you are now when I came in this morning." O'Brien indicated the uncomfortable metal chair Hyde occupied. "Said I should tell Commissioner Duggan or any fucking politician who sticks his nose where it doesn't belong that the major case unit has everything under control. But I should know, Al said, that he's working with Group Two, that Hyde won't be turning over the investigation…" O'Brien paused to knock a cigarette of his own out of the pack on his desk and extended his hand. "Need your lighter."

Henry dropped it in his hand.

O'Brien squinted at the red tip of his cigarette as he took a deep drag. Then he leaned back in his chair and recrossed his legs. "Mayor's all over Commissioner Duggan's ass. Hospital fire scared the shit out of him. Says he wanted to make sure that Horgan had taken over the case. Naturally Duggan said he already was, then gave me a jingle to make sure Al was into it. I said yeah he was."

Hyde grinned a tired grin and crushed his own cigarette. "Yeah, he is."

"Which reminds me," O'Brien said, "I got to make sure you and Jordan are never in the same room together. That interview a few days ago with Nomi Cram!" He fixed Hyde with a sad expression. "Do you get pleasure out of upstaging our city's leader?"

Hyde's eyes lit up. "Wasn't that great? I didn't plan it like that. The asshole fell right into it making those stupid statements. Nomi just led me down the path."

O'Brien shook his head. "Al loved it, too. Says he's going to nominate you for an Oscar. I told him I'm not going to let you do that again. And that's an order." But his expression began to crack when he tried to glare at Hyde.

"You mean you don't want me to call the mayor an asshole on live television?"

O'Brien snickered. "Oh stuff it, Henry. I'm trying to be serious. The mayor blames you for what happened to his kid, so you make damn sure you avoid him. Okay, next," he continued without looking up. "Al says you got a real mad on about what's happening with these fires. More than normal. So what do you know that you're not telling me or Al?"

Hyde was the picture of innocence. He pulled another cigarette from his pack and rolled it in his fingers, studying it carefully. "You know me, Chief. I don't talk unless I have something to say."

Hyde knew the chief, not to mention Al Horgan, would be bullshit if either one knew he'd kept quiet about those phone calls. For that matter, Fire Alarm recorded everything on the net and no one there had questioned that random transmission. It was odd how people forgot things like that in the middle of chaos.

"If you say so." The chief paused, looked at the cigarette Hyde was still rolling in his fingers, and took out another one of his own. "Fire, please," he said, sticking it in his mouth and tapping the end.

Hyde lit both. "Why you asking?"

"Al says you usually don't take fires so personally."

"Not until I see firefighters killed." Hyde shrugged. "I'll lighten up."

He didn't want to say that Leo Carmichael had contacted one of his less-than-savory buddies to arrange some wire taps on the unit's incoming lines. It would be hell to pay if any of the guys in the watch sections found out.

He knew that sooner or later he'd have to swallow his pride and come clean on those calls. It was just a matter of how to explain why he'd kept quiet.

•

Normal approach routes to Fenway Park were jammed. While Hyde fumed at the delay from the front passenger seat, Bobbie Scott switched channels on the radio trying to figure a path.

"Mass Ave's a bottleneck, Leo," Scott said. "Cops're are turning everyone at Huntington, but from there to Comm Ave's still a nightmare."

"How about the Fenway?"

"Jammed. College students are climbing over cars to go watch the fire. Carrying cases of beer with 'em."

Hyde was unable to contain himself. "God fuckin' damn it, Scott, I'm going to send you back to Fort Dudley if you don't find us a way..." But Scott cut him short.

They were at the corner of Ruggles and Huntington. "Cut down through the medical schools to Riverway, Leo, then swing back on Brookline."

"If I can get across Huntington," Carmichael sputtered.

The intersection was jammed with vehicles from both directions. Horns blared. Irate drivers screamed obscene threats at each other. Nothing moved.

"I'll get us the fuck across," Hyde snapped. "Pop the trunk, Leo. Get your ass out and give me a hand, Bobbie," he said as he climbed out of the car. The blue light was already flashing on the dashboard. "And scare the shit out of everybody with that siren, Leo."

Hyde took two helmets from the trunk, handed one to Scott, and plopped the other on his head. "Now we're going to play cops. Grab that big spotlight, Bobbie. We're going to teach these assholes how to drive."

In less than thirty seconds, with Leo's siren screaming, the blue light flashing, and Scott following his lead, Hyde had directed cars onto the sidewalk and backed others up bumper to bumper so that the ancient, black Arson Squad vehicle could squirm across Huntington.

Carmichael cut through streets and parking lots in the medical complex, dodged his way to the Riverway, then zipped through lighter traffic to the fire scene.

Smoke and steam rose through the glare of searchlights, blunting the dying red glow from Fenway Park's smoldering luxury box section. Ladder 15 and Ladder 26 were propped against the roof of the venerable baseball park. Engines 33 and 37 were pouring water up into smoking ruins. The water, filthy with dirt and soot, ran down through the broadcast booths and media boxes carrying dead Fenway rats into the grandstand.

Two chiefs were obvious in their white coats, but the one who stood out in the crowd of firefighters was Commissioner Duggan. His sharp features were outlined by the glare of bright television lights. He spoke into half a dozen microphones held out in his direction, but he broke away when he saw Henry Hyde lurking in the background.

Duggan draped an arm around Hyde's shoulders and eased him away from the media crush. "It's a clear case of arson again. Fucking arson!" he added with a snarl. "I've heard about three separate origins already and those reporters have already got wind of the same thing. It's going to be all over the eleven o'clock news and that means the mayor's going to be back on my ass."

Hyde grinned nastily. "Which means mine isn't worth shit, right?"

Duggan patted Hyde gently on the fanny. "You got that one right. I love your ass, Henry, but I'm going to be all over it if I can't give these flacks something solid." His expressive, black eyes reflected the flashing red lights of the fire trucks. "You can screw with just about anything in this city but the Sox, no matter how bad they are. Guess who's going to be crucified if you don't come up with something super fucking quick."

Fairchild struggled half-heartedly to control the grin spreading across his face. Dottie would be pissed if she opened her eyes and saw it again – a smirk, a dirty smirk she'd called it last time. He was lying on his back, pillows puffed under his head, and Dottie was riding on top of him. Her back was arched, her hands on either side of his knees for support. Long blond hair cascaded off her shoulders. Her lips were pulled back, her even, white teeth grinding. But what he got the biggest boot out of was how her ample breasts bounced.

"Ummm..." Her eyes scrunched tighter.

Fairchild licked his lips in an effort to wipe the amused grin from his face. Imagine actually being able to live your youthful fantasies! He studied her facial and bodily indicators as her pleasure increased. He'd have to get this on tape sometime. Call it *Women's Climatic Indicators,* sell it through womens' magazines. Stress how he could get a woman off better than any other man. Now wouldn't that bring them to his door! You'll have to get in line, ladies. No pushing or fighting now. I'll be happy to service each one of you. Oh shit! He could feel the grin returning.

Dottie leaned forward placing her hands just above his shoulders and increased her speed. With her eyes still shut, she whispered. "Come on, lover, time for you to get your hips in motion. I'm about to blast off for the moon."

Just at the moment, Fairchild happened to catch the flash of the digital numbers on the bedside clock changing – 11PM! He reached for the remote he'd placed just under the pillow and pressed the POWER button. Nicki Adams' attractive face swam into view on the big screen. "Good evening. This is Nicki Adams with the late news. We're going to switch directly to Bob Douglas live on Yawkey Way just outside Fenway Park where a multiple alarm fire has just been brought under control."

"You prick, Raymond, you no-good prick!" Dottie pounded on Fairchild's chest. "Why?...I was just about – "

"Sorry, honey, this is important." His eyes were fixed on the screen. "We can finish it up while we watch."

"Thank you, Nicki, I have with me here Fire Commissioner Frank Duggan, who can explain how his men were able to save so much of this venerable, old ballpark, one of Boston's world famous drawing cards."

Duggan's bright eyes were hard as he looked into the camera. "There's more damage than we would have liked, Bob, but we were able to save the luxury boxes and I'm told by management that they're already putting together plans that should have the Sox playing in Fenway by the time they get back to town."

"No!" That was the only word out of Fairchild's mouth as he twisted from underneath Dorothy Murray.

"Aren't we going to finish?" she wailed as Fairchild pressed the UP button to increase the volume as Commissioner Duggan spoke.

"You know I always give you the best fuck you ever had," he said without turning from the screen. "Just lie there and I'll finish you in a moment."

Raymond Fairchild was never one to comprehend human emotions. Life was a series of actions, almost all winnable. Human feelings were a totally foreign concept.

And then I'll finish that son of a bitch Grady for blowing the job.

6

"I wanted the owners' suites. When I say I want something, I mean..." Raymond Fairchild paused for effect and to allow his tone to rise slightly. "I mean I wanted them. I explained that. I was very clear."

He knew shortly after he turned off the late news that he should have left Fenway in the black man's hands. Jean-Paul didn't make mistakes.

"But..."

"You disobeyed me." Fairchild's voice mimicked the resonance of the Marine officer he'd been for a few years after college. He was one of those who never experienced combat but always gave the impression that he'd been there. "Leaving those suites intact may possibly make it look to the fire investigators like a friend of the owners might have been doing them a favor, and I don't want anyone coming around asking questions."

"Fenway's never empty, you know," Grady protested. "Just because there ain't no game being played don't mean there's no security. Jeez, do you think a guy can just walk in like jack shit and..."

"Shut up!" Fairchild's voice cracked like a whip. "I've never accepted excuses before and I'm not about to start taking any now."

"Shit, Mr. Fairchild, if I'd got near the owners' suites, I'd of gotten grabbed by the security people. They was having a party of their own in one of them suites while them mucky-mucks were on the road with the team. You saw for yourself on TV how much damage there was."

With just two words – Mr. Fairchild – two words spoken without thinking, Martin Grady had just assured two people of an early death – himself and the intermediary who'd paid him off.

Fairchild had never mentioned his own name, nor was his name ever to be used by those few who coordinated assignments for him. That was how Fairchild operated. If someone was well paid, there was no need to know the source of the money.

From now on, everything would be in Jean-Paul's hands.

There wasn't a pol in Boston more self-conscious about his image than Mayor Charles Jordan. His perception of himself mandated a perfectly cool image at all times. His unique sense of self-confidence, he assumed, was reserved for men in his lofty position to display just for the two women sitting across from him.

From the vantage point of Nicki Adams and Nomi Cram waiting patiently on the opposite side of his desk, the man was remarkably calm considering the proposition they'd just laid before him.

"That's right, sir," Nicki said with a smile. "Hermie feels this story should get national media attention. It could be super promotion for you and the city."

The general manager of Channel Seven, Herman Neubauer, had made the decision that morning to do a fifteen minute segment, the first time a full half of *Eye on Boston* would be devoted to a single story.

"There's a growing fear around the city about this arson wave," Nicki said. "We believe people are as terrified with fire now as when early man first discovered it. Fire is pain. Fire is disfigurement. Fire is at the heart of man's greatest fears."

"And Hermie feels the right words from you could help keep things calm," Nomi added. She leaned forward enthusiastically. "An interview right here." She slapped her hand on his desk. "With the man in charge. Boston needs to know how you're marshalling your forces to get to the bottom of this."

Jordan's media director, Dennis Campbell, had been quiet, but now he could sense a media coup here if everything were coordinated properly. "We, of course, want to mitigate the city's fear. How much time do we have to prepare?"

"I hope that's not a problem," Nomi answered. "We're already out of time. We have to do the interviews later today. Hermie will edit them tonight. We'll pull together anything questionable tomorrow. Showtime at seven PM tomorrow night."

"Not enough time," Campbell responded firmly.

"There's something you're missing here," Nicki answered. "This project belongs to Hermie. It belongs to the station. It belongs to Boston. We don't want the Mayor giving a canned speech. That's what the people hate." She smiled at Jordan. "He's most natural on an interview" – if he's not choking on his words, Nomi thought to herself – "looking out at each viewer and inspiring confidence."

"Nicki's right," Jordan agreed. "As long as you do the interview, Nicki." He turned quickly to Nomi Cram. "No offense intended, of course, Nomi. I just think Nicki draws me out better than anyone else in the city. So," he said with a smile, "now that we have that settled, who else are you interviewing?"

"Well," Nicki answered, "it's got to be mostly people at the top – police, fire, city council, some of the people who've experienced these fires, and, of course, the Arson Squad." She shrugged. "I can't tell you exactly who until after Hermie edits the tapes. We'll probably have a couple of hours of stuff that he has to boil down to fifteen minutes."

"Arson!" Jordan pursed his lips. "Who in arson?"

"Higher ups again," Nomi answered. She remembered Jordan's face from the other night when Henry Hyde had countered almost everything the mayor had said. "Probably Chief O'Brien. Maybe Al Horgan."

"Not that guy, Hyde."

It was Nomi's turn to shrug. "Depends on who Hermie wants or who the commissioner suggests. Never can tell."

That was when Mayor Jordan was unable to control his body language for the first time since the women entered his office. He squirmed.

"Want to have some fun, Henry?" Nomi Cram's voice drifted over the phone with a lilt that was simultaneously prankish and suggestive.

"Depends what you have in mind, Nomi."

When she'd called to suggest lunch, Hyde explained he only had time for a quick snack and she agreed to meet him at Sullivan's at Castle Island Park at noon. They bought hot dogs and root beer and carried their lunch out to the fish pier to watch the ships in Boston Harbor. All the park benches were full.

"Someone'll get up in a minute," Hyde said. "Somehow they always do when I arrive. Must be my intimidating countenance."

"Okay then, to your intimidating countenance." Nomi raised her root beer in toast. "How about to us, too."

Hyde raised his eyebrows and glanced curiously at her. "Okay. To us." Then he turned back to watch a bright red tugboat bump softly up against the hull of an inbound freighter. "You're sure this is a business lunch? Something I can deduct from my taxes?"

Nomi watched until the tug snuggled in and matched the ship's speed. "How about yanking Jordan's tail?" she finally asked.

"I'm a career employee of the City of Boston and a member of Boston Firefighters Local 718. I'm supposed to be loyal to whomever carries the title of Hizhonor." Hyde waited until the roar of a plane climbing from Logan Airport on the opposite side of the harbor diminished. "But our good mayor – I'm game."

A young couple got up from one of the park benches and passed in front of them hand in hand.

"See what I said. They're intimidated."

"Nice," Nomi said nodding toward the couple. "I like that." She put a hand on Hyde's back and directed him toward the vacant space. "Young love. Very nice." They sat down. "Remember when?"

"Yeah. Me, maybe. At least on those days when the memory's workin'. But you're the spring chicken. You've still got the time to do rather than just try to remember."

She squeezed his knee playfully. "You say the nicest things when you're exhausted, Henry." She giggled when he raised his eyebrows. "That's what attracts me to older men. But later for that. Back to Hizhonor. We're doing a major segment tomorrow night on *Eye on Boston* – fifteen minutes – and we need some insightful comments from the Arson Squad."

"O'Brien. He's the big cheese." Without turning his head, Hyde glanced at her out of the corner of his eye, then looked down at the hand that was still on his knee. "Not me. Why not Al Horgan? Al looks good on TV. Makes the squad look good, too."

Nomi squeezed his knee for emphasis. "You ought to be our main man. Nicki and I are going to hit the high spots. Duggan, O'Brien, Horgan – sounds like the Irish mafia," she said. "There's something going on with these fires that no one's saying. People are worried. The mayor's pissed. And you guys aren't talking. You know something and you're clamming up." She took her hand off his knee, turned her head in his direction, and waited until he was looking her square in the eyes. "I can see it in your eyes."

"You got a wild imagination, Nomi," he said.

"Nope. I can see it," she said with a nod. "There's something in the back of Henry Hyde's eyes that should scare the shit out of me. That's what I'm after."

Hyde put his root beer down on the bench and smoothed his mustache. "You're digging for something that isn't there, Nomi."

"I can see it, Henry."

"Then don't dig." He popped the remainder of the hot dog in his mouth and turned back to Boston Harbor. "Please."

Nomi said nothing. She finished her own hot dog and placed her cup inside the empty one that Hyde still held in his hands. "Good chow. How about if we do lunch like this more often?"

"I'd like that." His eyes remained fixed on a 747 dropping gracefully across the harbor toward Logan. "I'd like it more if we didn't talk business."

"Okay. Just hot dogs and root beer and small talk. I'd like that, too."

Hyde stood up and extended his hand. "Come on. Time for us both to head back to work." He pointed towards the harbor islands. "But let's take the long way."

They paused by the Korean War Memorial erected by the people of South Boston. The marble infantryman stared sightlessly toward Fort Independence rising behind them. There were brightly colored flowers surrounding the stone listing the names of the South Boston men who had died on that peninsula on the other side of the world.

Nomi counted the names on the stone. "I wasn't even born then," she murmured softly. "That's a lot of boys from a small part of Boston."

"There always are," Hyde said. "Ours was Vietnam. There's a memorial over on Broadway with a lot of names of Southie guys who bought the farm there." His eyes were fixed on something beyond the harbor islands.

"You knew some of them..." Nomi's voice drifted with the breeze. "...in Vietnam, I mean."

"You mean like guys I cut class with? Played football with? Chased girls with?" The harbor islands seemed to blend with each other. "Yeah, yeah...."

She locked her arm in Hyde's and turned down the sidewalk. "Come on, my friend. You've got enough to think about as it is."

He patted her hand and they walked arm-in-arm for a while before he steered them over to the firemen's statue at the far end of the park, freeing his arm as they stopped. "I'm fine now. Just got to pay my respects whenever I'm here."

They read the simple inscription on the Greene Memorial, Hyde for perhaps the hundredth time, for a firefighter who'd died in the line of duty.

Before they headed for the parking lot, Hyde stopped by the phone booth outside of Sullivan's to check his messages.

Nicki caught an unpleasantness in his eyes as he returned. "Problems?"

"Probably not." Then added, "I'll know better tonight."

As they strolled back to their cars, she put her arm through his again. "Small talk is a nice thing, Henry, gets a load off your mind sometimes. I think you could use some."

She stopped and waited until he was looking down at her. "I want to get to know Henry Hyde even better than I think I do."

She was rewarded by a softening in those eyes that always seemed to broadcast what was going through his mind.

He was going to say something smart like he usually did when someone expected him to be serious – maybe how his ex only wanted to know when his paycheck was due – but thought better of it. He squeezed her hand but let go quickly. "I'd like that, Nomi."

Hyde glanced at his watch as he locked the car door. A few minutes early. Was he going to meet that voice on the other end of the phone? The call had been short – no banter – just said that he could help himself by showing up at the Sports Depot at five thirty.

Hyde would always be a firefighter at heart. So it was only natural that he paused to analyze the building from the outside. It was an old New England railroad depot, ancient, steam-cleaned red and gray granite block on the outside, large windows, steep slate roof. The plaque by the front door said it was the Allston Depot built in 1887.

The entrance was a bastardized Georgian portico that had once extended well out from the building so passengers alighting from horse-drawn carriages could remain dry. Now a long red awning extended from the roof and a long, green Fenway Park style scoreboard covered much of the wall to the right. The Sports Depot was an Americanized version of an Irish pub. The current groupie drinking set in Boston satisfied their fantasies in such places.

It was anything but old New England on the other side of the center-entrance swinging doors. Hyde was struck by an avalanche of sound as he stepped inside. Too-close tables on both sides of the entrance were filled with customers whose clothing ranged from young single downtown types in designer outfits to college students in grunge. The din seemed to indicate they must all have been talking at once.

Hyde surveyed the room, lighted exits first. The beams supporting the high ceiling were festooned with tiny, white Christmas lights. Smoke from the main bar and smoking section near the bar drifted up through the fans hanging from the high-peaked ceiling. Television screens – there must have been thirty of them – were suspended about twelve feet high around the room. Most were tuned to different channels, although a few carried the same baseball game. But nobody seemed to be watching. Nothing could be heard above the din anyway. This was what Orwell must have envisioned, Henry thought.

Hyde decided he was too old for places like the Sports Depot. This was a drinking spot where people wanted to be noticed. He had no reason he could think of to see or be seen. Thank God his drinking habits had changed. Whenever he had spare time, his objective was peace and quiet.

A wooden bar, simulated to look antique, with a shiny brass rail snaked across the left side of the room. Hyde climbed onto a stool on the bar's left end. There were three bartenders, each of them with handle-bar mustaches, long-sleeved white shirts, red suspenders, and old-fashioned wide ties. He looked up at half a dozen TV screens, each tuned to a different channel, and shuddered. It was impossible to hear what was going on with any of them anyway.

"What'll it be?" one of the bartenders asked as he slapped a cocktail napkin down.

"Beer. Any draught?" He'd sip.

The bartender pointed to a collection of six long handled taps, each with the name and logo of an imported beer. "Nothin' but the best."

"The Irish one," Hyde said.

As the bartender was placing the pint mug on the napkin, Hyde sensed someone mounting the stool beside him.

"I'll have the same." The voice was deep with the soft lilt of the Caribbean.

Hyde turned slightly. He would never be able to describe the man as he looked up at him outside of his being very black and obviously very tall. A rather obvious hair piece of tight, curly, white hair looked out of place over a young, high-cheeked, smooth face. Reflecting dark glasses and a white mustache completed the disguise. The sleeves of his Harvard sweat shirt were cut off at the shoulder blades revealing muscular arms.

"You win. I couldn't identify you in a crowd of one."

"You're Hyde?"

"That's me."

"Let me see your shield."

Hyde hesitated. "Please?"

"I know you always carry it." The man's voice remained soft, the island touch still there. "Please." But the tone left no doubt he wanted proof.

Hyde showed his ID. "What do you carry?"

"Nothing, my man. I'm the one who shall remain a mystery."

"The first mystery is why you're wearing that white rug. Looks real bad, believe me." Hyde took a swallow of beer. "So you know everything about me and I'm stuck with someone who doesn't exist."

"Mr. Hyde, let's godown to the business I was sent here to conduct with you. It doesn't matter what I look like. We don't need preliminaries. And we don't need to discuss what has hoppen in the city up to now." Sometimes he seemed to use his accent to attract Hyde's attention, and sometimes there was barely a trace of it. It seemed a tactic to be turned on and off at will. This was not the guy on the phone. "I'm to tell you that you should be concerned with what might happen in the future if you don't cooperate fully. Do we understand ourselves, my man?"

Hyde stared hard at the face. The mustache was as phony as the hair. The dark glasses were so big, Hyde could see his reflection in them. There were no scars or special features in the black, impassive face. "I am not your fucking man."

Brilliant white teeth flashed in a venomous smile. "You will be anything we want you to be, Hyde. But because I like people like you, I'll accede to your ego. You are not my fucking man. Now let me be straight with you. The first thing you should know is why you have been selected." The white teeth gleamed momentarily. "First, you present our boss with the ultimate challenge. He believes you are the only man who could possibly stop him from destroying the city. That is, if he decides to."

Hyde drained half his mug. "I don't fucking believe this. This wacko sends you here to…"

"Please, our time really is limited," the man said glancing at a large, shiny, gold watch. "I be doing the talking. Secondly, it is well known within the tight group in City Hall that you and Mayor Jordan hate each other's guts because you sent up his son."

"I didn't send up that prick's son. I found the help for him that the kid couldn't find at home."

"It doesn't matter. You and Mayor Jordan will eventually enjoy each other's company."

Hyde knocked out a cigarette and lit it. "This oughtta be good."

"You see, absolutely no one would expect that Lieutenant Henry Hyde would become the mayor's bag man when Jordan raises half a billion dollars to save his dear city."

"Half a fuckin billion dollars." Hyde made a face as if he was sniffing the air. "Hey, what's a half a billion among friends? Easy come, easy go – right?" He stared into the reflecting glasses as if he could see through them. "You are in as much need of a lobotomy as the guy who's been calling me." Hyde sipped his beer, then pushed it away. "Tell you what. Since some of the good folk who work for your so-called boss end up very dead, why don't you become a free agent. Switch sides. You help me out and I'll make sure you get back to your island, wherever it is, with no hassle from Immigration. No one will ever know what happened. You'll probably have enough cash so you can start ripping off whitey."

"So far you fit everything I've heard about you, Mr. Hyde." The white teeth gleamed for a moment, but the man shook his head. "I guess you really aren't moved by money. I am." Teeth again. "Neither you, nor Mayor Jordan, nor anyone either of you know, can comprehend what people are willing to do for large sums of money. Believe me, there is nothing you can say to me." He eyed the gold watch again. "Now you will be patient and listen. Do we understand each other so far?"

Hyde slid off the stool. "People like you make me want to take a leak. Be right back."

"No, Hyde." The black man's voice was sharp but still low enough not to be overheard above the din. He had an iron grip on Hyde's upper arm. "Sit back down, my man" – he emphasized my man – "or I won't be here when you get back. And your fucking city will continue to burn, and you along with it."

Hyde looked at the fingers wrapped around his arm, looked into the reflecting glasses, then shook a finger as if he was scolding a naughty boy.

The hand released him.

Hyde climbed back up on the stool. "I'm still not your fucking man."

"As long as you realize that I am younger than you, faster than you, and stronger than you."

"I just had to take a leak."

"I don't want you to talk to a friend there. I don't want you to use a phone. You will spend just a few more moments listening to me."

"Go ahead."

The black man glanced at the big clock behind the bar. "Since you are a hard man to talk to, you are going to have to learn by example. You're resistant. I said it would take more before you'd fall into place and unfortunately for some innocent people, I was right."

"Listen, you and I are never going to consummate this affair. Why don't you call your boss and tell him I'll meet him anywhere, anytime. Does he have the brains – or the balls – to do that?" Hyde pulled some change from his pocket. "Here, I got a quarter. Let's give him a jingle and..."

The man shook his head. "We're getting nowhere, and we're running out of time. I have no idea who he be, Mr. Hyde. I've never met him. I've been told I never want to, and I agree wholeheartedly with that. But I am absolutely positive he'll achieve whatever he sets out to do. When you think back, remember that you were the one who wasted this meeting."

"Oh?"

The man slid off the stool. "Don't move from your place for a few minutes, Mr. Hyde. Perhaps you should have another beer, maybe a burger. I don't want you to get hurt. Oh, and the beer is on me." He was three or four steps away when he said over his shoulder, "You'll see how serious we are in a moment or so."

Hyde glanced down at the bar and saw a crisp hundred dollar bill tucked beneath the other mug. Looking over his shoulder, he saw a bushy white head ducking through the crowd and out the door.

He took another mouthful of beer, decided there was no need to finish it, and climbed off the stool. What did he mean? *You'll see how serious we are.* He was half way to the men's room at the far end of the Sports Depot when the hallway to the rest rooms was suddenly engulfed in fire. Raging tendrils of flame licked into the main room carrying shards of glass and splinters of wood as the fire exploded outward.

The two closest tables were engulfed in flame before anyone could react. An invisible canopy of heat burst across the broad, high-ceilinged room driving customers onto the floor. In seconds, they were scrambling for the front door and an emergency exit. The wail of smoke alarms added new urgency to the pandemonium. Sprinklers activated by the sudden heat gushed down on top of the terrified crush.

Hyde stayed low until the heat rose, then scrambled toward the far wall to avoid the crush. Instinct had taken over. There was no way he could ignore the flailing, burning bodies at the last two tables. Grabbing a jacket from the back of a chair, he smothered the burning clothes and hair on a girl rolling toward him. A second stumbled blindly in circles, a burning sweater melting into her flesh. Hyde whipped an arm across her ankles. She fell on top of him, screaming in agony. He tore off the remains of her clothes with his bare hands.

None of the four others was moving. Hyde knew from experience that you either survived a blast of flame like that in the initial seconds – by sheer luck – or you were dead. Hyde turned away from the corpses. Give the living a chance.

The girl with the melting sweater was sitting upright, naked, charred, mouth open, eyes staring sightlessly in disbelief. The other was crawling blindly toward the door bumbling into overturned furniture.

As Ladder 14's Lt. Mezey came low through the front entrance of the Sports Depot to evaluate the fire scene, his first image was of a man outlined by flames stumbling toward him. A naked woman was draped over his shoulder and he was struggling with a second under his arm. His blackened face was streaked with tears streaming from smoke-reddened eyes. Only after Mezey took one of the women did he recognize that the man was Henry Hyde, the officer who'd taken him under his wing on his first ladder truck

Outside, Hyde allowed the EMTs to take charge of the victims. Then he sank to his knees. Hands on his hips, he threw back his head and sucked in deep breaths of fresh air. Mezey saw his lips moving but heard no sound. He kneeled down beside Hyde. "What'd you say, Henry?"

"I'm going to find that fucker," Hyde said hoarsely, blackened mucous coating his mustache. "And when I do, I'm going to take him away by myself. He's going to be all mine." Red eyes stared deep into Mezey's. His voice was a whisper. "He's going to die very slowly."

Later that night, as Lt. Mezey lay on his bunk back in the fire station, he was unable to shake that look of Hyde's. He had never before seen hatred like that in a man's eyes.

7

The commissioner's office in Boston Fire Department Headquarters was plain, no nonsense, just like the commissioner himself – freshly painted white walls, photographs of himself with the right people, Dicky Newton's action photos of Boston fires, and flags. But there was one non-traditional aspect to Commissioner Duggan's office – golf clubs. His driver and aide made sure that their firefighting gear was always neatly laid out in the trunk of the official vehicle, which left no space for the commissioner's passion. So his golf clubs were always right by the office door, neatly polished golf shoes with ankle socks beside the bag, and a fresh outfit on a hanger above them in case anyone called him to play. Anywhere, anytime was his motto. There were even times when his aide had actually driven across fairways to pick up his boss for a multi-alarm fire.

Frank Duggan had made his desires absolutely clear to his secretary today. "No visitors. No calls. Not the mayor or any of his people. Not even the governor."

The governor had called twice in the past few days from his Beacon Hill office, the second time to explain that he was lending the State Police arson specialist to assist. Although Duggan had wanted to say he didn't want that asshole involved, he knew enough never to antagonize the governor.

"Okay, gentlemen, we're alone." Duggan leaned back in his chair and rested his feet on the corner of his desk. "No one to bother us. Everyone in this room is on equal footing. Say what you want, not what you think I want to hear." His eyes met Hyde's. "And, Henry, even though you kept that shit to yourself, you're my hero more than ever now. Does that make you feel good?"

"So I should've gotten in bed with you earlier," Hyde said.

Duggan allowed a slight grin, but his dark eyebrows peaked as he made his point. "When I see those pictures of you in the paper with those baggy eyes and cherubic jowls, I always say to myself, *What a great natural disguise.* Underneath that friendly St. Bernard look lies the toughest son of a bitch in the Arson Squad. And this morning when Chief O'Brien called me," – the characteristic grin was gone – "I realized you were so tough you were planning to get your man all by yourself." His voice rose emphatically with the final three words.

"I don't know who he is." Hyde was exhausted, in no mood for a chewing out. He sat back and held the commissioner's stare.

"I'm sure you don't. And I'm not going to get in a pissing contest with you. The only way we're going to find your man is to work together. All of us. You and your guys are still on the case like you were before you came in here. But from this moment on we're going to share all our information."

Hyde realized Duggan was waiting for a response. "Right."

"You're being used by a nutcase, a certified wack job who doesn't mind killing people. Probably has bundles of money since the cost of hitmen has gone up considerably these days. This is not your normal, run-of-the-mill arsonist like Willy Thomsen or Marty Grady."

"He killed them...or had them killed."

"That's right. Cold blood, too. And we don't know why he killed them. They were apparently doing a good job for him. He's also yanking your chain for some reason, but you're still alive. So we're going to let him continue to use you."

"That's why the city pays me the big bucks." After speaking, Hyde didn't know why he had to come up with a wise response to Duggan. The commissioner had always treated him well.

"That's correct, Henry. There's no other option. You and Leo and Bobbie are going to continue to operate together. Horgan's also going to work with you even though you told him you wanted this by yourself. After all, he is the department's major case investigator and this is a major case." Duggan wrinkled his forehead and tilted his head slightly as if he wondered if he was making his point.

Another answer was expected. "Yes, sir." Hyde nodded but held the commissioner's eyes. He was damned if he was going to be intimidated at this point.

"I'm shitting on you, Henry. But I'm also not shitting on you. You waited too long to tell someone the pressure you were under. I'm handing you shit because you were going to be a martyr. Martyrs don't work for me. You're not alone. No one's going to dump on your head. Plus you've already started to profile this nut, so how can I shit on you?" Duggan dabbed at an invisible spot on his cheek. "Tell me and everybody else what you have, even though we all know some of what you've got."

Hyde looked at his fingernails, then glanced quickly at the faces around the table – Duggan, Chief O'Brien, Horgan, Bobbie Scott, Leo Carmichael – then drummed his fingers on the hard surface. "Screw figuring out the fires," he said gruffly. "They were good ones. There's going to be more. Good ones. It might look like there isn't a pattern – a hotel, a school, Mass General, Fenway Park, the Gardner, the Sports Depot. But there's definitely a pattern, at least to me. Landmarks. He's destroying Boston's visible landmarks – old, new, culture, sports. He's got the public's attention."

"And he hasn't said a thing," Chief O'Brien stated. "No statements. No threats. No ransom. What? What's he want?"

"He told me he's coming to the specifics," Hyde said. "Soon, I hope."

"What's he going to do, torch the whole city first?" Duggan asked.

"He hasn't told me," Hyde said wearily. "He's made the point that he's in control, and we better believe that." He considered telling Duggan that the guy said that he – Henry Hyde – was going to work with the mayor to raise half a billion big ones to save the city. No, not yet. Better idea to wait on that one. "Let's face it. We're dealing with an exceptionally bright individual. He uses people. Thomsen and Grady are dead. We haven't figured out the one at the Gardner yet. From out of town, I guess. I may be a toy but at least I'm alive. He used them and for some reason knocked them off. The black guy made it clear he could have done me, if he wanted to. Said I was going to deliver the city, but he didn't tell me how. Then boom!"

"Boom is right," Duggan said.

Hyde nodded. "The voice doesn't get his hands dirty. Willy Thomsen was an expert at his trade. Grady, too. They mostly used gasoline. Who knows why he had them killed. But he's got other pros. Twice he's used magnesium. There aren't any guys I know around Boston using that stuff now. That means pros from out of town, like the black guy."

"Your voice is a twisted mother," Horgan muttered.

"Twisted maybe, but one really bright son of a bitch. He knows what's precious to us so he's been around the city for a long time. The only fire he's been at was the first one, the hotel. I've looked at Dicky Newton's photos of crowds at all the fires and no face stands out. He's still one step ahead of us."

"Even with hints," the chief said, "yanking our chain."

"One of Leo's buddies helped me tape and trace his calls but all we got was a pay phone down by the harbor.

Why there? Don't know," he answered himself. "And then there's the way he talks. No hard Boston accent, not what we're accustomed to anyway. You can tell where someone comes from around here – Southie, Chelsea, Brookline, white or black, public school or private school. Leo, play the tapes. It's almost like he's playing a game with his voice and accent, trying to throw us off."

They listened.

"So you see what I mean," Hyde said. "No hard accent. That could mean our man is probably educated and knows how to throw us off. Maybe he didn't go to a city school, but I don't think he went anywhere real fancy either. Nothing preppy in the way he talks, like our beloved governor."

"You've got so much in that head of yours, Henry, I want you to get everything down on paper. Sit down with your section guys. Each of you make a profile. Then compare. Every time something new comes up, add it on."

Hyde smiled nastily. "If our man decides to take me out, at least you've got my brain on paper. Right?"

"Right," Duggan said. "And there's something else you guys are going to have to get used to." He retrieved a box from under his desk and opened it. "Help yourselves."

Hyde reached in and came up with a cell phone. "The department's getting fancy. Didn't know these were in the budget."

"Neither does the mayor," Duggan said. "There's one for each of you and everyone's assigned number is on the back. Learn how to use them."

Carolina Fairchild shook her wet head angrily as she shrugged the bath towel to the dressing room floor. The prick! She could feel unwanted tears welling up in her eyes as she strode purposefully across the carpeting to the full length mirror. Pride was everything. Tears angered her. They were alright for weak women, but not for her.

"Asshole!" she snarled at the naked woman who stared back at her. "Whatever made you think the arrogant son of a bitch would remain Simon Pure forever?" Not someone like Raymond, not an ego like that. Sex was a driving force for the man, his personal victory over women.

She remembered how insatiable he'd been before they were married, and she could still hear his words as clearly now as they'd been when he proposed: "While I truly think I love Carolina, the person, I want to be absolutely honest and tell you up front that my first love was that gorgeous machine you call a body. I wasn't drawn to your mind. If you keep all your gear in perfect working order, keep it looking just like it does today, we can have a wonderful life together."

"And what can I expect in return if I keep the machine exactly as it is?"

"You can have anything you want, Carolina. You can have things you can't even imagine today. We will be Boston's most beautiful couple."

Since he'd never been an easy person, she acknowledged to herself that it was his money that had initially attracted her. She cared for Raymond, or at least she had at one time. That was when she thought he needed her.

In recent years, however, she'd found that trying to love him was increasingly difficult. His personality had changed. His treatment of her sometimes grew ugly. More than in the past, he was possessed by money, by winning out over everyone – even their few remaining friends – and by getting even with anyone he thought might have crossed him.

Carolina studied the woman in the mirror, spreading her feet until they were more than a foot apart. "That's what he fell in love with, babycakes. And he told you that right from the start. But he also said as long as you followed the maintenance program you and he would be an item." She saw tears at the corner of her eyes before she could tough them back. "Why the hell are you jealous?"

Why was she jealous? The man had literally confessed that he was a sexual animal before they were married, that he needed sex like other people needed oxygen or food. And no man like that can ever be satisfied with one woman. She'd always wondered about a guy like Raymond, a sex addict basically, like that Red Sox player a few years back. But his attentions had never flagged. Always steady. Until now...

"You knew it would come," she said to her reflection. "You just wouldn't admit it could happen to you until now."

She stared at the perfect body in the mirror, the machine she had worked so hard to maintain. It had been expensive to take care of the machine with the life style they followed, but she'd done it.

Why don't men feel it's important to keep their end of a bargain? It was the dumb, little things the past week that convinced Carolina, the things you'd think a guy would know enough to cover up. The clincher last night was a strange aroma, a trace of perfume she'd noticed when she nuzzled his neck. It was a new brand, one she knew permeated the skin no matter how hard you scrubbed.

Raymond was treating her like an asshole. If it was so obvious to her, then others would notice it, too, and envious people who really weren't the close friends they claimed would laugh behind her back.

"Don't let him take you down," she said out loud to the Carolina in the mirror. "You've paid your dues."

The fire alarm bell coming over the speaker at the Arson Squad had been for District Three. The familiar voice of Leona Blake, Fire Alarm's blond bombshell, told Engine 32's lieutenant a follow-up call to the alarm had come in just as the bell was striking. A resident across from 46 Mystic Street reported smoke showing.

"Engine Thirty Two." Leo said, looking up from the yellow tablet he was writing on. "Charlestown. Your turf, Henry."

Hyde kept writing. "The city's my turf." He ground his cigarette into the overflowing ashtray, tore off the sheet he'd just filled, and began writing on the next page. "Charlestown's where I sleep."

Bobbie Scott pushed back from the table and went over to the coffee pot. He was about to pour when he looked in his cup. "Dammit, Henry, you flicked your ashes in my cup again. Don't you look when you're doing that?" He rinsed the cup under the faucet.

"Ashes are healthy. You're a fire eater, one of Boston's unsung heroes." Hyde never looked up from his writing. "You're a man who lives with ashes. You know, you find origin and cause in the ashes when you do your job, you get your ashes hauled when you hop into the rack with your old lady, and it's ashes to ashes when you answer the final alarm." He looked up at Scott who was sitting back across from him with an amused expression. "So what's a few ashes in your coffee?"

Leo pointed at Scott with his pencil. "Let that be a lesson to you. Never complain to Henry because you always get a ration of bullshit. The man will not shut up even when he's doing something brilliant."

A scratchy voice with a fire siren in the background came over the wall speaker. "Alarm, this is Engine Thirty Two on scene with Ladder Nine. We have a working fire – flames from a second floor window at one one six Elm Street."

"Roger Thirty Two. Switch to channel two."

Leo picked up the Motorola and switched it to circuit two. "You may not give a shit if your place is burning down, Henry, but I'd like to hear if Ladder Nine rescues any naked broads from your bedroom."

Hyde looked up from the report he was preparing. "What are you talking about?"

"Listen up, Henry. That's a working fire. One one six Elm Street. Beautiful, naked women are leaning from the windows screaming for brave firemen to save them. Don't you live at One One Six Elm?"

Hyde's eyes opened wide. "Son of a bitch. No. But I'm one twelve." He was already moving toward the hallway. "Come on. That fucker's trying to burn me out!"

8

"The fucker," Hyde said as Leo pulled their black Crown Vic up on the sidewalk behind a chief's car. "He's already got my attention. Why this? Why's he pissing me off even more?" Hyde leaped from the car and trotted up the hill, hopping over hose lines that snaked toward 116 Elm Street.

Hyde had chosen a neighborhood where the tumbledown structures of pre-Revolutionary Charlestown had been torn down and rebuilt as condos or town houses intended to look rustic. The tightly packed neighborhood, a mixture of brick and wood, lay under the spiky shadow of Bunker Hill Monument. It was clean, the drug dealers had been chased across the Tobin Bridge to Chelsea, and it was home to Henry Hyde. Not fancy, but a man's home is his castle.

And now that home was endangered.

An extension from Ladder 9 lay against the roof. White smoke belched from a vent that had been chopped through the roof. Hoses curled inside the wreckage of the front door. Filthy water poured from that same door and ran down the sidewalk.

The district chief watched Hyde's awkward approach with amusement. "You guys must be mind readers. I just called Fire Alarm to send you over here." The chief's white coat set off his black face. "Commissioner Duggan got a stop watch on the squad these days?"

"Cut the shit, Wally." Hyde pointed at 112 Elm Street. "That's my home there, one twelve. Was there any damage?"

"Naw. The boys contained it pretty quickly to the place next door."

"So you called for the Arson Squad. What've you got?"

"Well, for one, there was no one home..."

"They both work days."

"And the front door was chained so we had to break it down. When we checked the rear, the back door lock had been jimmied. The fire started on the second floor in a hallway. No electrical equipment nearby, no plugs, no nothing. And, since there was no logical reason for a fire to start, we noted a strong gas smell and there's a burn trail on the floor near what I'd say was the point of origin." The chief grinned. "Think I can qualify as a fire investigator?"

"An investigator drawing a district chief's pay." Hyde shook his head. He turned to Leo and Bobbie. "This esteemed district chief says he's already figured out how the fire started. If you two will step inside and take the trouble to agree with his conclusions, I'm going to check out my place and see how much smoke I took."

Only a rear bedroom window had been open in Hyde's condo. The wind had been blowing away from his place and there was virtually no smell. But as he came down the stairs and rounded the corner into the kitchen, he saw a neatly addressed business envelope on the kitchen table.

TO: LIEUTENANT HENRY HYDE, CFI

It hadn't been there the last time he'd been in the kitchen – when? Two days ago? He snatched up the envelope, ripped it open with his index finger, and unfolded a sheet of business paper. This, too, was typed in capital letters:

WELCOME HOME, BRAVE ARSON INVESTIGATOR. JUST TO SHOW YOU WHAT A FINE PERSON I AM I DIDN'T TORCH YOUR PLACE. THIS NOTE SHOULD

LEAVE NO DOUBT IN YOUR MIND THAT I'M IN CONTROL. I DO WHAT I WANT. I GET WHAT I WANT. I BELIEVE I NOW HAVE YOUR COMPLETE ATTENTION. THE NEXT TIME I CALL YOU CAN CONFIRM THAT TO ME. THERE HAD BETTER NOT BE A PHONE TAP AGAIN BECAUSE YOUR PLACE BURNS IF THERE IS ONE AND MAYBE YOU'LL BE IN IT. ALSO THE NEXT TIME WE TALK YOU WILL BE WORKING FOR ME. THE CITY OF BOSTON WILL STILL BE PAYING YOU AND YOU'LL STILL BE LOOKING FOR ME BUT YOU'LL NEVER CATCH ME BECAUSE I'M SMARTER THAN YOU. I MAY TELL YOU WHAT I WANT NEXT TIME, HYDE.

A fruitcake! Absolutely out of his ever-loving tree. A true...no, wrong. Not even overkill from his point of view. This time a gut reaction wasn't the right approach. Hyde remembered the mind-wrenching school he'd attended in Quantico run by the FBI's Behavioral Science and Investigative Support Units. Some of the lecturers had written books about criminal profiling. Not only had he read all of them, but he'd insisted that Leo and Bobbie read them, too. That was why the commissioner had asked his group to develop their own profile of this arsonist. Their methods were admittedly crude, novices' imitations of a unique professional talent, but it had been a beginning.

Now as he reread the letter, he was certain that he was correct about one thing. He was head-to-head with a brilliant psychopath, maybe one who was over the edge – but brilliant! The man needed to control, knew he was in control, and wouldn't stop until he achieved his goal. The trouble was a psychopathic mind was never satisfied. It never stopped killing, never stopped burning...it just never stopped. There was always one more level to attain, more people to control, or more people to kill if he couldn't gain control. There was no such word as enough.

Was it the black guy – the one from the Sports Depot – who'd been in his place?

How did he get in? Hyde had installed dead bolts on both doors and the rear kitchen door was chained. He glanced up and saw the chain, which he'd checked the last time he left, hanging loose. Printed neatly on the door frame in pencil were the words: DON'T BOTHER CHECKING FOR PRINTS.

"You fucker!" Hyde bellowed. As those same words he'd just shouted at the world silently repeated themselves in his mind, he understood they represented his own frustration as much as anger. The son of a bitch has you by the balls and he's loving it.

Al Horgan's holstered gun landed on his desk with a thump. He could feel the exhaustion in every muscle. Four hours sleep in the past forty eight no longer worked at his age. A decent meal at home and maybe six hours in the sack would improve his outlook on life. He was just slipping his worn, brown belt back through the belt loops when Chief O'Brien knocked on the door frame.

"Always open. No door."

O'Brien stepped inside. Noting Horgan's tired eyes, he nodded at the gun and said warily, "I hate to ruin your dreams, Al, but it would mean a lot to me if you put that back on."

"My wife has a thing about me coming in the kitchen with one of those things on my hip." Horgan frowned. "What's up?"

"Why don't you stay and enjoy dinner with Henry and his boys. Leo's doing his famous meatloaf. If I remember right, that's one of your favorites."

"When my wife isn't cooking, yeah."

"Maybe you'll be willing to tag along, too, if they get a call."

"Since we both know they're the best team we've got, and they don't need any help, what's up your sleeve?"

"Intuition." O'Brien cocked his head to the side. "Intuition makes a great fire investigator, Al. I'd join them myself but I don't want to piss Henry off more than he already is. You're a good friend of his." The chief raised his eyebrows. "Just as a favor to me, why don't you see how he's handling the pressure."

"Henry's a tough mother."

"Very tough. But he's getting a load of pressure from this nutcase. Bobbie Scott tells me that arson job next door to Henry's condo was just to get him to see how easy this guy can get to him."

"Yeah, he told me. I don't know…" Horgan shrugged unhappily.

"Do me a favor, Al. He doesn't need his chief on his ass. He needs a buddy who cares. Just see how he's handling it tonight. He can't get too personal in this or he'll lose the picture. If he's having a problem, talk to him. You can get through to Henry better than anyone else."

Raymond Fairchild had always considered women as toys, man's fitting reward for hard work. He'd picked Kai out of a choice selection, and choice it had been. She'd seemed to jump out at him. Once she'd taken the secretarial job, it was just a matter of time on his part. Patience. A lunch. A drink after a bit of overtime. Then dinner. A little here, a little there. It was subtle. Her free time became his until gradually her time was dependent on his whim.

The final step was bringing her to the lavish apartment on Beacon Hill. Once he'd asked for her suggestions on redecorating and her ideas were incorporated into the apartment, she became an integral part of it – and finally of Raymond Fairchild. She was his. So subtle. His.

And now was as good a time as ever to study his new toy in more detail.

With extra care, he gradually pulled the sheet down until it reached the sleeping Kai's knees. Exquisite! A delectable Eurasian mix! He closed his eyes, then opened them slowly so that she would gradually swim into view. Yes indeed, she's real, every luscious inch. And her responses in bed – where had she learned to handle a man like that? Or was it just that she'd never had a man like him?

Score one for the good guy!

He decided in college, when he could still remember the girls who'd come before, that he would keep track of all the women he screwed. But that had lasted only until his first child was born – a girl. That's when he admitted to himself that sheer numbers were no longer important. Perhaps in acquiring money, yes. But with women, why not concentrate on quality?

Women, money. Money, women. They were one in the same. That's why you busted your ass, along with everyone else's that got in your way. Women and money were much the same thing. That's how you kept score. You can't tell the winners without a scorecard.

He was certain Carolina had only suspected him once, and even then she'd never been able to prove anything. It was a dumb mistake on his part, a mistake he vowed never to make again. It had been just before Christmas a year or so after they'd been married, and he'd been able to convince her that he'd gone off with some office friends to drink. They ran into some secretaries in a bar, but all they'd done was dance. He lied to her with a straight face and begged for forgiveness, actually squeezed out some tears, for doing something like that and said it would never happen again.

Then, just to show her he hadn't been messing with anyone, he'd screwed her four times that night – and she swallowed his story hook, line, and sinker. Christ, every woman thought she was superwoman, that she could outscrew a guy anytime. But not old Raymond Irondick! He was a performer. If he was going to be better than any other man, he had to outperform every other man.

He had no doubt women compared their husbands, and he was certain every woman who knew Carolina probably wanted to steal him away for a night – that is if she was honest about her sex life. But a good dog never shits in his own backyard, and Raymond never looked at any female they both knew. Let the neighborhood women lust after him from a safe distance.

Fairchild closed the bedroom door behind him and decided that he deserved a drink, a toast to one more conquest. If he was going to arrive home from work late – a business dinner, of course – a little alcohol on his breath wouldn't hurt. He poured himself a snifter of Remy VSOP and sat down in front of the floor-to-ceiling window that looked out over the Public Gardens.

What a magnificent view! Beacon Hill was a long way for a kid from Southie to come, and he still had a long way to go. Bright lights outlined the walkways through the beautifully manicured park. The reflection off the waters of the duck pond rippled through the trees. If he concentrated hard enough, maybe he could see the solid brass mother duck and her eight brass ducklings frozen in time at the edge of the pond. Or the majestic swan boats nestled against their pier for the night. Or even the young lovers who kissed beneath the lowering willows.

What a day he had in store for himself tomorrow. Start early, too, around 2:00 AM. Don't wake Carolina – of course, she never woke up after a goodnight tumble – when you call to yank Hyde's chain. Then catch a couple of hours while the Arson Squad was working overtime. Tickle Jordan's chin the first thing in the morning before he can get to me.

Wonder if Hyde will fall into place now, or will he tough it out a little longer? He was tougher by far than the turkeys Fairchild encountered on a daily basis. Thought they were tough guys because they'd made a little headway in the rackets. What a bunch of pussies! Thought they were all going to become Whitey Bulgers. Sorry troopers. There was only one Whitey, and even the feds couldn't catch up to him. But, he acknowledged with a nod of his head, there was no one as smart or as tough as Raymond Fairchild.

Fairchild tossed off the last of the Remy and slipped out of the apartment. What a pad! And he deserved it.

Bobbie Scott rolled over and decided he wouldn't get back to sleep without a head call. He climbed quietly out of his bed against the far wall of the bunk room and slipped into his shower clogs, then moved softly across the room toward the sliver of light under the door.

"While you're in there, take one for me."

Hyde's hoarse whisper startled Scott. "You awake, Henry?"

"Haven't been sleeping."

"Too much coffee?"

"One asshole too many," Hyde said, followed by a disgusted sigh which had been wrapped around the word shit. "Go on and take a leak before it runs down your leg, Bobbie."

The phone in the main room rang as Scott pulled the door shut behind him. He picked it up before the second ring. "Arson, Scott speaking."

"Lieutenant Hyde, please."

Scott glanced at the wall clock – 2:16. "Is this a fire matter, sir."

The voice was strangely muffled. "Why would I call Arson headquarters and ask to speak to the famous Lieutenant Hyde if it wasn't a fire matter?"

"I'll have to wake him." Scott checked to make sure the automatic recorder was functioning. "May I tell him who's calling?"

"A friend."

Scott sensed Hyde behind him before he heard his voice. "I'll take it, Bobbie." He was standing in the doorway in his shorts absentmindedly scratching his belly.

Hyde paused to fart, grunted satisfactorily, then sat down in one of the scratched, faded metal desk chairs in his shorts. He closed his eyes in anticipation of the voice he would hear. "Lieutenant Hyde here."

"Caught you sleeping, didn't I?"

"Like a baby."

"Let's not waste time, Hyde. Remember my note?"

"Yeah."

"Do I have your complete attention?"

"Yeah."

"Who do you work for?"

"The poor overtaxed citizens of Boston."

"That's who pays you, Hyde. If you want to be stubborn, I'll let you play that game for a while because..." The pause was magnified by the wail of a distant siren at nearby Boston Medical Center. "...because I control you."

"Now listen, asshole..."

Scott could hear the voice that boomed through the ear piece. "Shut up."

Hyde looked up at Scott and shook his head, index finger to his lips.

"You can't afford to be a big mouth or a wise guy, Hyde. I've got you by the balls and you know it. The only way the fires are ever going to stop is when you do what I tell you."

"Fires! You're talking fires?" Hyde's fist shot out, knocking a coffee mug into an ashtray. Cigarette ashes curled up around the surface of the cold, beige coffee. "Why not talk about murder? It doesn't make any difference whether people are killed in one of your fires or you pull a trigger. You're murdering innocent people. Stop burning. Start talking. Where? When?"

The soft, cool laugh that followed sent a sharp chill down Hyde's spine.

"Ah, you do understand. You're coming around. People are indeed dying. But, you see, I don't care about them. Really – I honestly don't care. More are going to die. You see, people get in the way – in my way. That's their fault, Hyde, not mine."

"You're out of your fuckin' mind," Hyde said softly, more to himself than the other.

"Not what you think, Hyde. I am the most brilliant man you will ever encounter in your miserable, salaried life. If you were me, you'd be a millionaire already." The voice rose slightly. "You know, you've just given me an idea. Since you're a man who's put his life on the line for so many years for peanuts, maybe I'll share some of that money with you."

Leo and Al Horgan, wearing T-shirts and skivvies like Scott, had entered the room quietly. They watched as Hyde's face contorted in rage. "Talk to me. Just talk to me. How do I start saving those lives?"

The response was jocular. "Not quite yet, Hyde. You're ahead of yourself." There was a background chuckle. "I don't trust you yet. Just to make sure you follow instructions perfectly, I'm going to have to lead you on a treasure hunt. If you do well..." – more chuckling – "...well then eventually we'll reach the critical point of our relationship."

"Go on."

"There's going to be another fire shortly."

"Go on."

"Who is Boston's famous silversmith? You know, the one who said *The British are coming! The British are coming!*"

"Paul fucking Revere."

"Very good. And where is his house?"

"The North End."

"Excellent. I won't ask the alarm number because I know you never served there. But I'll bet you'll never forget it because you're going to hear that alarm any moment now." Mocking. "Fire Alarm will send Engine Nine and Ladder One."

The familiar electronic beep of the alarm started from the loudspeaker before the sentence was finished.

"I can hear it coming over the phone now, Hyde. Go get it. But wait a minute." Now the voice was taunting. "There won't be much damage, just enough to piss off your favorite mayor a little more. When you and your men get inside, look in the trunk in the upstairs bedroom, the one looking out over Prince Street."

"Why?"

"Because there's a personal message for you there. We'll see how well you follow instructions. If you screw up, you'll find a lot more dead people. And each one will be your fault." The phone went dead.

Hyde whirled and pointed at Leo. "What are you fucking standing there for? Come on, get your fucking clothes on and get that car ready. We got a chance here. Whatever piece of shit is starting that fire for him is going to tell me who he works for."

9

The Paul Revere House in Boston's North End is five doors down from the corner of two narrow streets, Prince and North. The brown wooden structure, built in 1680, a renowned tourist attraction, has been well maintained right down to the old-fashioned Dutch door facing a small courtyard and the tiny panes in the leaded glass windows. The men from Ladder 1 had been careful to smash only the modern lock on the ancient front door.

Although it was after 2:30 in the morning, Leo was forced to park the car on the sidewalk a block away. A large, curious crowd filled the cobblestoned street and flowed into Gus P. Napoli Square and the Sacred Heart churchyard. Hyde pushed through the throng, ducking under the police line. "Who's running the show tonight?" he asked one of the firemen rolling hose.

"Chief Lucas," he said, pointing at a white coat exiting the courtyard gate of the Revere House.

Hyde hopped nimbly over some hose lines and was heading in that direction when a face in the crowd stopped him in his tracks.

Horgan almost bumped into him. "What is it, Henry?"

"Shit." Hyde scanned the crowd. What the hell? That face? Who? "I thought I saw someone...I don't know..." His eyes stopped on each face, half in shadow, half illuminated by the quaint North End street lights. "I thought it was..."

Mug shot! "Harvey..." What was the last name? "Harvey..." He snapped his fingers with frustration.

"Harvey Rothstein?" Horgan asked.

"Bingo!" Hyde said.

"I thought he was supposed to be in the slammer."

Horgan followed as Hyde moved along the edge of the crowd, his eyes searching. "Naw. You're not reading the bulletin board, Al. The chief got a notice from the DA's office a couple weeks ago saying Harvey'd been paroled." Where else would an arsonist go for entertainment but a fire? And why would he be up at this hour unless...?

"Hey, Paul." Horgan beckoned the fire chief to join them.

Hyde's eyes scanned the crowd once more before turning back to Lucas. "What do you know, Paul? Looks like you saved a little bit of history tonight."

Lucas nodded to Horgan. "Not much to it, Henry. I can't figure this one out. A neat little package designed to create smoke mostly. Not a hell of a lot of fire damage."

"A designer fire maybe?" Hyde was looking away from the chief as he spoke, still scanning the crowd for that face he thought he'd seen. "Do we have a little case of arson?"

"Go on in and have a sniff for yourself," Lucas said. "Whoever set it didn't seem to want to cause much damage. Actually moved furniture away from the accelerant."

Hyde's eyes remained on the crowd. "Could you smell it?"

"Oh, yeah. Place smelled like a dry cleaning shop. Benzene's my guess. You know how fast the stuff evaporates. Set it over by a front window to burn some curtains. Even opened the window so someone would see the flames. Hell, you're the fire investigator, Henry, so you tell me why the setup was so obvious." Lucas turned to Horgan. "What're you doing out tonight, Al?"

"Slumming more than anything..." Horgan stopped as Hyde whirled and suddenly darted into the crowd. "Henry!"

"Move!" Hyde screamed. "Move! Get outta the way!" People drew back from Hyde as he lunged for a man who had turned away. "Hey, Rothstein! You fuck!"

The man was pushing people aside in a frantic attempt to avoid the wild-eyed Hyde. He elbowed a large, much younger man whose thick arm came back hard across his chest in anger. "Where you headin', man?"

Hyde's right hand landed on his target's shoulder, gripping a handful of jacket. Then, with his other hand, he got a firm hold of the jacket collar. "What's the matter, Harvey? You scared of me?" He dragged his man backwards. "Come on, let's go see if you were inside the scene of the crime."

Hyde hauled the stumbling Rothstein backward through the circle of people to the spot where the other fire investigators were standing. "Hey, Al, look what I found." He released his grip on the collar and spun Rothstein around, then dug the fingers of his right hand hard into either side of Rothstein's neck beneath his ears.

Horgan had seen that look in Hyde's eyes just one time before. "Take it easy, Henry. We got a lot of people watching here." Hyde had been suspended that other time after a civil investigation for excessive force.

Hyde's mouth was inches from Rothstein's ear. "I want to know who paid you for this."

Rothstein's eyes were bright with fear. "Mr. Horgan," he said, trying to turn his head, "I just got out. I didn't have anything to do with this..."

"You're a lying piece of shit." Hyde's knuckles whitened as his fingers dug into the man's neck. "Give me his name before I really hurt you, you fucker."

Rothstein winced. "I just came to watch after I heard the sirens. Honest. I live here, just up the street. I got a room with my cousin on Fleet Street."

"Tell meeee..."

Rothstein grimaced as the fingers dug deeper into his neck. "Shit, that hurts." He tried to wiggle out of Hyde's grasp. "Lemme go..."

"Henry." Al Horgan moved close to Hyde. "You're attracting attention. People are watching."

"Tough." Hyde moved slightly to his left, never letting up on his grip, to cover Rothstein from curious eyes. "Don't give me any shit, Al, not now. The whole scene follows this fuck's standard method. Set a fire. Hang around to watch the fun. That's how he ended up in the slammer last time. Wanted to watch his fucking fires. Got yanked right out of the crowd then, too."

"Henry," Bobbie Scott moved closer, "Al's right. A TV truck just arrived. We're going to have a problem in a second."

"Fine. Great. I don't give a shit. Some asshole calls me and tells there's going to be a fire here. Someone has to set it. Right? We arrive and do what we're supposed to do, part of which is studying the crowd for suspicious faces. I see one. Right?" He was speaking fast and backing away from them as he did. "I grab a convicted felon here at the scene of a fire who loves to start fires and then watch them, and you guys want me to be sweet to the prick."

"Henry," Scott persisted, "Al's right. You..."

Hyde's features reflected an unnatural fury. "You're a new guy, Bobbie. You don't know how these things work. Sometimes you gotta bust some nuts." He turned away and trotted toward Baker's Alley with a wriggling Rothstein stumbling along beside him. "Come on, Harvey, we don't want to make a scene."

Scott appealed to Horgan. "Has Henry been like this before? I mean..." He paused, searching for the right words.

Horgan shook his head. "Come on, let's save Henry's ass before he does something stupid. You guys get Rothstein out of the way. I'll handle Henry."

Hyde dragged Rothstein into the alley and spun him around. He smashed a flat hand into the man's chest, knocking him back into the brick wall. "Okay, Harvey, tell me about the creep who hired you to start your little fire in there."

"I didn't have anything…"

Hyde slapped him with his free hand. "Don't lie to me, you fuckin' son of a bitch."

"You gotta believe me…"

Hyde's hand came back, his knuckles tearing lips across teeth. "That fire was arson, shithead, and you were hanging around enjoying it, just like you always did." His hand wrapped around the man's throat. He drew his fist back. "Come on, tell me, tell me all about it. Who paid you? Who's behind this?"

"Hyde, believe me. Please. You're choking me. I swear I didn't have anything to do with it."

Hyde's fist smashed into Rothstein's nose. The man screamed in pain as blood gushed onto Hyde's sleeve. His knees buckled.

"Don't you go down on me, asshole." Hyde tried to yank Rothstein up by the shoulders, but he slumped sideways to the ground. "You chicken shit bastard." Hyde dropped to his knees and slapped the bloody face twice. "Do you like it, Harvey?" His voice was shrill. "Is it fun to get the shit pounded out of your sorry ass because you're a lying sack of shit? Tell me the guy's name and you can walk. That's all I want is his fucking name."

"Please," Rothstein mumbled through torn, swollen lips, "Please. I don't know anything." He covered his face with his arms.

"You shit." Hyde was screaming now. "I'll tear your nuts off." He drove a hand into the man's crotch and squeezed.

Rothstein let out a cry of agony. "Noooo…please…"

"Give me his fucking name." Hyde's voice echoed through the alley into the street.

Rothstein's scream echoed off the alley walls into North Street.

"Henry!" Horgan was behind him now, bent from the waist, wrapping his arms around Hyde. "Are you crazy? Let him go, Henry, let him go." He tried to pull Hyde away.

Hyde kept a death grip on Rothstein's testicles.

Leo chopped down on Hyde's arm.

"Leave me alone," Hyde bellowed. "I'm gonna' make this prick talk." He shook his hand up and down.

Rothsteins's screams intensified.

Leo chopped again and again until Hyde let go. Scott had Hyde's other arm. Horgan heaved with all his strength and they fell backwards as two policemen rushed into the alley.

"You bastards! Let me go, you bastards," Hyde shouted, struggling to break free. "All I want is that name. Let go... you bastards..."

"Henry...Henry...take it easy. Get control of yourself, Henry." Horgan was whispering softly into his ear. "We got cops here. They don't like what you were doing. They write reports on things like that."

Cops! The pricks! Hyde allowed his muscles to go slack. "Shit," he said softly. "Shit, shit, shit."

"It's okay," Horgan cautioned the police. "It's going to be okay now. I've got everything under control." He turned back to Hyde. "That's better, Henry. Relax. We're not going to let go until you calm down."

Hyde's voice was so soft, they could barely hear him. "All I wanted was a name." He spoke between deep gasps. "I'm going to find the bastard. I'm really going to find the bastard." He looked up at Horgan, then at Carmichael and Scott. "I'm sorry, guys." He looked back at Horgan. "I snapped there, Al, went crazy. I'm sorry. Leo...Bobbie...I'm sorry." He took a deep breath and exhaled slowly. "I guess I blew it for a second there." Then he saw the police who were still watching uneasily. "Hey, don't you guys play games like we do in the fire department. It's a lot of fun for everybody." He pointed at Rothstein who was whimpering. "Except for the bad guy."

Horgan relaxed his grip on Hyde and got to his feet. "Game's over guys, back to work." Then he looked over at Rothstein. "It's going to be fun trying to explain him to the chief."

"You're going to have to try and explain it to the media first," said one of the police. Cops didn't especially care for fire investigators – they weren't police but they had the same powers. "They saw you chase him in here and they'll see what he looks like when he comes out."

Hyde rose to his knees and glanced over again at Rothstein, still doubled up, clutching his crotch, whimpering, blood covering his face. "I suppose," he said, "a really smart lawyer might try to push for excessive force." He climbed to his feet and turned to Leo. "Read him his rights so these guys see how much we respect human rights. We should book him for attempting to evade arrest. But for now, we'll just place him under protective custody and take him in for questioning."

"You gotta be kidding," one of the cops said.

"Naw. The people out there are mad." The old Henry Hyde was once again in charge. "One of our city's most famous historical sites was almost burned to the ground tonight. The crowd out there is an animal, hungry for blood." He ran an imaginary knife across his throat. "It's our sworn duty to protect this man, who does indeed have a history of lighting fires, from a possible lynch mob." He gave the closest cop a twisted smile and said, "Thanks for your help guys. We'll take our prisoner into custody now."

Leo was on his knees, reading Rothstein his rights. Hyde turned to Horgan and Scott. "Come on guys, there's one more thing we have to do. Let's give Mr. Revere's house a once-over before we take Harvey back and clean him up."

No one objected when Hyde climbed the stairs to the bedroom facing Prince Street by himself. Just as he'd been told, there was a chest by the window. As promised, another envelope was inside.

TO: LT. HENRY HYDE, CFI

What's with the CFI bullshit? But he realized, at the moment his anger was rising, that it was simply one more way of yanking his chain, a means of finding his breaking point. *Fuck him!*

NOW THAT YOU UNDERSTAND WHO IS IN CONTROL, WE ARE READY TO WORK TOGETHER. BOSTON WILL CONTINUE TO BURN UNTIL I HAVE HALF A BILLION DOLLARS DEPOSITED IN A FOREIGN ACCOUNT, NUMBER AND INSTRUCTIONS TO FOLLOW WHEN YOU REPORT THAT THE MONEY IS READY FOR TRANSFER. HOW DO WE GET THE MONEY? STAND BY. FROM YOUR FAVORITE MAYOR! WHERE DOES HE GET IT? FROM THE DEEP POCKETS WHO PUT HIM IN OFFICE AND PROFESS LOVE FOR THE CITY. I KNOW YOU WILL SUCCEED, HYDE, BECAUSE YOU CAN'T STAND TO SEE TOO MANY MORE PEOPLE DIE. WE'LL TALK SOON.

This was personal – real personal – making him the fall guy for innocent people who were dying horribly. He closed his eyes and sucked in half a dozen deep breaths until he was certain he had control. Then he crammed the note into a pocket and headed downstairs where the others were collecting evidence samples and taking photos.

Scott saw the look on his face when he paused at the bottom of the stairs. "A ten spot for your thoughts, Henry."

"I was just wondering if our distinguished mayor is ready to bend over and grab his ankles."

Raymond Fairchild finished reading the Boston *Globe* article for perhaps the fifth time that day. Then he went back to the photograph above the article's lead headlines. Beautiful! The photo clearly showed that the victim's right eye was already shut and there was no doubt blood was running from his nose. His shirt was spotted with it. If only the photographer had gotten a picture of Hyde actually pounding the guy. But it was enough. The article said it all. Excessive force. The fire investigator, Lt.Henry Hyde, had beaten the suspect. The commissioner would hold a hearing on the matter.

Why did they have to put it on the front page of the Metro section? Why not the front page of the paper? Wouldn't the *Globe* ever understand what the average reader was looking for when it came to news?

But it was still wonderful reading. Fairchild could feel himself shaking with delight. Hyde had gone overboard. He was stretched to the breaking point!

You are mine, Hyde!

Fairchild imagined Hyde's fist smashing into Rothstein's face...the sound of bone on bone...the sight and smell of blood. He could feel his whole being tingling. It had to be almost as good as sex.

That was when the idea came to him that sex was the way to honor the occasion – cracking Hyde's image. But it must be something different. How do you celebrate a beating? Try something that would really be...

Carolina Fairchild felt a chill from the past when she heard Raymond's voice over the telephone. If asked, she couldn't describe its tone, just something intimidating, frightening...threatening, although he'd never hurt her because she'd always acceded to his demands. It had been how long since the last time – a year? More than that. Almost a year and a half since he'd started a conversation like that? The words were always different, the orders he issued to her varying, but the end result was always the same.

"Carolina, did you hear me? I want you naked when I get home tonight. In the kitchen. If necessary, you may wear an apron for protection while cooking. And I want you wearing the pearl choker I brought you from Hong Kong." His orders were always so simple, but they were also authoritarian, leaving no doubt that there was an implied threat if she ever failed to cooperate.

"Uhhh...Raymond, it's a little late to...I mean, Nicole...she's home now." She had to admit that he'd been more careful once their daughter had started going to school. "I can't just..."

"Carolina, I'm going to fuck you in every room on the first floor tonight. I don't care what you do before I arrive home. Send her to stay overnight at Marsha's. Do you understand me?"

Carolina's naturally tinted complexion had become ashen. When Raymond talked like that there was no avoiding him. There never had been. Something had happened today to bring this on. She'd never been able to understand the cause, but whenever it occurred he assumed a dominant role. He wouldn't hurt her – he never had hurt her. Ever since the first time it had occurred, he'd said that the last thing he ever wanted was to hurt her. It was just that he had these compulsions, completely unpredictable, and she had to satisfy them. Besides, she'd never fought back. What once had been a fascinating sex game that she eagerly accepted was now a period of fear and anxiety for Carolina because she thought that one day Raymond might snap completely.

These impulsive couplings had begun a few years after they were married and at that time Carolina Fairchild had considered them trysts. Actually, she'd been amused by them before they had children. Each occurrence was bizarre and simultaneously exciting. Sometimes he'd surprised her away from home – camping, in the backseat of three successive taxis in one night in Paris, in every room over a two day period in a neighbor's house they'd been watching while the owners were on vacation.

Her husband's imagination had been both outlandish and hilarious at the same time. Once he'd told her to meet him at the Ritz-Carlton across from the Public Garden. They enjoyed an evening of dinner and dancing on the roof and then, after the Ritz had closed down for the night, they'd crept around the hotel making love in outrageous places – an elevator, in the darkened first floor bar, in one of the kitchens, even in front of a window looking out on deserted Newbury Street.

In those days, it had all been almost as exciting for Carolina as for Raymond. But as years passed, especially after Ray, Jr. had been born, it sometimes bordered on the insane. When she tried to talk him out of his weird follies, he became all the more determined.

The excitement and challenge faded as the children grew. Then it became a sneaking, embarrassing thing. Eventually, Carolina realized that it was no longer a joint experiment by two people living an outrageous sex dream. It was Raymond using her as his tool to satisfy something deep inside himself that seemed to eat away at his very soul if he couldn't satisfy this urge.

At one time, she confronted him. "You're not making love to me any longer. You're screwing every women you ever imagined. I just happen to be convenient."

And he had answered coolly, "You have everything a woman could desire, Carolina. And you are everything I desire. You have money, clothes, a perfect escape cottage on the Cape, vacations all over the world. With all that, you can accept one little deviation in my make up. I've never hurt you. Never. I know myself, and I'm telling you right now, I'm not asking anything of you that is beyond everything I give you." His eyes had hardened in a manner she'd never seen and his voice dropped so low that she could barely hear him. "Don't ever refuse me."

As the children entered school, he showed restraint and practiced a control that he said she would never understand. But there were times when he seemed to snap, times when she'd been forced to do things to protect the children that made her hate herself.

Now, tonight, when she'd least expected one of these breaks with reality, he'd called and there was no choice but to accomodate his wishes. *"Do you understand me?"*

She shivered at the prospect.

•

Carolina had said little since Raymond came into the kitchen that evening. There was a look on his face she couldn't ever recall seeing before, something behind his eyes, something deeper than she could plumb. Even when she pirouetted for him, wearing nothing but the shorty, French apron he'd given her years before, there was barely a smile on his face. If anything, it was more like he'd just come up with the right change for a newspaper.

Without warning, he'd taken her on the kitchen table, roughly, appearing pleased when some dishes crashed to the floor. But he never laughed at the mess, something he'd often reveled in after wild sex.

Dinner was silent, eaten naked in the dining room at his insistence. When they'd finished, she asked innocently, "How about some dessert?" He grabbed her by the hand, pulled her into the living room, and literally raped her on the couch after turning on all the lights. *Assault...rape.* Those were the words that came to mind after he was finished. At one time, these madcap games had been mutual, fun for both. Tonight, he wasn't involving her. Tonight, she was the toy – a piece of equipment.

After that, it had gotten rougher, meaner.

"You're hurting me. Please, Raymond. Why?"

Raymond Fairchild had done some weird, often kinky, things during their relationship, but mostly they had been laughable. At least Carolina had concluded at those times that it was better to go along with Raymond's funkiness than chance fighting him. This was different.

An hour later, in their bedroom, he had become worse.

"Please, Raymond. Stop for a moment. You're hurting me. Please, think about me, Raymond." She tried to move forward, away, but there was no place to go. He had her arms behind her back and increased the pressure when she attempted to wriggle away.

"Relax, my love. You've always found new ideas fun. It's not going to hurt if you relax." That voice she was hearing wasn't really Raymond's, not the man she'd lived with for more than fifteen years.

Over the past two hours, the sex had been odd, one-sided, but it had been normal sex. Now, Carolina had been forced onto her knees on the bed. Her head was jammed up against the headboard. "No...Raymond...no...you're hurting..." she whimpered.

He tightened the grip on her arms. "You'll learn to like it." His voice, strange and high, frightened her. It was as if he was talking to a stranger. "He thinks I'm an asshole...thinks I'm scared of him." Fairchild's voice suddenly dropped until it seemed a distant growl. "I'll show him."

"Raymond!" She screamed in pain. "I can't...please..."

He released her arms and shoved her head into the pillow. She struggled, but he was too strong, too heavy. "I'll show him who's scared."

Fairchild was relentless until he'd been satisfied – and asleep within seconds after he'd rolled away. He never saw the damage he'd done, never heard her weeping, had no idea how long she lay in pain in the hot, bloody water in the bathtub.

10

Herman Neubauer didn't just understand news in Boston, he knew it like Ted Williams knew pitchers. He had a sixth sense for it, but he would never be an anchor man or a media star. Chunky, balding, thick glasses, a high, whiny voice – all were traits that kept him behind a desk producing news for the city he loved. He could smell a story where his competitors remained oblivious. Neubauer's most unique talent came in assigning the right reporter and the best cameraman for each story. But at this moment he was confused.

"You're kidding me, Nomi...you're kidding me," Neubauer repeated after a moment's thought. "You say you want me to put you on special assignment. But, you're junior here. A talent, yes, but junior. Nicki, maybe, yeah. She's got five years seniority on you and she's not even ready to anchor."

"I'm a great talent. Maybe hidden's a better word."

Neubauer turned his head and studied her out of the corners of his eyes. "You're not hidden, Nomi. But you're going to improve with age."

She mimicked him, looking out of the corners of her eyes. "I don't have time, Herm. No one makes anchors out of middle-aged broads, and that's what I'll be by the time the honchos decide I'm ready. I'm no kid. I want it all now and the only way to get it is to get that big story."

"Fires? Arson?" He blinked curiously. "Seriously?"

"Right. Fires. Arson."

"What makes you so special?"

"That talent you just said wasn't hidden."

Neubauer made a face. "You're trying to take advantage of me, Nomi. I got bosses, too."

Nomi removed her glasses and looked at him again out of the corners of her eyes, then saw the stubborn expression spreading over his face. "You've got to believe me, Herm. It will pay off. I just have to get my face off the screen doing interviews and work on my own if I'm going to get this story. Trust me or...or I walk." She'd made this decision after watching the morning news. Henry needed help. Outside help. She didn't have to keep her job to help him.

"Okay, I trust you. I'm going out on a limb. If you make a mistake, I go down."

"I don't expect to go down on this one." She smiled. "Thanks."

"Keep me in touch."

Carolina Fairchild had made an effort to be strong, but it had failed completely. The physical pain, as bad as it was, was tolerable. But after all those years – to be treated like a slut. Until last night, all of Raymond's kinky habits had been bearable, unpleasant but bearable. But he'd gone beyond that last night.

She shook with an inner rage during the examination, eventually breaking into tears of pain before the doctor was finished. The whispered words between the doctor and her nurse, though primarily clinical, were audible at times and Carolina understood that she'd been badly damaged. Now as she sat across from the doctor's desk, she could feel the tears welling up again.

"Mrs. Fairchild, I can explain everything medically to you, but first you have to talk with me."

Carolina Fairchild talked. And as she did, spilling out the events of the previous night, she already knew what she would do.

Don't get mad, Carolina – get even.

Hyde pulled back the curtain just enough to see who was ringing his doorbell.

When Nomi saw the curtain fall back in place, she banged on the door with her fist. "Come on! I know you're there. Let me in."

The door opened. Hyde looked like hell. "Hi." Before she could respond, he continued, "I'm under orders to keep away from the media. I..."

Nomi carried a shopping bag under one arm. She pushed in and shut the door behind her with the other. "You look like hell, Henry."

Hyde shrugged. "People tell me that's always the way I look." He pulled out a cigarette and stuck it in the corner of his mouth.

"When's the last time you had a square meal?"

"Coffee's a meal."

"You need something to eat."

"Why?"

She came up on her tiptoes and grasped his face in both hands, kissing him lightly on the lips. "Because I'm hungry, too, and I want a man well fed and strong before I go to bed with him."

Nomi was unable to keep her eyes from Hyde's plate. The process he employed before eating his baked potato was priceless. First, he cut it precisely in half. Then he carved neat x's with his knife across each piece. A slice of butter was deposited in the middle of each half of the potato. He happened to notice Nomi watching him, chin cradled in her palms, as he reached for the salt and pepper.

"Hey, I don't get a chance to have baked potatoes often. Don't know how to cook them." The butter was melting into the potato. "There's a reason for this, you know. See how it melts into the potato when you cut slices into it. Doesn't slide off onto the plate."

She smiled. "Fascinating. Go ahead. Don't let me interrupt you."

"You won't." He sprinkled salt and pepper evenly across each potato half. Then he spooned a dollop of sour cream and chives onto each one, spreading it gently with the bottom of the spoon. Looking up again, he saw that Nomi was still watching. "Aren't you going to eat?"

"After the ceremony."

"Single guys get set in their ways you know."

Hyde sprinkled bacon bits carefully on top of the sour cream, making sure that they covered each half equally. Satisfied, he picked up his knife and fork and sliced off a bite of steak. "Perfectly cooked. Just like the Ninety Nine. I never could figure out how to master a broiler myself."

Nomi took a bite of steak and washed it down with her red wine. "Do you ever have a square meal when you're off duty?"

"Restaurants sometimes." He was hungry and ate heartily. "You know, this may be the first time a bottle of wine has ever been on this table." He sipped it, then took a mouthful. "Nice."

"If you owned a candle, it would also be romantic."

"Do you know how many fires are started by candles every..." But he stopped himself and grinned. She'd left the kitchen light on and she'd turned the shade on a lamp in the far corner toward the wall to dim it. "You didn't do a bad job on the lighting either. But a man's got to see his food," he said lamely.

Nomi poured more wine into their glasses. "Drink up. That should loosen you up a little. You're just as nervous now as when I came in the door."

Hyde looked down at his plate, then at his wine glass. He sipped the wine thoughtfully before he looked again at her. Her brown hair, which once before an interview she'd said was mousy, had been let down and swept back behind her ears. Her glasses were on the side table. When she smiled, her eyes seemed to sparkle in the dim light. She tilted her head to the side waiting for him to speak.

Hyde dabbed at his mustache again in an effort to smooth it. "All this," he said indicating the dinner with a sweep of his hand, "is very nice, very nice indeed. But let's go back to the beginning – I'm a little slow sometimes. Must be my advanced age. Still back at the front door when you came in here and, ahhh, made your announcement." He licked his lips.

"Go on."

"Ahhhh...are you really planning to stay here tonight?"

She winked at him. "Want me to call my mother first and ask permission?" Her smile was enticing.

"That's not what I meant." Hyde twisted his head, stretching his neck nervously.

"Talk to me." Nomi reached out and placed a hand over his. "What do you really mean? Is the toughest son of a bitch in Boston having a hard time accepting a reasonable offer?" She was enjoying his embarrassment. "I mean, do you want to run right upstairs now, or would you like to finish your dinner first?"

"Shit, Nomi, stop yanking my chain. I'm old enough to be your father."

"Not unless you knocked up my mother in high school. Besides, what has age got to do with it." She winked at him again. "You're not, ummm...I'm trying to be gracious...unable to perform, are you?"

"Of course not. Come on, I'm being serious. This sort of thing doesn't happen to me every day, you know."

"Why I was expecting to have to chase the women out of here with my broomstick." Then she saw the strained expression on his face. "Hey, come on. I'm just teasing. And I'm just trying to be honest with you. How long has it been since a woman has been honest with you, Henry?"

"Honest? What's that?" When he held her eyes, his expression was totally serious. "It's not that I'm not attracted to you. We both know that. It's just that...oh shit, I can make a fool out of myself if I really try. It's just that..."

"It's just that it's not anything. I'm a big girl. I've been having a difficult time letting on that for some unknown reason I really am attracted to you. We agree on mutual attraction. Okay?"

"Okay."

"When I heard about what happened in the North End last night, I called Al. He said the cops had already called the EMTs and they showed before you could get this guy, Rothstein, into your car. He told me Chief O'Brien had no choice but to place you on a paid leave of absence." She got up and came around the table. She bent down so that her face was level with his and turned his head to make sure he was looking into her eyes. "Hey, listen to me. I understand how you feel. I understand what made you do that to Rothstein. I understand what you're going through with this arsonist. I want to let you know that someone cares about Henry Hyde." She kissed him on the forehead. "But I don't do charity gigs. I came over here under my own free will. Do you follow me so far?"

Hyde nodded.

"Fine. I want to finish my dinner. I want us to finish that bottle of wine, too. I fully intend to clean up the kitchen so there's no mess tomorrow morning. If you want, I'll go home afterward. Do you want me to do that?"

He shook his head.

Boston's mayor preferred lobster to beef, especially when Raymond Fairchild was buying. Charlie Jordan always chose Jimmy's Harborside rather than the upscale and touristy Pier Four – "More my kind of people, the ones who vote for me. Not as many limos. You can smell the boats, too, even watch 'em clean the fish sometimes. Remember your origins, Raymond."

"I do."

Jordan had suggested they meet after the evening rush because he wasn't getting the answers he wanted from his City Hall clique of advisors. He knew Fairchild would suggest dinner and ask where they should meet, and Jordan, as always, would select Jimmy's. He could always get that table in the far corner by the water where you could hear each other talk. The same efficient, discreet waiter was always their server and the mayor was rarely bothered by favor seekers.

"I'm beginning to think this fruitcake has the city by the balls, Raymond." Jordan poked his own chest with his thumb for emphasis. "I had the fire commissioner on the carpet this morning. Wouldn't let the sucker sit down. I said, *Does he have to burn down Faneuil freakin' Hall, the Old North Church, and maybe Fire Headquarters, too, before you get a handle on this?*"

"I would imagine he wasn't too happy," Fairchild said quietly.

"Happy? You shoulda' seen his eyes. Christ, if looks could kill I'd be dead meat now. There are stories about Duggan's temper. But I had to let him know who's in charge." This time Mayor Jordan tapped his forehead with an index finger. "I didn't wise off. I used the old noodle. I said he was not only supposed to put out fires, he was supposed to stop the bastard who was setting them. He says he's got every fire investigator in the city working on this. I said he didn't have that prick, Hyde, working today. So he says, sort of nastily, that Hyde's on leave with pay pending an in-house investigation. I said, *What's to investigate?* The son of a bitch was pounding on an innocent bystander in public."

"You mean the one he put in the hospital? The convicted arsonist?" Fairchild sipped his chardonnay and licked his lips appreciatively. "By the way, you ought to stop for a minute, Charles, and enjoy this wine more.

—118—

Magnificent. Might calm you down a tad also." He raised his eyebrows. "Your voice carries, even from the corner here."

"Hey, I'm pissed enough that maybe I don't care. This is like war, Raymond. Son of a bitch's burning the goddamn city and I'm the one in charge. I got to find someone to stop this shit."

Fairchild could almost have written the mayor's last words before he heard them. The man was already more pliable than he'd anticipated. "Frank Duggan's been a good commissioner and he's got a lot of friends all over the city. It might be wise to stay on the right side of him." It was a relatively simple matter to keep Jordan properly oriented and under control so that he wouldn't do anything rash.

Jordan shrugged. "Hey, like I say, I'm the guy in charge. Duggan works for me. When he starts raising his eyebrows and firing back at me, I got to keep him in his place."

Fairchild raised a hand for the waiter. "I'm going to have them bring up another bottle of this chardonnay. I can see we're going to need it. The food's not even on the table and we only have a glassful left." He leaned back in his chair. "Lighten up for a moment, Charles. Smile."

After the lobsters and second bottle of chardonnay had arrived, Fairchild indicated to the waiter that they wanted privacy. "We have a great deal to discuss this evening so we'll be happy to pour our own wine."

Jordan raised his new glass to Fairchild. "I'm glad you were free to join me this evening, Raymond. I need some advice, some fresh ideas beyond City Hall."

Fairchild touched glasses. "Glad to, Charles." Employing a full given name rather than a nickname was an indication that you had arrived on Boston's upper level, that you had moved beyond your roots, that you could rub elbows with those born into a higher strata. When you came from Southie, you showed them you could not only fight bare knuckles, you could take them head on in their own arena. "You can rely on me to keep my mouth shut also."

"Well you're the only sealed lips in the whole goddamned town. The front pages are spouting more garbage and rumor than the sports pages. The media's having a field day."

"I've seen the papers."

"That's just the tip of the frigging iceberg. The *Globe's* Spotlight Team is off and running, new series starting tomorrow. Wouldn't surprise me if they even have quotes and inside scoops from probational firemen. Neubauer's people are running all over the city putting together another fifteen minute segment. Even the goddamn radio – WBZ has started a series of sixty second editorials that are repeated four times a day."

Fairchild nodded, using a lobster claw to make a point. "What has gotten people riled up, Charles, is the loss of life. Fires are forgotten by everybody but the fire department. Deaths are not forgotten and they are your problem. People don't give a damn if the insurance companies take it in the ear, but the authorities are supposed to protect lives. You are supposed to protect lives. That's why they pay taxes. Forget the garbage collection. Forget snowplowing. Tragedy stays in their minds. When people die, the buck stops on your desk at City Hall."

Jordan was defensive. "People die tragically every day in car accidents, and no one seems to worry too much."

"But people are driving those cars, Charles. Unless they're clobbered by a drunk, most people are actively involved in their own death. Innocent people being killed by an arson fire becomes a different matter. And a fire department funeral, wow." His eyes never left Jordan's. "All those marching firemen from around the country after the fire at the Gardner. Flag-draped caskets on fire trucks. The bagpipes. And all that TV coverage. Come on."

Mayor Jordan said nothing. His only reaction was to lick his lips.

Fairchild took a sip of wine and leaned forward. "This time, it's not going to go away overnight. Someone's got to stop it. Every time there's another fire, that's another nail in your coffin as far as re-election is concerned. And don't forget the governor's office. The people look to their elected leader for a solution."

Charles Jordan wasn't enjoying his dinner with his old friend nearly as much as he'd hoped he would. He expected sympathy along with the advice he hoped he would. "Sounds easy, Raymond. Christ, you make it sound like a pushover. But how the hell are we going to stop it all? I mean, I don't just go on TV and say, *Hey, stop it, you're killing innocent people.* Come on, I need help, not another bucket of shit thrown at me."

Fairchild looked across the harbor and watched the lights of a big jet descend onto a runway at Logan. "Maybe your arsonist wants something."

"All he has to do is say so. What? A statue? I'll commission one for City Hall Plaza, whatever size he wants. A guarantee to get out of the country? I know enough people who can arrange that with no questions asked. Christ, he can have my wife. All he has to do is ask."

"I think you can cross that one off the list," Fairchild said with a wry grin.

"Up yours, too." The mayor dipped his napkin in his water glass and daubed at some melted butter on his tie.

Fairchild waved his hand. "No, don't do that. You'll just smear it." A serious look came over his face. "Listen, I understand what you're going through. I'm available anytime, day or night, to help you. You've got to make a statement. Say your door's open to everyone. You're willing to discuss this anytime, anywhere, with anyone. You're going to field a lot of crackpots, but maybe the guy will get in touch with you."

"Sure, with some harebrained demand."

"You've got to listen to him, Charles, no matter what he wants. Like I said, use me. Bounce anything off me. I'm your friend. I'm here to help."

That's what Jordan had been looking for, a little sympathy. "I appreciate that, Raymond. I really do."

Horgan perched uneasily in the single available chair he'd found in the hospital ward. Boston Medical Center had been reinvented from a down-on-its-luck city hospital to a respected medical institution after a series of mergers. But some of the large, ancient wards that had once served the indigent still existed, although they had been upscaled to support the institution's new reputation. This was where Harvey Rothstein had been placed when EMS delivered him early that morning.

After the standard repairs due anyone who might have been the loser in a street fight, Rothstein was allowed to sleep until later that afternoon. At the insistence of a senior advisor in the mayor's office, two Boston police officers were the first to wake and interview him. Rothstein said he preferred not to file charges against the fire investigator, even after he'd been promised that the charges would stick. His answer was the same when they threatened to bring him in on parole violation. He knew Hyde too well and he also knew Hyde had friends outside the traditional circles. If Hyde went down, a convicted arsonist might just be found floating off Castle Island.

Horgan studied Rothstein's face for a moment before he began his pitch. Henry was good when he was bullshit. He could still work over a suspect faster than anyone Horgan knew, but this time he'd been so pissed he'd made some mistakes. Rothstein's broken nose had created deep, purple bags under his eyes, and his upper lip had expanded like a melon from the ten stitches underneath. The duty nurse said his testicles were also melon-like, a fact not evident to the casual observer.

Rothstein, disconcerted by Horgan just sitting there staring at him, spoke first. "Mr. Horgan, I told the cops I'm not going to press charges." He sounded like a man whose face had just come out of a deep freeze. His words were slurred and he drooled when he spoke because he couldn't bring his lips together. "I'm no dummy. I know you guys would love a reason to..."

Horgan interrupted him. "No, you're wrong, Harvey." He'd learned to use a guy's first name when you wanted to appear friendly. "Just shut up and listen for a minute. You sound like a faggot when you talk and someone else around here might pound you if they hear you. Okay? You going to be quiet?"

Rothstein nodded.

Horgan glanced around to see if they could be heard and lowered his voice. "I know you're aware of the arson fires around the city. We know you haven't been involved, at least not so far. When Hyde saw you last night, he was just arriving at another arson fire he'd been tipped off about. He's been under a lot of pressure. He sees you in the crowd, right? Of course, he has to assume you may have been involved in this one, right?"

Rothstein raised his arm and waved it because it hurt to shake his head. No, he wasn't involved.

"Hey, calm down. Remember what I said? I just said we knew you weren't involved in the others. We don't suspect you on this one. But at the time..." Horgan shrugged his shoulders. "You shoulda known better, Harvey. What're you hanging around fires for? When you get released from here, stay away from anything burning. Don't light a cigarette. Don't eat where there's candles on the table. Don't stop near any of those gas lamps in the North End. Just don't. I'll guarantee we'll take care of you if you stay clean."

Rothstein frowned through his pain. The cops said they would, too.

"Yeah, I know what you're thinking, and you're right. We expect something from you. You're a known commodity. You're good at what you do. There's a shortage of guys like you these days because someone's knocking off the guys who do so well at setting the fires." Horgan didn't know if Rothstein followed where he was going, but it was time to lay it on. "Yeah, you're right. Your name is on a short list, Harvey. It's just possible that someone may get in touch with you to see if you're looking for a little work."

Again Rothstein waved his arm and his pained expression took on new meaning.

"I know," Horgan said with a grin, "guys like you all insist you're retired from the business. Martin Grady claimed he had, but he was willing to take one more deal. El zappo. Willy Thomsen had been clean ever since he got out of the slammer. He got his at the English High fire for some reason. You know what we found under his name in Bank of Boston? Fifty big ones." Horgan was amused when Rothstein's eyes bulged through his pain. "That's right, and all deposited in different branches in five grand increments so there'd be no reason to trace a ten plus deposit. But he never had a chance to enjoy it."

Horgan could tell by the expression on Rothstein's face that he was taking in everything that was said. None of the guys who set fires for a price had ever heard of money like that.

"So, Harvey, you'll be out of here in another day or so. I understand you might not be using you're pecker for a while, but at least you're alive. And there's a chance you might be able to show the little fellow some interesting places to visit in a couple of weeks, providing you and he are still alive."

"Hey, Horgan..." Rothstein mumbled.

"I said to let me do the talking, Harvey. You've never seen my Mister Nice Guy routine before. Now, if you get a call and the promise of a big bundle to pull off a job, I want you to get in touch with me."

"Not Hyde!" Rothstein's words were sharp when he said that.

Horgan was on his feet now. He placed a comforting hand on Rothstein's shoulder. "Don't worry about Hyde. He and I are buddies and I promise my buddy won't touch you again, not if you let me know if you receive an offer that sounds too good to refuse."

Rothstein frowned.

"Why don't you just have a talk with your pecker, Harvey. Hyde's real sorry about what he did. Promised me he'd never touch it again. Said he'd apologize the first chance he got. And we both figure you'd much rather be alive so you and your bruised buddies can pay some visits again."

"You're a prick, too, Horgan," Rothstein sputtered, wiping the drool from his chin.

"You know our number." Horgan was walking out of the room, but he turned to add, "Protection, Inc. Our aim is to keep retired arsonists alive."

11

The bedside phone rang twice before the answering machine picked up the call. Hyde's voice could be heard on the recorded message.

Nomi snuggled against Hyde's shoulder. "I don't like phones either, especially when I'm having fun." They waited for a response on the other end.

Bobbie Scott's husky voice came over the machine. "Pick up, Henry, pick it up goddamnit."

Nomi hooked a leg over Henry's. "Aren't you going to talk to Bobbie?"

Hyde ran a hand down her thigh. "I thought we were just about to start something here."

"Well, yeah, I thought it was a nice idea." Nomi glanced over at the clock on the bedside table – 9:56 AM. "Christ, look at the time." She tried to pull her leg back but Hyde rolled slightly toward her, enjoying a better grip on her thigh. "I should make some calls, Henry, at least to Herm."

"Henry!" Scott's voice was loud and insistent as it crackled over the machine. "Leo and I checked out your car. You have to be there."

"Why not just a quickie?" His hand slid up her leg. "You'd feel guilty if my bad guy killed me today and you'd denied me my final piece of tail."

Nomi giggled. "That's the same line you used at five thirty this morning when I said I needed my beauty rest."

"Well, it was the perfect sleeping pill, wasn't it? You slept another four hours until Bobbie's call."

"Henry!" This time it was Leo's voice. "We're off today. We're right down your street. Either you pick up or we come up and break down your fuckin' door."

"He will, too." Hyde released Nomi and picked up the phone. "What a bunch of assholes, waking a suspended firefighter who had his first chance to sleep in for…"

"Stuff it, Henry. You never did know how to sleep in. Bobbie and I have all the stuff you wanted. How about we get some Dunkin Donuts and coffee? You jump in the shower and wash up that aging body of yours and we'll be there in twenty."

"Bring enough donuts for four."

"Whoeee. Henry's got some bimbo with him." Scott's voice in the background was loud enough for Nomi to hear.

She grabbed the phone. "Like hell he does. You better bring me a couple Boston cremes." She held her hand over the phone. "Listen to this, Henry." Then she added, "You can apologize when you get here, Mr. Scott."

She could just barely hear Scott's voice in the background. "Shit, Leo, that chick's voice sounds familiar."

Leo bent the top of the box of doughnuts back underneath and placed it on Hyde's kitchen table. He pointed in one corner of the box and mumbled sheepishly, "Two Boston cremes, right here." But he'd yet to look Nomi in the eye.

Bobbie Scott removed the coffees from the holder one by one and set them in front of the four plates Nomi had placed on the scratched wooden table. "I know you can't tell just by looking at me, but I am blushing," he said to her. "I hope you aren't too mad at me. We were both just pissed…I mean, unhappy with Henry not answering his phone when we knew he was here. We know he does that sometimes, even to the only friends he's got."

Nomi placed four pieces of paper toweling on the table. "As you may suspect, Henry has no napkins." She reached into the box and removed her two Boston cremes. "Perfect breakfast." She looked up at Scott with a big smile. "Do I really look like a bimbo to you?"

"No," he answered humbly. "I never had that impression."

"I didn't think so. It must be the company I keep." She never looked over at Hyde. Instead, she grinned and her eyes danced while she was speaking to Scott. "Your apology isn't necessary. I just have to get used to the man I've chosen to hang with."

She noticed they were still standing. "Oh, for heaven's sake! Sit down, the two of you. You're going to have to get used to me because I've come to help Henry, too, and I'm not leaving unless he tosses me out."

Hyde bit into a doughnut and spoke through a cloud of powdered sugar. "Well, that's it then. You guys are going to have to get used to her. Me, too, I guess." He washed down his donut with a mouthful of coffee and winked at Nomi. "And you're going to have to get used to them. They're ugly but they're my brothers."

Hyde pointed at the large briefcase Leo had brought with him. "What's in there?"

"Tape recorder. All the tapes you wanted. The profiles we worked on first thing this morning again. And our weapons. Never can tell when we'll need them hanging with you."

"Well I'm shocked," Hyde said with a snicker. "I was always told you're not supposed to have those off duty. Chief O'Brien'll have your ass if he finds out."

"Chief O'Brien's got enough trouble with the mayor and the commissioner without worrying about whether or not we're carrying," Leo said. "All he said this morning was – *I don't want to know where you're going. I don't want to know who you're seeing. Give Henry my best.* Al said the same."

"Nice of them," Hyde said through another cloud of powder. "Sorry you can't give them my love. Nomi, here, is sort of in the same situation as me. Her boss doesn't know where she is. You haven't seen her either."

Scott smiled at Nomi and said, "I know you're not here, Miss Cram, but I sure am glad to see you. I liked you from the first time Henry introduced us over at City Hall."

"Don't be too complimentary, and don't call me Miss Cram. I'm Nomi. I like my name. It's different. It makes people remember me."

Scott smiled.

"I'm carrying a lot of baggage, too," Nomi said. "Being a part of this, I get the edge over all the media hot shots in town. That's the only way Plain Jane gets ahead in television. You guys and Henry are sort of a dividend. And time's wasting, Henry. Never know what's going to happen next. People may be dying again tonight. Let's get on with it."

"You're the expert, Henry," Leo said. "You start it out. We'll react."

Hyde closed his eyes and massaged his forehead as he began. "White male. Must work in Boston because a bunch of his calls have originated during the day from downtown. Age – late thirties, maybe early forties."

"Why forties?" Scott asked.

"Tough question." Hyde opened his eyes. "Maybe there's a little personal opinion there. His patience. Definitely no one in his twenties. Had to be at least thirties. He maintained control when I lost mine. Turned it around and stuck it up my ass because he knew he was still a step ahead. He's learned control, which hardly ever shows before thirty. I think you'll see what I mean when we get deeper into him."

"Education?" Nomi asked.

"Beyond high school," Scott said. "No street talk. Speaks like a college guy."

"At least," Hyde said. "Since we know he's called from pay phones around Atlantic Ave at least twice, he probably has an office around there. That could mean anything – real estate, insurance. Hell, with all the restaurants in the North End, he could own one or be a chef or a bartender, maybe even be an artist from one of those lofts on the piers. But I think it's more likely business because he sounds like he's educated."

"Accent," Leo said. "Almost none. Definitely not foreign. No Haaaavuhd Yahd. No Chelsea. No Southie. Probably not from our turf."

"Hey, Leo, you'd be surprised the number of people from around here who don't talk like us. Take a spin around the North Shore sometime. Or any of the burbs for that matter, anywhere there's money. The kids don't pick up an accent unless they hear it at home or at school. His voice has been purposefully muffled, but I thought I almost heard a preppie touch a couple of times." He held up his pinkie finger and wiggled it. "You know, a touch of culture. I definitely sensed brandy and cigars when he talked, not beer and Luckies."

Leo looked out of the corner of his eye. "I guess that pretty much says where we're from."

"Play one of the tapes for me," Nomi said. "I know what Henry means. I worked over at Channel Two for three months. There's a bunch of those types in public television."

Leo played a tape over twice. Nomi made a couple of notes and when they were finished, she said, "I see what you mean about muffling his voice, but Henry's got something there. His terminology – like *excellent* or *indeed* to preface a sentence. I think he's trying to impress. You can't muffle habits. What do you think he's doing, talking through a handkerchief?"

"My friends got to that pay phone before anyone else picked it up," Leo said. "No prints. Wiped clean. So a handkerchief is as good a guess as any."

"There's another thing I noticed in that recording," Nomi said. "He's emphasized that he's smarter than Henry, which means he sees a contest in intellects. He was playing word games with the Isabella Stewart Gardner Museum and the Paul Revere House to see if he could fool Henry. He's definitely showing off. And what about the fact that he says he's already a millionaire?"

"That cuts out a lot of people," Hyde said. Then he shrugged. "But the calls aren't coming from the financial district where I'll bet we'd bump into a dozen millionaires every time we walked a block."

"So," Scott said, "I got a forty year old, white, male millionaire from the Boston area who has at least a college degree, and has more going for him than anybody I ever grew up with. He probably operates around Atlantic Avenue, but I think we've eliminated the trades. He makes a lot of money and he could do it honestly, but he's an arsonist, a murderer, and we know he has other people do his dirty work for him. So that makes me think he's in the rackets no matter how he talks. Where does he get his contacts?"

"And why does he kill them?" Leo asked.

"More likely has someone else kill them," Scott said.

"And he's a shakedown artist," Nomi said. "He says he's going to use Henry – another person again – to get him whatever it is that he wants."

"More money. Wants to be right up there with Bill Gates – without working, of course."

"Henry, you've gotta control your temper when he calls the next time." Scott leaned back in his chair, arms folded across his chest. "Me and this guy are from two different worlds. I don't know what to look for. Nomi already pointed that out. I know people by size, shape, what they drive, what their women are like, what sports they're into. You know what I mean? If I can get into those things, I can figure him out better." He looked over at Nomi. "I figured out you and Henry were hitting it off."

She wrinkled her forehead. "How?"

"Don't ask me how. It just seemed right. I'm pretty good at figuring out people." Scott squinted, like he was straining to explain what he was thinking. "You see, where I was brought up in the city, ma'am, we played basketball. That's all we played. All you need to play is sneakers, one ball, a hoop, and it's no trouble finding guys. If I get a guy in conversation about basketball today, I can probably tell you what part of the city he came from. If he played in school I'll figure out who coached him and that'll tell me how old he is, and I'll know what position he played. It ain't hard to figure all those things."

Nomi looked curiously at Hyde.

"Bobbie's right," Hyde said. "Hardly a guy who won't talk sports. Next time I got to be nice to the asshole."

The call came that afternoon.

"Hyde, you're going to have to learn how to control yourself. I understand you picked on the wrong man the other night."

"Is Rothstein the wrong man?"

"After hearing from a little bird what you did to him, I have to protect the poor man from additional damage to his privates. Indeed, I never heard of the man before."

"I guess I'll just have to make up to him the next time he starts a fire. I'll spring for beers."

"It sounds to me like he deserves champagne. VSOP at the least."

Damn, Nomi was right. The words he used. The tastes. "You know, you're a cultured guy. College and all that. You said you were smarter than me. Did you go to college around here?"

"Will it make you feel better if I said I did?"

"What were you? An Eagle? A Terrier? A Husky?"

"A man like you would think city colleges, Hyde. Enough of trying to learn about me. I have someone I'd like you to talk to about our next step."

"Not you?" Hyde asked.

"Certainly not yet. I think you've met the gentleman before. He is rather striking."

"The black guy."

"You do remember him. Keep in mind that he's as dangerous as ever."

"I'm disappointed. I wanted to meet you."

"Not yet."

"Where do I meet him?"

"The Grand Canal."

"That the place near the Fleet Center?"

"And on Canal Street no less. Just a slap shot away."

"Hockey game tonight?"

"No. Bruins are in Toronto. Celtics. Crowd will be coming out of the Fleet about ten. My man will fit right in with the fans."

"I'd much rather meet you."

"Not yet."

"You know what, asshole," Hyde said softly, "You're scared of me."

The line went dead.

But now he knew their man went to a college in the area – and there was no doubt that he had played hockey. It wasn't a hell of a lot to go on, but there was a profile developing and it wasn't someone who'd turn up in the picture files or the post office wall.

12

The Grand Canal was another British pub designed for the Boston night scene groupie. Actually, Hyde decided after he'd perched himself at the bar, Nomi might even like the place, and she was no groupie, not even a yuppie.

There was a warm fireplace. The bar, down the stairs to the right as one entered, was a large wooden affair, much more elegant than the pubs the youngsters liked. There were leather couches near the fireplace, attractive waitresses handling the tables, the food coming out of the kitchen was appealing, and there was no stink of dead beer. That was when he noticed a number of customers were wearing ties and dresses.

Yeah, she'd like the place.

Hyde sipped a ginger ale and was beginning to think that there would be no meeting when the man entered along with a group of Celtics fans. This time there was no disguise, and there was also no reason to think he'd been to the game. When Hyde realized the black man was moving in his direction, it was as if he'd materialized rather than entered through the door. The man was a presence. He was dressed in a suit customized to hide the gun that Hyde could tell he was carrying. The suit was a dark, double breasted, pin stripe and looked elegant on a man that size. But, once again, what really caught the eye of women as he crossed the room was the shiny black face, striking smile, and high cheek bones. Very dark glasses added to his mysterious appeal. Hyde noticed that even men noted his entrance – but they also looked away as he passed near them. He was elegant in every respect, but he also seemed to radiate defiance to each person he passed.

The man came directly to the bar stool beside Hyde.

"And what are we drinking tonight?" Hyde asked.

"Nothing. I'm not planning to waste time tonight, my man."

"I am not..."

The man's right hand snaked out and grasped Hyde's wrist with an iron grip. He twisted his hand slightly, his thumb intertwined with Hyde's. "One more word and I'll break it. Understood?"

Hyde nodded and blinked. A little more pressure and a quick twist and he would hear the snap of bones.

"You are to make an appointment with Mayor Jordan tonight. Not his office. Not anywhere you can be seen together right now. His home would be a good choice."

"You think he's going to invite me to dine with the wife and kiddies? That silly shit will hang up on me. Besides, it's too late."

"Not if Miss Cram initiates the call."

Hyde froze. Then he pulled the ginger ale closer with his free hand and took a mouthful. He could barely swallow. He turned to look at the man next to him, but there was nothing to be seen through those dark glasses. "You prick."

"Not under my control, Mr. Hyde. We know everything you do. Perhaps you should be more discreet about your sexual liaisons." The dark glasses were again turned so Hyde could see his own reflection in each one. "You have Miss Cram make that appointment. If she says the right words, Mayor Jordan will make some time regardless of the hour."

"You're so damn sure of yourself."

"You will show up at Mayor Jordan's home with her. You will not play games either because we know everything you're doing every minute."

"So I pay a social call on the asshole. Then what?"

"You explain that the city is going to keep burning until he arranges for half a billion dollars to be deposited in a foreign account, details to follow."

"Half a billion? Just half a fuckin' billion? Why not a billion? Why not go for two. Hey, get real. The asshole will simply call the cops. Then he'll have me locked up, probably after the bozos kick the shit out of me."

"That won't happen. Take my word for it."

"Where in the fuckin' world does your boss think this city is going to get that kinda bread?"

"My man, this is the end of the century when people make bushels of cash overnight. Times have never been better. You're going to tell the mayor that some of Boston's dot com kings and Internet princes are going to bail him out. He can do the dealin' after that."

"And afterwards – what happens next?"

"Show some patience. Someone be in touch."

The black man rose from the stool without another word and moved up the stairs quickly to the door to Canal Street.

Hyde could feel his face turning red. It was instinct that made him jump from the stool and run after the man.

The black man was already outside, but he turned just as Hyde hurtled through the door. Before Hyde could gather himself, he knew it was already too late. The man took one step in Hyde's direction, his right arm lashing out at the same time. The fist caught Hyde hard on the left cheek. It sounded like a gunshot. He fell backward as quickly as he'd been going forward. Hyde hit the front wall of the Grand Canal and slid down onto the sidewalk, too numb to move.

The black man knelt and lifted Hyde's chin until their eyes were level. "You're a hard case, my man."

All Hyde could see of the man's face was the streetlight reflecting off the dark glasses. "Your boss must be quite a man if he thinks he can pull this off," he said through the pain. "And I'm not your fuckin' man either."

"As long as he's making me rich, my man, he can pull off anything he want."

Hyde drove Nomi's car because he knew every street and every construction zone in the city, even the latest short cuts better than she did. It wasn't difficult to find Mayor Jordan's home, the perfect residence for a Boston politician, a well-kept two family in South Boston on one of those neat, secluded alleys off Broadway.

Charles Jordan's greeting, like his smile, was practiced. When he opened his front door that night, the smile was painted and the words were from memory. "The pleasure is all mine, Nomi, and..." The remainder of his sentence stuck in his throat when he recognized Hyde standing behind her.

Hyde was neatly dressed in a sport coat and slacks, his hair was combed, and his own smile was a mirror of the mayor's. He was trying very hard and would have been perfect except for the small bandage on his left cheekbone. Hyde held his own slightly cordial smile even as Jordan's disappeared.

Jordan pointed at Hyde but his eyes were fixed on Nomi. "Why? Is this a trick? I wouldn't have expected you to..."

"I'm guilty, sir. I specifically didn't mention Henry when I talked to you." Nomi was on the top step. "I can explain everything if you'll allow us in." She lifted one foot and placed it on the WELCOME mat. Her next words came quickly. "You probably don't want anyone seeing Henry standing at your front door, and both of us understand why. I promise we'll leave in sixty seconds if I can't make it clear why you should at least listen to us."

Jordan stepped back, ushering them in with a wave of his hand. He glared at Hyde, then pulled back his sleeve and held up his watch. "Sixty seconds."

This time it was Nomi who'd rehearsed what she intended to say. "The series of fires in the city have been set by a number of different individuals, some of whom have been found dead at the scene. They were murdered to cover the real source. Four Boston firefighters died at the Gardner. Boston is developing an ugly reputation fast. There is one person behind all of these fires. As you have been informed, there have been absolutely no clues and no means of tracing him. But he has established contact with one person."

She indicated Hyde. "No one has any idea why Henry is the one he's selected. He intends to shake down the city and he intends to use you and Henry – only the two of you can deal with him. Apparently no one else. If you don't allow Henry to stay, I can't begin to guess how many people will die in Boston. Think about the media. If you refuse to talk with him, the city will eventually hold you responsible."

Nomi looked at her feet and took a deep breath, looked up at Hyde, then at Jordan.

The mayor frowned, then sucked in his lips until they disappeared. He finally looked back at Nomi. She was staring at her feet again, refusing to say anything more. Finally he turned to Hyde.

The cordial facade on Hyde's face had turned to one of absolute seriousness. "She's not bullshitting you...sir." The last word hadn't come easy. "I won't bullshit you either."

Jordan bit his lip as he made his decision. "Let's go into my study." He ushered them into a high-ceilinged room toward the rear of the house, making sure to pull down the shades before he turned on all the lights. When he turned back to them, he was no longer the Mayor of Boston. The canned words and expressions were gone. "I don't want anyone to die on my account. Believe me."

"We do understand, sir," Hyde said.

"Sit." Jordan pointed to a couple of worn, overstuffed chairs with crocheted doilies on the backs and arms. "These chairs are family heirlooms. My grandmother's.

But they're comfortable." He moved behind an ancient wooden desk. "What do you drink?"

Hyde turned to Nomi with a surprised look on his face.

"Coffee...I guess," she answered.

"I've got stronger if you'd care to indulge."

"Coffee would be okay," Hyde said.

Jordan opened a cupboard behind his desk. "I intend to have a little Bushmills myself." He glanced at them over his shoulder.

"Coffee...with a dash of Bushmills would be nice," Hyde said. "It might relax us all."

Mrs. Jordan brought the coffee. She was gentle and sweet when introduced. After telling Nomi how much she enjoyed her on television, she politely excused herself.

Jordan took his Bushmills neat in a water glass, sipping before he spoke. "Your sixty seconds worked. Now you have thirty minutes to explain, especially why the two of you are here."

Hyde nodded. "I like that approach better. If you were too nice, I'd be suspicious." He grinned nastily. "After the thirty minutes, I want forty-eight hours more or you can have my shield and run my ass out of town." Then he relayed the message – half a billion dollars – and reveled in the alternating expressions on Jordan's face as the mayor began to comprehend the whirlpool he was being sucked into.

13

Ray Collins was drunk, about as drunk as one could be and still navigate. His hair, once neatly trimmed when he was a marine, had thinned over the years so that unwashed and uncut it hung over his eyes and ears in an ugly mat. The dark green uniform sweater from that long-lost era was now stained and ragged at the cuffs. For a man whose classbook listed him as "the most handsome boy in Charlestown High School", it had been a long fall. There was no longer anyone who thought Ray Collins had life by the balls. His existence had become a blur.

The bartender at Dorgan's had shut him off that night after counting Ray's money on the bar. "That's it, boyo. You're shut off. Find a place to sleep. You got enough here for a cot and some donuts in the morning." Recognizing dull resistance in Ray's eyes, he extended a hand across the bar and grasped the man's shoulder. "Ray. Go save a life, maybe your own. Go on, get out of here."

Where was...what street was this? Ray stumbled, fell against a parked car, then looked both ways up the dark street. The cars were mostly old, some of them stripped and left on the street for junk. The few that were new and fancy with smoked windows belonged to the dealers. No one would dare touch those. Trash littered the streets, the sidewalks, the alleys.

I know where I am...I do. Shadows of long-deserted breweries stood out like ghosts. *I'm in a shithole. It's where I belong.*

He remembered that there was a place a couple blocks up Parker Street where he could get a bed. A dump. He couldn't afford a room. That was an extra five bucks. But he could afford a cot in the dormitory with the other...with the other drunks. He knew it would stink of vomit, but so did he. No one would notice.

Ray was almost to the corner when he lurched to his left, recovered momentarily, then tumbled to the right into the alley that ran behind the flophouse. He struggled to his hands and knees, mumbling angrily, "Stupid son of a..." But fear cut off his words as the sound of running feet was suddenly on top of him.

A form reared up in front of him out of the darkness. Before Ray could move, someone knocked him backwards, then landed on top of him.

"What the fuck?" It was a male voice, loud, angry. "Arnie, look out. Flashlight."

A beam came out of the darkness, searching, holding for a second on the person who had just rolled off Ray.

"You okay, Woody?" The beam landed on Ray.

"Yeah. Surprised me." Woody got to his feet. "Who's that?"

"Fucking drunk."

Woody kicked Ray in the side. "Let's get going. No time."

Ray lay on his back in the garbage, struggling to catch his breath. Then he vomited across his chest. Only when he stopped and could breathe regularly again could he feel the pain in his ribs magnified by each breath. It reminded him of one of the times he'd been wounded in Vietnam, a chunk of shrapnel in his side. His life had probably been saved by the ribs that stopped the hot metal from tearing into his guts.

Ray finally rose to one elbow, gritting his teeth at the sharp stab in his side, and wiped at the vomit soaking into the front of the green sweater. He was struggling to his knees when he heard a loud popping sound followed instantly by a brilliant light that illuminated the entire alley...*like night illumination flares.* Ray watched a sheet of flame race up the back side of the structure.

No...like napalm.

And like napalm, Ray realized, the old, wooden structure was absorbing the flame. Fire billowed outward and up as the dry shingles seemed to explode. He could feel the heat intensify with each passing moment.

Ray knew vaguely why he leaped to his feet, the pain forgotten in the terror of that moment. His buddies were inside. No, this was different from the helicopter. These guys weren't really his buddies. No one who flopped there really cared about the others. But there were some like him, some who had served over there and survived the horror of the jungle, and they didn't deserve to die now in a place like that after everything they'd endured.

Ray wasn't certain of what he was going to do as he rounded the corner until he saw the red light on the pole. Fire alarm! He fumbled for the handle, yanked, then yanked again to make sure.

Then he turned and ran through the front entrance into the wide hallway that served as a lobby. The clerk was asleep behind the grillwork cage. "Fire," Ray screamed. "Fire! Fire!"

The clerk's head popped up. "Where?"

"Out back, alley. The whole back of the building's burning." There was no time. Ray ran over to the stairway. The grillwork door was locked, controlled by the clerk. "Push the button. Push the fucking button. I've got to warm them."

At the first sound of the buzzer, Ray had the door open. He raced up the flight of stairs screaming, "FIRE!" with each painful breath.

•

The sound of the box interrupted a quiet night for the Group Two watch in Fire Alarm.

Dave Kennedy looked at the red light on the board behind him. "Box Two Three Six Six. Near the corner of Tremont and Parker." He checked the location. "By the Fiddler's Inn."

"What's that?" Vartanian asked.

"Kind of a dormitory for down-and-outers. Had false alarms there before."

Leona Blake glanced at her computer screen. The lights would be going on in the fire house. "Engine Thirty Seven, Ladder Twenty Six, Box Two Three Six Six," she announced into her microphone. She looked toward Tim Carver. "No calls?"

"Nothing."

"By Fiddler's Inn," she continued. "No calls yet."

"Engine Thirty Seven on the way."

"Ladder Twenty Six following."

The second floor was already filling with smoke when Ray ran down the hall banging on doors. "Fire!" he screamed. "Fire! Fire!" When someone stumbled into the hallway, he shouted, "Get 'em up. Get 'em out. I'm going up." He gestured toward the ceiling and disappeared back down the hall through thickening smoke.

Somehow, even though the smoke was choking him, Ray knew he'd make it to the third floor. He kept his head down, crawling as he reached the top of the stairs.

He climbed to his feet and ran blindly down the hall screaming the same word over and over again, "Fire! Fire! Fire!" until his voice choked to a gurgle from the smoke.

A red light signified the end of the hall – FIRE EXIT. He couldn't breath. *Open the door.*

He pushed down on the handle but it wouldn't budge. With a final desperate lunge, he hurled himself against the door. It flew open.

With a howl like an attacking cat, a gout of flame licked in through the opening. In an instant, Ray felt his eyebrows and hair burning, his face blistering. And, unable to hold his breath, he coughed, then inhaled. The heat surged down his throat. His chest burned. Ray fell to his knees, tried for a second breath, then a third. His lungs had to be working because there was so much pain.

Ray turned and headed back. He was on his hands and knees, blinded by smoke, forcing himself back toward the stairs when his hands touched something – something soft. A body! He had to help, had to bring it with him, like he'd done before.

He tugged. The body wouldn't move. *I'm stronger than that.* No, he wasn't. His head was spinning wildly. He couldn't see. *Get out. You've done all you can.*

A hungry tongue of flame licked over his head. Ray began to crawl, but his arms gave way.

Take a breath...get up...

But he couldn't get up. He couldn't breathe. He couldn't see. He couldn't...

"Fire Alarm, this is Thirty Seven. Just turned off Tremont onto Parker. We have fire showing. Structure is fully involved. Strike a second alarm on the orders of Lieutenant Medall, Engine Thirty Seven."

"Striking second alarm."

Less than twenty seconds later. "Fire Alarm. Thirty Seven on scene. We have many civilians down. Request a third alarm, Rescue Two, and EMS backup."

Boston Fire Alarm was a flurry of activity as additional units were called out. Lights snapped on in other firehouses to send cover to empty neighborhoods.

Before the Fiddler's Inn fire was under control, two more alarms were sounded. Within the first half hour, Commissioner Duggan took command and was backed up by the deputy commissioner and the operations chief. Every media center in Boston was also at the scene.

Ray Collin's body was discovered shortly after Commissioner Duggan declared the fire knocked down.

Nomi Cram lived on the third floor of an old three decker in Brighton. The building was in decent condition but far enough from Commonwealth Avenue to still be awaiting gentrification. There were as yet no yuppies searching for hidden values where she lived. Instead it was a combination of young marrieds not yet on the way up, singles like Nomi who could afford a safe neighborhood, second generation Hispanic families, and a large gay population that in many ways made the area safe for women.

A couple named White, who had changed their name from Blanco after moving in, lived on the second floor with two school age children. A gay male couple occupied the first floor. When Nomi had time to cook, she sometimes invited the guys up because they were responsible for the flowers that bloomed in the small yard and the hanging baskets on the front stoop.

Nomi had selected her apartment as Hyde's base of operations because, "Only my boss knows where I live, my number's unlisted, and no one can get you by phone, Henry, unless you want them to."

"I like this place," Carmichael said. "Real curtains. Not the plastic sh...crap like Henry's."

"And there's actually food in the fridge," Bobbie said. Nomi had taken a coffee cake out of the freezer and heated it in the oven before they arrived. "And we didn't have to bring our own coffee."

"You can both stuff it," Hyde said irritably. "I didn't sleep much last night and I don't need to listen to that crap."

"Suspended firefighters are supposed to sleep like babies," Carmichael retorted snappily. It was the wrong comment and Leo knew it before he'd finished the sentence. "Sorry, Henry. That was my superb sense of humor screwing up again."

Hyde looked into his coffee. "Not a problem. I was thinking more about what to do for Ray Collins."

"The guy that woke everybody up? The drunk?" Leo said.

"The Ray Collins I knew went to Vietnam after high school, just like the rest of us. He was a marine. Wounded twice. First time he took a bullet through his ass cheek, flesh wound. A buddy of mine ran into him at the hospital in Danang. It was so minor he was back with his unit in three weeks."

Hyde looked out the window before speaking again. "His unit was at Khe Sanh...during the siege." His voice had become as soft as any of them had ever heard. "It was a different Ray Collins then. He won a Bronze Star in action, and then a couple of days later he got his second Purple Heart and the Silver Star for saving three men trapped in a burning helicopter, including his CO."

Hyde got up, walked over to the window, and lit a cigarette. The room was absolutely silent.

"That was the Ray Collins I knew." He turned around. "I lost track of the older one. I know he married Lucy Wilson, who was in our class, and I know they had a couple of kids. Someone told me not so long ago that Ray was never able to adapt after he came back. He was one of those guys who tried like hell, but I guess he could never hold a job. I ran into him once and got him to take the exam to get into the department, but he never followed up on it. Probably already too far gone on the booze."

Hyde sat down again in front of his pack of cigarettes and lit another. He sighed. "That's why I wish I was there last night. I would have liked to help bring Ray out."

Bobbie said, "Someone ought to get hold of the marines, let 'em know one of their own..."

"I called the commissioner before I came over. He was in Nam at the same time. LRRP patrols. He went through a lot of the bad shit, too. Duggan's still got a lot of military contacts. Said he'd take care of it." Hyde looked at the others. "Come on, let's get on with it."

Scott turned to Nomi. "You know, Nomi, none of us would object if you wanted to set up a no smoking policy here. We'd actually help enforce it."

Hyde grinned slightly. "Stuff it. Give me your coffee cup for an ashtray, Bobbie."

"Henry's entitled to his habit as long as the pressure's on." Nomi offered the plate of coffee cake around the table again. "Come on, eat up or I'll have to take this downstairs to the guys."

"What guys?" Hyde asked. "I didn't see any guys when I came in." He was reverting to his old self. "Couple of fairies maybe, Homer and Jethro, but no guys."

"Be nice. They're my security blanket," Nomi said. "How about that fire at Fiddler's Inn. Let's concentrate on the bad guys."

"No description," Leo said. "Bartender at Dorgan's said he went outside to make sure Collins was heading for Fiddler's Inn when two guys ran by. Heard the sirens shortly after. Coulda' been them. Two white males was all he could give us."

"Probably was them," Bobbie said. "All the corpses have been identified. Street people. None in the alley. No one we could tie to the point of origin."

"We don't even know if our man was involved in this one," Hyde said. "No calls from him before or after. What would torching a flop house do for him?" He shrugged. "Maybe he'll tell me when he decides to let me in on the rest of his plan." Hyde looked expectantly at Carmichael. "How long before we have that breakdown of Atlantic Ave. businesses?"

Leo wrinkled his forehead thoughtfully. "I'm using another old buddy, a guy who had a little trouble once. He owed me one. By the time he finishes, I'm going to owe him big time. He works the phones for a telemarketer. When things are quiet, he's playing with the computer, trying to break into the demographics for the district, but it's not the same as a residential area. His company mostly hits purchasing agents, human resources people. They got the names of the independent businesses, but not broken down like you want."

"Can you at least get a list of names?" Hyde indicated the others with a sweep of his hand. "With four of us, we can start breaking them down. Nomi's got sources, too. We got the beginnings of a profile if we can work with some names."

"Where's your phone, Nomi?" Leo asked.

"Bedroom. Make believe I picked up everything."

Leo got up. "Let me see what he can do."

"I got about thirty six hours left before that asshole, Jordan, owns me," Hyde said. He lit another cigarette. "I suppose we may just piss off a lot of big money names before we're finished."

Bobbie noted Hyde's twisted grin. It was hard to be both irreverent and black at the same time in Boston, but it was something to work for. He wanted to be the next Henry Hyde.

Dennis Campbell, Jordan's media director, sat quietly on a couch in the mayor's office. His legs were crossed and he was making a major effort to appear nonchalant. As he listened to Jordan's part of the phone conversation, he thanked whatever god might be foolish enough to pay attention to him that it was Raymond Fairchild on the other end.

"That son of a bitch, Hyde, has big balls, Raymond. Acts like he's the commissioner. Big as life right in my own house. Got his foot in the door with that broad, Cram, from Channel Seven. As much as told me that he was so close to nailing this arsonist that I could fire his ass if he didn't have the bastard in forty eight hours."

Amusement was definitely evident on Jordan's face at the idea of canning Hyde.

"Yeah. Me, too, Raymond. Total surprise. From no leads at all to total confidence."

Obviously neither one could fathom Hyde's attitude.

"No, I can't figure either. But the little prick acted like it was just a matter of time." There was a neutral expression as Jordan nodded his head. Then satisfaction at the prospect of wrapping it up.

"Yeah, you've been my most loyal supporter from day one, Raymond. I'll let you know the moment I find anything out from Hyde."

Jordan hung up the phone and came around from behind his desk. "Dennis, I want you to schedule a news conference at the end of the day, just in time to break for the six o'clock news."

"Nothing that's going to put us in a corner?"

"Nothing of the kind. We're going to announce that we are following a trail and may be able to bring in suspects in the arson case within twenty-four hours."

Raymond Fairchild stared at the shiny, black object in his right hand. He was squeezing the life out of the telephone, but the inert instrument was resisting him. Who the fuck did Hyde think he was? Forty eight hours? He glanced at his watch. More like thirty six – and counting, you shithead!

And Jordan – that arrogant prick! Who did he think he was acting so high and mighty?

After a moment's hesitation, Fairchild pushed the buzzer for Dorothy Murray.

"Yes, Raymond."

"Mix me a drink and get yourself ready for the ride of your life. I'll be back in five minutes."

Then Fairchild made two phone calls. That was all that was necessary. Both of them, Hyde and Jordan, deserved a lesson.

14

Women. They should be seen...used...enjoyed...but...

Raymond Fairchild uncrossed his legs and shifted on the park bench. Too hard. There was no comfortable position. It was a cloudy day and the wood was as cool through his pants as the breeze coming off Boston Harbor was on his face. His cell phone, open, rested on his lap. A passenger jet sweeping down over the harbor briefly attracted his attention.

That bitch!

He turned his right hand over and stared at the black and blue skin swelling around the torn flesh on his index and third fingers. He tried to make a fist but had to stop before the tips of his fingers could touch his palm.

Dogs were allowed one free bite – but not Dorothy Murray. *First bite, last bite, bitch.*

She'd gotten spoiled. Must have thought life was all milk and honey, that she was home free. Bullshit! Sometimes you have to pay the piper, pay the sugar daddy who foots the bill. Did she really think she was too good for a little kinky stuff? Too goddamn high and mighty? Couldn't remember what it was like just to be a secretary?

When a broad was suddenly lifted to the top of the heap by the big guy, she should know – she had to – that you did what you were told and enjoyed it.

On the other hand, it was a damn good thing it was just the fingers she got. A sudden chill coursed from his groin to his belly at the thought. That bitch! Close call, little Raymond.

That was the end of it. Dorothy Murray was history. That was something else Jean-Paul could do for him.

The park where Fairchild sat was a green strip on the harbor side of Commercial Street by the Marriott Long Wharf, a great location for girl watching at lunchtime on a nice day. Today was too cool. The women were all in coffee shops munching on salads covered with nuts and fruit. There wouldn't be a chance of finding a replacement for Dorothy today. But that wasn't the reason he'd come out to the park. Still – Fairchild smiled inwardly – the idea had merit. Just pick out a chickie strolling by. *Hey, honey, how'd you like to live like a real queen?* That should be a hard one to refuse.

But not today.

Fairchild held the cell phone in his right hand and punched the number awkwardly with his left index finger. Then he shifted hands and heard the first ring on the other end as he brought the instrument to his ear.

Second ring.

Third ring.

"Yes, sir." A familiar voice, a face he'd never seen.

"I've changed my mind," Fairchild said.

"Hey, man, I work fast. Just a couple of hours ago, you..."

"I said I changed my mind."

The person on the other end had been recommended by an intermediary and had no idea who was giving the orders. "I'm going to have trouble calling off my guy. He's already on the road. Since talent in this trade generally work at night, they have to be extra careful in the daylight. My guy is off to case the place, put together a plan of attack."

"I assume he has a beeper."

"Yes."

"Stop him."

"You mean cancel everything?"

"I mean stop him. I've changed my mind. I want him to do a car instead."

"Just a car! After what we hired him for? I mean… that's a lot of bread and…"

"The pay remains the same." The message was all that mattered.

"Same address?"

"No. There's a detached two car garage down the street." Fairchild explained how to find it.

"So, if there's two cars, which one do you want?"

"The Cadillac."

"Do you want it to blow when it's started?"

"Christ no. I don't want anyone hurt. I just want it torched." Fairchild shuddered at the idea of Jordan, his fatted calf, going up in smoke.

"Okay. Then my guy's got to use a timing device so he can be somewhere else when it goes."

"I don't care how. Just do it."

Fairchild snapped the phone shut and studied his throbbing fingers. That bitch. He hadn't really been hurting her. Perhaps he should have his doctor look at the wound. The last thing he needed now was an infection. But, no. Time was short. He couldn't afford turning up in familiar places either. Later maybe.

He flipped the phone open, punched in the secure number for Jean-Paul, let it ring three times, hit the off button, then hit the redial.

The response came as the first ring died away. "Yes." The creamy-rich voice was full of sleep.

"I have a woman I want you to take care of."

"Ahh. Women thank me when I take care of them."

"She's Hyde's girl friend."

"The TV lady. White women especially like me."

"She's going to be a part of one of your fires."

"That is so sad. I hate to waste them. Maybe she could love me first."

"That's your privilege. All I want is the job done."

•

Leo and Bobbie had gone. Nomi stood before a seated Hyde. She tipped his chin up with her finger tips, bent from the waist, and kissed him softly.

"That's nice," Hyde said. "Have I said that before?"

"You have." She kissed him again.

"I can't remember the last time a woman treated me like this. I might get used to it."

"You're going to get a lot more of it." She nodded toward the bedroom door. "We haven't used my bed yet."

"No, we haven't. It sounds like fun. Of course, so does the sofa, the bathtub, the kitchen sink, the hall closet... the..."

"I've started something."

"I promise we will, your bed." Hyde pursed his lips. "But..."

"You're going to say you don't have time for a little tumble?"

"If a little tumble is like I think it is, it's usually not so little and it usually turns into more than one." He shook his head slowly. "I can't believe I'm saying this but I don't have the time."

"Whatever you say."

"I did just say it and I can't believe it." He stood up and patted her on the rump. "In another couple of days, you'll either spend the day in bed with a guy who's earned back his job or a guy who doesn't have one. I might even become your dependent. Right now I'm going to try to keep that job."

"Where are you going?"

"Al Horgan said he'd make a copy of every file on every incendiary fire I've investigated in the last few weeks. Since I'm not supposed to be near my office, I'm going to call him on your phone and ask him to meet me for a cup of coffee. While I'm gone, you can finish keying all our profiling notes into your computer. When I come back, we'll add Al's stuff, too."

•

Nomi installed the last of the profiling data into her computer then scrolled back to the beginning to proof her input.

"What? What am I proofing this for?" she asked out loud. "It's not the six o'clock news. We're not trying to please advertisers." She punched the necessary keys and watched as the new document rolled out of the printer, one copy for each of them.

Her doorbell was a faint irritant in the background above the sound of the machine.

"It's open." Her voice was unnecessarily shrill. "Try turning the knob."

Nomi was still watching the printed lines roll up when she heard the door close behind her. That was when she first looked over her shoulder.

"I have upset your plans." The accent when he said *your plans* carried the mellifluous song of the islands...the accent that Henry had mentioned.

Nomi froze. Her eyes recorded shiny black skin, white teeth, flashing eyes – then a gloved hand clapped over her mouth. Black leather covered her nostrils. She couldn't breathe. She clawed at the hand.

"Drop your arms to your sides." Her head was yanked back against his chest. "You are going to hurt yourself if you fight me. Drop them – now!"

Nomi let her arms fall to her sides. The pressure eased. She drew air into her lungs.

"That's betta. Now you can make things easier for both of us if you listen to me. Do you know who I am?"

A brief flash of Henry's description of the black man at the Sports Depot, again at the Grand Canal, flashed across her mind. But she shook her head – no.

"I think you do. Your friend Hyde, he probably mentioned me. You are involving yourself in something that you be better off not knowing. If you agree to what I tell you right now, I will take you away from your work here. And you have a good chance of remaining alive."

The man's soft accent was lilting, almost sweet. But his tone – deadly. He didn't care what he did to her.

"If you don't agree, then you be dead. I'm really not offering you a good choice, am I? Now, will you cooperate with me and live?"

Nomi nodded.

"I'm going to remove my hand. If you make any noise, you will be dead quickly. There is nobody in the apartment below. If you do anything to attract the attention of the gay men on the first floor, you be responsible for their deaths."

He removed his hand and turned her chair around as if she were weightless, then bent from the waist so that she was looking into his face.

The eyes! Nomi again was struck by those flashing, black eyes – but they had no depth. Without saying a word, those eyes reinforced what he had just explained to her. She was certain there would be no change in his expression if he killed her at that moment.

"Our Mr. Hyde is brighter than I gave him credit for." His smile was a slight parting of the lips, a quick flash of teeth. "You have been hiding your beauty, but I can see it. Jean-Paul sees beauty everywhere. I could enjoy you."

Nomi closed her eyes.

He straightened up. "We are going out of here together. Let's get your coat so you will appear normal."

He removed a long-barrelled gun from his black leather coat and held it under her nose for a moment. "I want to tell you that this doesn't make any noise." He slipped it back inside. "And you must remember that if you attempt anything that displeases me you will die along with anyone who happens to witness the event." So little accent, coy, almost as if he was putting it on.

Nomi rose slowly to her feet. She intensely wanted to be brave but she knew her voice was shaking. "Can you tell me a good reason I should go with you?"

"Being alive better than being dead."

The Mercedes that she entered, like the man, was shiny black. The windows were tinted.

No one saw her leave. No one would see her in the car.

"Arson. Inspector Carmichael speaking."

"Leo?"

"Yeah."

"This is Sully."

"Just what I need is you calling me at headquarters."

"You weren't home. This is important."

"This phone may be tapped."

"Then that would make two of us tapping it. I'm at home. Find a pay phone and call me."

Leo left Bobbie Scott to mind the squad phone and walked down to the McDonald's at the corner of Mass. Ave. and Southampton. He inserted a quarter and dialed Johnny Sullivan's home phone number.

"You know, Sully, I could have job problems if someone knew you were calling me."

"Don't sweat the small shit, Leo. My kid plays hockey, got a scholarship offer from BC, the commissioner's college. That must make us asshole buddies. I'll put in a good word if you run into a problem. Okay?"

Leo smiled to himself. That's how the city ran. "What's so important?"

"Coupla things. That black cat you told me about's on the move. He grabbed some broad."

"Who?"

"Don't know who yet or why. I'll give you a jingle when I got an ID. Before I could locate you, the job was already done. And the action's gonna get very hot and heavy super quick. Your bad guy's sending some heavy messages."

"Shit! Where?"

"Sorry, buddy. These cats don't fuck around. Real pros. They use more than one cell phone. All I got is that a job was changed. Gonna hit someone's car instead of a building. But I don't know who's pulling off the job or where. All I know is that the guy that was called gives orders to a guy who arranges the job."

"Shit! What've you got on the guy giving the orders?"

"Not a hell of a lot. I recorded everything. We got a voice. Hell, you got that voice, too. I traced one phone. It's a dummy corporation as far as my guys can find out. Leo, believe me, I'm working on it."

"I'll tell you what..." Leo paused. How to explain to Sully? "Things are getting a little involved...I mean... Sully, we got a problem with politics."

"Because of my sterling reputation?"

"Not so much that. It's just that some things that are going down need to be kept in the department. Better that people don't know you're involved – yeah. But also better for you if we make a mistake. Shit, Sully, Henry and I talked it over. I need to do the cellular stuff that you're doing now. Believe me, it's the best idea for all of us – believe me," he said tentatively.

"Okay, I believe you."

"We been together through a lot of..."

"I said I believe you. I'll do it. Okay?"

"How tough is it going to be for me to learn?"

"It isn't. You and me, I'll show you how to use my scanner, how to program the data into a unit I'll loan you. You don't have to understand the electronics, Leo. I'll make you a part of the network."

"I didn't want to do this." Leo was apologetic. "I know how it is. I owe you."

"Hey! Better you don't know all of my business – better I don't know all of yours. Still friends. Okay?"

"Still friends."

Franny Jordan pushed the button for the garage door. Even before she could see the cars, she was playing an old game. "Eenie, meenie, minie, mo..." Her index finger bounced from her husband's Cadillac to her own reasonable Chevy convertible.

The Mayor of Boston, her husband was fond of telling her, had to put on a show. A Cadillac sent a message to the voters – class. Although he was driven to and from City Hall by a chauffeur in a city-owned car, he often showed up at events on nights or weekend in the Cadillac.

His wife's idea of class was a convertible. The make didn't matter. If you wanted people to understand who you were, you put the top down and let your hair blow in the wind. The Jordans remained a happy couple because they indulged each other's whims.

Today Franny Jordan's index finger stopped on "this very one" – her husband's Cadillac. The weather was questionable anyway, cloudy and cool, a good day to leave a convertible inside.

She followed the familiar side streets until she turned south on Dorchester Avenue. Each intersection became more familiar as she approached the neighborhood where she'd grown up. More than half of the small businesses and corner bars still carried the same family names, even though they were run by another generation.

Some of the names near Fields Corner were unfamiliar. New cultures were taking over whole blocks of the ancient streets as the previous owners moved to new sections of the city or to the suburbs. Irish, Jewish, Black, now Vietnamese. Movement meant rising status.

As the Cadillac came to a stop at the light at Freeport Street, she heard a single loud click. A split second later, the front of the car heaved up in the air at the same time a gush of flame seemed to surround the outside.

The car came down on the two right wheels, teetered for a moment, then righted itself. Before Franny Jordan could react, flames flowing from beneath the dash ran up her legs. Her skirt disappeared. Her nylons melted. She could actually see her flesh blacken.

It was sheer instinct that let her find the door handle. Smoke and flame filled the auto's interior as she tumbled into Dorchester Avenue, her remaining clothes and hair on fire.

One of the neighborhood's new residents, a Vietnamese launderer yelling excitedly in his own language, was the first to get to Franny Jordan. She was screaming unintelligibly, pain controlling her, when he rolled her in wet sheets.

When Engine 17 arrived on the scene moments later, the Cadillac was fully engulfed. The victim had been moved away from the car just before the gas tank had gone, but two other cars were now also in flames.

When the first Boston EMS vehicle arrived, an immediate call for backup was sent to assist the Vietnamese cleaner and two bystanders caught by flaming gasoline.

The first police unit on scene recognized the Caddy and the license plate.

When Mayor Jordan emerged through the door from the emergency room at Boston Medical Center, Commissioner Duggan was already there.

"Find Hyde for me," Jordan demanded.

15

Hyde hated limos, particularly this one. He felt small in the plush back seat at a moment in time when he wanted to feel and act big. Even stretching, he couldn't touch the window that separated him and Charles Jordan from the driver. The side and rear windows were heavily tinted but he could see out. No one could see in.

Hyde had been brought over to Boston Medical Center in a deputy chief's car to meet the mayor. City Hall was less than a dozen blocks from the hospital, an easy ten minute walk, but Jordan preferred the privacy of his limo and now they were stuck in traffic on Cambridge Street. The trip would take half an hour and Hyde needed every minute as much as he needed a few hours sleep.

"I'm sorry. Very sorry. Your wife's a fine woman." Hyde tried to remember what Mrs. Jordan looked like. He was embarrassed because he couldn't remember her first name. The only time he'd met the mayor's wife was when she brought the coffee into Jordan's study. That was... when? Yesterday? Last night?

"The doctors say she'll survive." For once, Jordan's voice was subdued, his manner reserved, almost apologetic. "It's going to be a long haul for her." He closed his eyes. "Agonizing, they said."

Hyde had seen too many burn victims. He'd been able to feel their anguish when he looked into their eyes. Shock was a blessing in disguise; shock nullified the agony. He'd experienced burns before, but nothing like Mrs. Jordan's. Hers were third degree. Over fifty percent of her body. It wasn't so long ago that her survival odds would have been limited at best. Now she'd make it, but survival was almost as bad as the alternative.

He glanced over at Jordan, who was staring into his neatly folded hands. The mayor couldn't imagine what was in store for his wife. The desperate medical battle to stave off infection would take weeks, perhaps even months. Then there was the agony of the scrub tub where it felt like crushed glass on raw flesh when dead skin was scrubbed off. The daily changing of bandages was equally painful. But what they never told a victim about until the last moment was the innumerable surgeries when thin slabs of live skin were sliced off like cheese to cover the raw, burnt flesh and become protective, healthy, new skin.

Hyde had heard the unearthly screams, still heard them in his sleep, as hardened firefighters pleaded for more drugs.

How tough was Franny Jordan?

Poor woman. He couldn't remember what she looked like but – poor woman.

"Yes, it is painful," Hyde answered weakly. "But Mrs. Jordan is a fine woman. She's tough. She'll make it." She'd make it better if her husband gave his one hundred percent to helping her.

"It's the same person – the arsonist, I mean – isn't it?"

"It has to be. The methods vary, but so do the guys he's hired," Hyde said. "Inspector Sullivan from our Auto Arson Unit, our best guy, is at the scene now. Although cars are something different than we've…"

"What's different about it?"

"Everything we've had so far from him has been structural. There were different methods used to ignite them. We found the bodies of two different people who set fires, and each one had a completely different method. We don't know why they were murdered. But there haven't been any cars torched."

"It's the same person. I know it is." Jordan leaned forward, balancing his forehead in his hand. "We don't have any choice. I got to call in all my ducks." His voice was barely audible. "And I'm going to have to convince those ducks to call in theirs." He glanced over at Hyde. "Funny, a lot of the new money people are learning something from the old money – hold on to it, don't spend it if you don't have to. The really savvy ones realize it's easy come, easy go. They aren't running around in their old preppy clothes like the old money, but they haven't learned how to wear a coat and tie either." Jordan shook his head, realizing he was circling his subject. "We have to pay...we have to pay."

"If we can't find him by tomorrow." Hyde was amazed at the weakness of his own voice.

"I've already raised a lot of the money. No problem with the rest." Jordan straightened his back, and stared straight ahead as he said, "So how do we do this?" His eyes were suddenly angry. "You're the messenger boy. What next?"

Messenger boy. Fuck him. "I don't know. I haven't been told."

The mayor mirrored his own frustration. "So – what?"

It was a good question. Where was the end? "We haven't given up. We have leads," Hyde said. "A lot of people are working on this. We really do have some things we're chasing down and..."

The high-pitched ring of a cell phone interrupted.

The chauffeur answered and, after a moment's hesitation, pushed the intercom button. "Mr. Fairchild for you, sir. Should I tell him you'll call him back?"

Jordan shook his head and reached for a phone set into the console dividing the back seat. "Hello, Raymond."

Hyde studied Jordan's reactions.

"I appreciate your concern. She's critical but the doctors say she has a good chance for recovery."

A softness around the eyes.

"No...no...they can't say for sure. But I was told it was obvious something exploded. They don't know how yet." Jordan grimaced. "Probably meant for me."

"Yes, it is depressing. I see no alternative but to go along with what I told you during our last conversation. I'm going to have to hold you to your promise of..."

"Believe me, Raymond, I never thought it would come to this. Maybe" – Jordan glanced at Hyde – "the Arson Squad will come up with something. I have the investigator, Hyde, with me right now and he says he has some solid leads."

"Yeah, that's right. Right here. He says there are people working on it right now...right now. Christ, I'd kill to get my hands on that son of a bitch." Somberly. "That was meant for me. No reason to hurt Franny. If he wants to kill me, I want to kill him."

"No, I'm going right down to the wire with Hyde. If he says they've got solid leads, I'm not going to authorize that transfer until the last minute."

Behind them, the urgent bellow of fire sirens overrode all other sound.

"Jesus, not another fire."

Jordan's driver pulled the limo up on the curb of the median to allow a ladder truck and an engine to squeeze by.

"What are you so angry about, Raymond? You were willing to help me out. I hope you're not going to back out on me now. I don't know what I'd do without your support. Not just with the money, I mean. With everything. You've been my best friend."

The chauffeur had pulled in directly behind the fire engines and was using them for blocking as they headed for City Hall.

"Yeah, of course I'll keep you informed. Anything that happens, any little thing."

Hyde saw the column of smoke as they came over the rise above the Kennedy Federal Building. It was still black, still feeding on fresh fuel, still out of control.

Revolution, American independence, and Boston's Faneuil Hall were synonymous. The ancient structure was as close to sacred as a building could be. It was America's "Cradle of Liberty". Boston's mayors had always given their State of the City speeches from Faneuil Hall's second floor where fiery Sam Adams had railed against the British king more than two centuries before. It was a symbol of Yankee steadfastness and independence.

The pall of dark smoke that rose over the ancient structure mirrored the glum expressions of the onlookers.

Hyde remained slightly behind Jordan as the mayor strode across the brick and cobble to Commissioner Duggan's side.

"How bad is it?" Jordan asked Duggan.

"Under control." Duggan wasn't looking at the mayor.

"Do we know what caused…"

"It started on the second floor, above the retail stores." Quaint stalls on the first floor housed small shops as they might have appeared three hundred years before. "No one was up there."

"You mean it didn't start by itself…"

The commissioner continued to avoid Jordan's eyes. "I mean no one knows yet. Cause unknown at this time." Duggan moved quickly from Jordan's side as his chief of operations, listening to a hand radio, waved him over for a private conference.

Jordan looked over his shoulder for Hyde, who was a few feet away talking with the district chief. The mayor gestured irritably to Hyde.

Hyde exchanged a few more words before he ambled over beside Jordan.

"Duggan says the fire started on the second floor. Then he says there wasn't anyone there. He said the cause was unknown. What's he mean?"

Hyde stared straight ahead. *Why me?* Why was he all of a sudden Charles Jordan's buddy? "He means that all they know is that the fire started on the second floor. Until the fire is out, fire investigators can't get in to determine exactly where it started on the second floor and what caused it."

"But that son of a bitch did it!" Jordan slammed a fist into his palm. He glared up at Hyde. His cheeks shook with rage as he spoke. "It's the same son of a bitch who hurt Franny. And you can't find him. All the shit that he's pulled today...and you can't find him."

Hyde said nothing.

The commissioner appeared beside them. "I've got to steal Henry," he said to the mayor. "This fire's under control. We got another that's causing some bigger problems." He regretted his last words before he was finished.

Jordan eyed Duggan, waiting expectantly to hear about the new fire and, when it wasn't forthcoming, said, "Where and what problems?"

"Old South Meeting House." Again, Duggan's eyes were looking away. "It's hot. White hot. Just like the hotel."

Jordan's face was reddening. "The son of a bitch. The son of a bitch. He's got me by the balls." He grabbed Hyde's arm. "He's destroying history, making me look like an asshole. You said you've got leads." He was shaking Hyde's arm now. "You better get that son of a bitch or I'm..."

It took Duggan less than a second to see the pressure building in Hyde. He grabbed Hyde's arm, pointed toward the operations chief, and pushed him on his way before the mayor could finish

Voodoo. Black magic. Those were the first thoughts that came to Hyde. It was as if the man had materialized out of thin air. One moment Hyde was talking with a lieutenant from an engine company. Then the lieutenant turned to answer someone, and Hyde felt instant pain. His right arm was suddenly twisted behind his back, then jammed upwards. The pain was intense. The pressure was steady. He was being pushed rapidly from behind and his body was complying. His feet seemed to move by themselves, almost as if he'd been carried behind the truck.

"My man, oh my man, you are one hard son of a bitch."

Hyde knew that if he moved even a little the bone would snap. "You're pushing your luck, asshole. What if someone sees this."

"They will indeed see two friends talking, so hoppily talking," Jean-Paul said with his island lilt, "because you know that you will come out of this second best. And, my man, I will fade away."

"What do you want?"

"You are supposed to be working with the mayor to help end these fires. I be told that is not the case."

"I don't understand. I was just with him."

"Oh, but you do understand, my man. Jean-Paul hears everything. And what I hear is that you need some convincin.'"

"I'm not your fucking..."

"You are whatever I want you to be."

The pressure increased ever so slightly. Hyde winced.

"Just a little more and you be badly injured. Am I getting your attention, my man."

"What else?"

"You don't seem to understand that when you are ordered to do something with the mayor, that is all you do. From this moment on, my man, you will."

"Fine. That's all I'll do." How the hell does someone hear that...? Who was Jordan talking to on the phone back in the car? Raymond. Raymond who?

"There's someting else. Your lady friend has decided to stay with Jean-Paul until this be all over."

Hyde's head swiveled around in an effort to look at the man. "Listen, you mother..."

"Shut up." Another slight increase in pressure. "You be about to use a racial slur, my man, and that always gets me excited." Jean-Paul's voice grew softer, more threatening. "Now you listen to this. Your Miss Cram be one fine lady. I know women. Oh yes I do. And that lady has a great deal to offer...to make a man happy."

Hyde's muscles tensed.

Jean-Paul's lips were next to Hyde's ear. "No more. You can't help anyone with a broken wing, little bird. Yes, she likes me. I see it in her eyes. If you don't do exactly as you be told, she's going to love Jean-Paul. Don't move a muscle, Hyde. Don't even think bad thoughts now. Because if the lady learns to love Jean-Paul, that young lady will never come back to you."

Hyde closed his eyes. If he moved or even said what was on the tip of his tongue, the black man would hurt him badly.

The voice was soft, taunting. "You know what they say about white women and black men. They never go back home once they've enjoyed us. You don't want that to happen now, do you?"

Hyde shook his head.

"Do what you be told, my man."

It was perhaps a second, no more than two, before Hyde realized the man was gone. He allowed his arm to drop to his side. The pain was real now. It had been so close to the breaking point. He could barely wiggle his fingers.

He turned and thought he saw the tall form moving through the crowd, but before he could move in that direction it was gone.

"Henry!"

Hyde turned. Bobbie Scott was coming toward him.

"Henry." Scott recognized the pain in Hyde's face. He reached out and squeezed his shoulder. "Are you alright?"

Hyde shook his head. "Nomi – she's been grabbed."

16

Carolina Fairchild lifted her hand tentatively and touched the corner of her right eye with shaking fingers. It was tender, but also dry. No more tears. The skin was raw, and she knew a glance in the mirror would exaggerate the redness. And ugliness.

She hated crying women. It was a sign of weakness. Women who felt sorry for themselves and cried until their eyes were puffy and sore usually deserved what got them to that point. They had no positive self image. No respect for themselves. Just self pity. Balling bitches.

Did anyone ever accomplish anything by feeling sorry for themselves? Not in the least.

Carolina looked down at the water glass on the table. Straight vodka. The ice cubes had melted. She picked it up, holding the glass to the light. Go ahead, take a good hit. It's clear, just like water. No kick there. What the hell. She took a mouthful, held it momentarily, then swallowed as unpleasant fumes infused her nose.

Shit! She coughed involuntarily and suddenly the liquid was coming back up and it was burning. Jumping quickly to her feet, her hand covering her mouth trying to hold it back, Carolina stumbled to the bathroom. Just in time. The vodka and what little she'd eaten in the last twenty four hours splashed out in a rush.

Carolina didn't realize she was on her knees until she was finished. That hadn't happened since college. She remembered the phrases – driving the porcelain bus, making love to the toilet bowl. So original and funny then. Forget it. Not funny now. She rose to her feet and moved over to the sink to wash her face. The creature she saw in the mirror was one she'd always detested – red, puffy eyes, yesterday's mascara running down her cheeks, age lines that on a normal day were carefully covered, messy hair.

Frumpy.

"You are the perfect harridan," she said. She eyed the sorry creature staring back at her. "Time to get your act together, babycakes."

Carolina leaned into the shower and turned on the water. First shower. Then pamper.

After a long, hot shower, she did her hair in a way she hadn't done in years – because Raymond didn't like it that way. Then, dressed in jeans and a sweatshirt, which Raymond also hated to see her in except in the garden, she headed downstairs and fixed herself scrambled eggs, toast, and fresh coffee.

Food tasted wonderful. "Beats the hell out of booze anytime," she said aloud.

By the time the frying pan had been washed and the dishes rinsed and put in the dishwasher, she knew what her next step would be. Raymond, perfect Raymond, had to have made at least one mistake. It might take time, but Carolina would find it.

She went through each drawer in her husband's dresser, carefully lifting each item one at a time, searching for whatever he might have inadvertently left.

Nothing in his dresser. The bastard was fastidious.

Each of the Fairchilds had a walk-in closet of their own. Carolina started at the rear of Raymond's, going through every pocket, then hanging each item back up as precisely as it had been before. She found what she was looking for in the second-to-the-last suit, in the tiny pocket inside his left hand coat pocket.

A slip of paper. A phone number neatly written in ballpoint pen. No name. Just a number.

One of his whores?

Carolina really didn't care. It was a start.

She went downstairs to the den, sat at her desk, and opened the phone book to the exchange code section. It was a number in the city. She placed the scrap of paper on the surface of her desk and smoothed it methodically with the palm of her hand until she was certain that this was what she wanted to do – had to do.

The phone line was her own, a personal number because Raymond didn't like women yakking when he needed to talk business. The thought struck her that she had no idea what her first words would be. But who cared? Whatever, the words would come.

She punched 1, then more slowly the 617 area code. Do it! The next seven numbers were a blur. She closed her eyes. It would be a woman's voice answering. Carolina was certain of that.

The phone on the other end rang once, then again. She opened her eyes. There were two more rings before she heard the ominous click, an unexpected pause, then an answering machine – A man's voice! No name. No introduction, just a dull monotone: "Leave the time, the date, and phone number." Not even a please.

She listened to five short beeps – five other messages? After the long beep, she said, "Why does my husband have your phone number?" Her voice was strong. "If you want to nail the miserable son of a bitch as much as I do, call me at..." She hesitated for just a second then gave her phone number. Even if Raymond happened to be home, he never answered her phone.

If someone called back and she didn't like the sound of the person on the other end, all she had to do was hang up.

Hyde tucked the mail under his arm and pushed his apartment door open just wide enough to snake his hand inside. His free hand rested on the grip of his pistol. He snapped on the wall switch. His eyes swept the room as he stepped inside. Nothing seemed to be out of place, no hint that someone had been there, was perhaps even still waiting.

He cocked his head but heard nothing. Then again, he thought, all those years of screaming sirens and the chaos of multiple alarm fires had dulled his hearing anyway. He could probably apply for disability some day, and the commissioner would tell him to stuff it because every firefighter had a hearing problem.

All that he noticed was a lingering pungent aroma. It was his own stale cigarette smoke combined with the stench from the fire next door. He went into the kitchen and dumped the mail on the table with the last pile he'd left there.

It was only when both arms came to rest at his sides that he realized how much the right one ached from his most recent run-in with the black man

But the real ache, the pain that wouldn't go away, was in his heart. Nomi.

Messages! He went directly to his bedroom and checked the display on his answering machine. Six messages.

He pushed play.

One. Silence. Click. Probably a telemarketer.

Two. "We want you. We need you. We love you." The girls down at headquarters. Lousy vocalizing but he could feel a grin forming. "Henry," they continued together, "we are bereft. We are lost. Hurry back to your lovers."

Hyde felt himself actually smiling. Good broads. They deserved flowers for that effort...if he ever was allowed back in the office.

Three. "Daddy, call me please. I got a ding on the car and...oh, just call me as soon as you can." His daughter.

Four. "Mr. Hyde, this is Ms. Tracy at Travelers Insurance. Your daughter was involved in an auto accident with one of our insureds involving personal injury. The police file indicates the vehicle was registered in your name. Would you please contact me at..." Some ding.

Five. "For Christ's sakes, Henry, would you get back to me?" Leo.

Six. "Why does my husband have your phone number? If you want to nail the miserable son of a bitch as much as I do, call me at 978-293-0655."

Hyde hit the replay button and listened again. What caught his interest was the way she spoke – that was one tough broad. He hit replay again.

"If you want to nail the miserable son of a bitch as much as I do..."

Hyde winced. Just a few short years ago that could have been his own wife. Who was this lady and who was the guy in such deep shit?

Better yet, why did the miserable son of a bitch have Hyde's phone number in his pocket? He looked up the exchange. North Shore. No women on the North Shore called men in Charlestown. But she didn't know who Henry Hyde was from Adam. She was just calling a number she found in her husband's pocket...and she was bullshit.

What the hell. Take a chance. Give the lady a jingle, then he'd get hold of Leo.

The phone on the other end rang just once before it was answered. "Hello." The voice was the same as on the machine but this time it was softer, tentative.

Hyde decided she must have been waiting for this call. "I'm not sure whether we both want to get the miserable son of a bitch or not, but let's give it a shot."

"Who is this?"

"This is the person you left a message with about your husband who is supposed to be a miserable son of a bitch, and I really don't have time to play games." Hyde decided he had the upper hand the moment he heard her ask who he was. She wasn't comfortable doing this. Don't give her the edge. "Tell me your problem, lady."

"I...I was expecting a woman to call me back."

"Your husband's girlfriend?"

"I suppose so."

"I can promise you that as much as I might welcome the idea, there are no women living at this number."

"None?"

"My daughter spends occasional weekends, mostly when she needs money and wants to butter me up. Now, I said I don't have time. I'm not kidding. What's your husband's name? And why should it mean anything to me?"

"You've taken me by surprise, Mr...."

Not bad. She was trying to turn the tables. "My name is Hyde. How's that?"

"What do you do for a living, Mr. Hyde?"

What did it matter? "I'm an arson investigator for the Boston Fire Department."

He heard a sharp gasp.

"Does that help you at all, lady? I mean, does that explain why your husband has my phone number."

"I can't imagine it would."

Why not take a shot in the dark? "Does your husband work in Boston?"

"Yes."

"Around Atlantic Ave?"

"How did you know?"

"Did he play hockey in college?"

"You do know my husband."

Bingo! "I may. Maybe we can help each other. Can we get together?"

"Perhaps." She wasn't going to give up anything.

"I know by your number that you live on the North Shore." Hyde glanced at his watch. A trip there and back, talk for a while – two hours plus. Too much time for a shot in the dark. "Listen, I'm really sorry, but I don't have the time to come out your way. My work right now is keeping me in Boston. Can you come in town?"

"I suppose so."

"I'm serious. You name a place, a place you feel comfortable, and I'll meet you there – any time you say."

"I usually meet people at the Ritz Bar, but if..."

"Great. How soon?"

—173—

"I guess I could make it in...two hours?"

"Two hours. I'll be there in less than that. Try to make it sooner."

"I'll do that."

Hyde studied himself in the mirror. A quick shave was definitely in order. Shower, too. Shirt and tie. After all, the Ritz had its standards. You meet a lady in a high class place, you gotta look like a gentleman.

The phone rang.

He turned and glared at it. Who knew he was here? Who cared? Let the machine take it. But he changed his mind and picked up.

"Hello."

"Hyde, do you understand now that you do what I say?"

That goddamn taunting voice. "I am doing what you say."

"I don't think so, Hyde. Not really. You're still trying to find out who I am. Your big mouth is even telling people you're going to find me. Don't you know any better? You're not good enough. And I know you're not diddling your girlfriend right now because I know where she is."

"You calling me from your office on Atlantic Ave or..." – why not take a shot at it – "...your home on the North Shore?"

There was an instant of silence. "You're off base, Hyde. You don't know who I am. You're too dumb."

"You live on the North Shore, shithead? Your wife called me from there. Told me what an asshole you were. She's bringing me a picture of you."

"You got my message, Hyde, delivered in person. My man should be very persuasive. You do anything but what I've told you you're supposed to do and your girlfriend will never fuck you again."

The line went dead.

Hyde put down the phone and looked back toward the mirror. He saw himself, and right beside him was Nomi. They looked good together. They wouldn't try to kill her yet. She was their ace-in-the-hole. They didn't dare do anything to her until they were sure of him and sure of the money.

And he'd scored when he mentioned the North Shore.

You're getting closer, Henry. You're getting closer. Now just keep your cool.

Nomi watched every move the man made. Very soon, she realized that he was as aware of her movements, even when he was out of the room. It was an eerie sensation, almost as if he were telepathic. Once, when he'd gone into the bathroom – and she heard the lock snap – she got up and tried to open the door to the outer hallway. It was double locked with a deadbolt, and only a key would open it. He came back into the room with a smile. Although she was back sitting in the chair he'd pointed her to when they arrived, he said, "You had to make sure Jean-Paul wasn't stupid." He pulled a key from his pocket. "This what you need, little lady. It be the only thing to open that door. And now you know." His broad, white-toothed smile indicated that he wasn't worried about her escaping.

Later, when he was in the kitchen of the small apartment, she tried one of the windows. The building was ancient, the window frames a dark-stained, water-mottled wood, the panes old, distorted glass. The bottom could have been lifted if a club lock, like those used on auto steering wheels, hadn't been in place.

She was again sitting when Jean-Paul came back into the room with a tray of food. He nodded toward the window. "You had to try that, too. You got to know that Jean-Paul thinks of everything." Sometimes he spoke with a heavy island accent, sometimes it was barely noticeable. It seemed to depend on his mood.

He placed the tray on a low table near her chair. "Jean-Paul has a big appetite, but I can't eat everything on that plate." He pointed at the tray as he pulled up a chair. "You want something, you bring your chair over here. I'm supposed to keep you healthy for time being, but I don't be babying you."

Nomi watched him eat. The food was tempting but she was damned if she'd give in to him.

"What are you going to do with me?"

Jean-Paul leered at her. "What you like Jean-Paul to do with you first?"

Nomi looked away.

"Many things," he said with a laugh. "We got a couple more hours. We can do a lot of things. You choose."

She didn't look back. "What happens in a couple of hours?"

"I'm not really sure." No accent now. "He'll call and tell me exactly what has to be done."

"Who will call?"

"Man who pay me."

"Does he have a name?"

"He have name, little lady. But it doan matter. Maybe he say you have to die. If so, you don't want that to happen before you and Jean-Paul have fun, do you now?"

"Believe me, you'll be sorry if you try..."

"Little lady, do you know where you be?"

She looked up. "No."

"Nobody help you here. You alone with Jean-Paul."

The cell phone rang. Nomi counted three rings. Jean-Paul didn't move to answer. It went silent. But now Jean-Paul was holding the phone to his ear. When it began to ring again, he answered instantly.

Nomi watched his eyes as they flicked about the room. Then they settled on her.

"Yeah, she be looking right at me."

Most of the short conversation was a series of one word answers until she heard Jean-Paul say, "You want her brought there alive?"

After an answer, the only other word Jean-Paul said was, "Okay," before he put the phone in his pocket.

When she looked up, he was staring at her intently. "You should want to have fun pretty quick, little lady."

Nomi closed her eyes and gritted her teeth. If he touched her, he was going to have his hands full. When she opened her eyes, he was staring at her. "If you try anything with me, I can assure you that you won't have fun."

"Hey, you have fun with that fireman fella. What's wrong with Jean-Paul? I'm bigger than him, better looking, a lot tougher." He broke out in a broad smile. "Hey, you must have seen some of the bruises I give him."

She didn't respond.

He rose to his feet. "Little lady, Jean-Paul is fire." He held out a hand. "Come with me."

17

Hyde had a key to Nomi's apartment but he tried the knob out of curiosity. The door swung open. Why lock the door if the occupant has been forcibly removed? He stepped gingerly into her apartment in a semi-crouch, swinging his stubby gun from one side to another. Moving silently from room to room, he found exactly what he anticipated – nothing.

The last room was Nomi's bedroom, the one place he'd purposely avoided before. In a way, he noted, their habits were similar. The bed was made but rumpled; his own was usually unmade. Clothes were thrown over a chair. She used the closet floor for dirty clothes, too.

It was an odd feeling being in a woman's bedroom like this, sort of sneaking in a way. But he wasn't really sneaking, or peeking, or anything like that. He was looking for...what? Clues? What kind of clues? Or was he just looking for a part of Nomi he didn't know?

Nomi wasn't strange to him, not anymore, but the room was. It was so different. Feminine. That was it – feminine. The aroma was different, the frilly things, the woman herself. Nomi was there even if she wasn't. And at that thought, he found himself shaking.

Hyde was shaking because she wasn't there, because she had been grabbed by a thug who enjoyed burning things, enjoyed beating the shit out of people, enjoyed hurting Henry Hyde, and who'd told Hyde how much fun he would have doing kinky things to Nomi. The Black guy hadn't said exactly what he was going to do – he'd just hinted at it.

Back in her living room, Hyde saw that her computer was still on. She'd been compiling all their profiling data. He sat down and studied the text on the screen. He was there – the arsonist, the extortionist, the killer. It fit so neatly, a profile that matched almost every aspect of the pure psychopathic personality. All he needed was a name, a photo. A woman he'd never met might deliver this man in the next hour, a man who had everything and needed nothing. A pure psychopath.

He scrolled back to the beginning and was trying to figure how to print when Nomi's phone rang. Once. Twice. Three times. When the hell did the answering machine take over? After the forth ring, he heard the robotic click. Hyde stared at the inanimate machine on the table beside the computer as Nomi's voice told the caller to leave a message after the beep.

"Henry! You there, Henry?" Bobbie Scott's voice. "Pick up if you're there. Leo and I've been trying everywhere. Don't screw around. This is important."

Hyde picked up the phone. "Yeah, Bobbie."

"Leo's guy got a breakdown of names along Atlantic Ave. We got it down to an even dozen and…"

"Where are you now?"

"Southie. At Leo's."

"Let me speak to him."

"He's paying some IOUs. Ought to be back in less than an hour."

"Okay." Hyde paused. "Okay. Those even dozen – there's only one we want. How many of those do you two think make a good fit?"

"Three. All of them are out of their offices, not expected back. One's been in the Far East for the last ten days so that lets him off the hook."

"Do either of the other two live on the North Shore?"

"Both of them."

"Perfect."

Raymond Fairchild spread his suit jacket and brief case across the park bench he occupied. It was a not-so-subtle message that the occupant of that bench wanted privacy.

It was a pleasant enough afternoon in Boston's Public Garden. The surrounding flower gardens were perfectly manicured. A light breeze rustled leaves in the tall trees that surrounded the pond. The swan boats, long, narrow, flat-bottomed craft with sterns shaped into giant swans, moved slowly about the pond with their cargo of children and an occasional parent. Fairchild remembered the first time his mother had brought him into Boston to ride the boats. She'd been upset that he didn't pay attention to the lovely gardens or the ducks or even the other children. He'd been more interested in the drivers sitting inside the swans pedaling the boats.

Nothing had changed since then. A mix of ducks, all fat, followed after the elegant swan boats. They put on a noisy show quacking for peanuts tossed by the equally noisy children riding the boats.

For Fairchild, it was a safe place to think, to celebrate imminent victory. No matter what the asshole, Hyde, had said on the phone about the North Shore, about his wife. It was a fishing expedition. Even though Carolina hadn't answered when he called, it didn't mean a thing. The bitch wouldn't speak to him anyway. Probably balling on someone's shoulder.

The city was in his pocket because its icons were burning. There was one way, and only that one way, to stop that.

Thank God Charles Jordan hadn't been in his own car when it blew, or there might not have been a mayor to shake down. After this was all over, Fairchild would make sure one incompetent arsonist wouldn't survive to screw up another job. However, Charles Jordan was now neutralized. Even though his wife hadn't been an intentional target, that was now a moot point. Her accident had crushed the man. Jordan was pliable. When Hyde provided Jordan with the final instructions for transferring the money, it would be done without argument.

And Hyde, the tough old maverick. To break a tough guy, you find his weak point. If there was nothing obvious, then you usually looked for a woman. Guys like Hyde got attached, went for that one-woman garbage. That's how women got the upper hand, how they pussy-whipped you.

Raymond Fairchild knew he had the upper hand. Now that Jean-Paul had the Cram broad, Hyde would grab his ankles. He would do what he was told if he thought it would save her.

Moving the money was the easiest part. It was now all a matter of timing. His overseas banking arrangements had evolved over the years through his contacts. Laundering money was a simple process. Countless seemingly respectable bankers would look the opposite way when you were talking gobs of money. They became silent partners operating in a similar manner to the street names used in the financial marketplace. Under his guidance, his so-called investors had become wealthy commercial real estate speculators in America without involving their names.

In return, the least they could do was create a secure and equally silent banking relationship for their mentor. As a result, while the bank routing numbers for Fairchild's half a billion might eventually be traced by the pros, all the investigators would find would be a dead end. Naturally, they'd think Switzerland and go after their financial institutions. But Swiss bankers could be compromised these days. Not so the Arabs. Their value systems were so different, literally bullet proof, impossible to crack.

Fairchild bought a bag of peanuts and strolled down to the pond's edge. He cracked open a few shells and munched on the peanuts. When he tossed the empty shells in the water, a few ducks turned their attention to him, but the birds knew their territory well. They rejected the shells, quacking for the sweet nuts instead.

An object lesson. Just like our city's power structure, Fairchild thought. Greedy. *Show me the money!* How trite those words sounded. Tacky. That's why the mayor of the City of Boston was shortly going to cough up a bundle in order to save his city.

Fairchild cracked open some more shells until he had a handful of nuts. He tossed them in the air above the waiting ducks and watched them scurry across the green water, stirring mud to the surface, biting, pushing, anything to beat the next duck out of its share.

Show me the money, Charles!

Power was a wonderful reward. There was nothing in the world quite like power over your fellow man. Sex might be a close second, but that was only if you had a collection of women to pick and choose from. Power, sex, winning, keeping score, beating down everyone else.

He tossed the remainder of the peanuts into the water and went back to the bench. Opening his brief case, he took out his remaining cell phone – something had malfunctioned on the other – and went through the usual process to contact Jean-Paul.

"Yes?"

"The girl?"

"Scared. Angry. She doesn't care for Jean-Paul."

"Where's Hyde?"

"He was at her place. My man say he left a while ago. Do you want to know where he be next?"

"No time now." Let him go fishing. "I have things to do. I'll call you again when I'm ready."

Fairchild put the phone back in his briefcase, slipped into his suit jacket, and looked at his watch. Where to go to finish the details? He looked across the Public Gardens to the Ritz rising in the background on Arlington Street. Maybe he should stop at the bar for a celebratory drink.

No, he might see someone he knew and there was really no time for small talk.

He decided on Kai's apartment. Not a soul knew about that place. And if Kai was there, well maybe he'd try something new with her. There was nothing she'd refused up to now. And there was always time for a little creative sex.

Leo had a puzzled expression on his face.

"What've you got now," Bobbie asked.

"Our guy's used the same cell phone for a couple of hours. I think Nomi's okay. What we figured but weren't absolutely sure about is they got a tail on Henry. They know where he is just about all the time."

Shit. They'd see the lady Henry was meeting. "Where's our bad guy?"

"In Boston."

"I thought Sully turned you into a genius. You can't do better than that?"

"The guy had two phones. One was an early model, easier to trace. He's not using it now."

"Can you..."

"Give me time. If I can't figure it out, I'll call Sully."

Hyde stopped on the sidewalk outside the Ritz. A fully uniformed doorman was helping an elderly woman from a chauffeured Mercedes. He steadied her before assisting her to the door, discreetly signalling a bellman to retrieve some packages from the back of the car.

Behind the Mercedes was a Jaguar, and behind that was a BMW. A taxi waited patiently behind the BMW. It was one of the few times Hyde had seen a Boston cabbie who hadn't cut in front of the others. Nor was he sitting on his horn. Strange how the Ritz affected people.

To his right was the Ritz Bar window that looked out on the Public Gardens. The customers could look out on the lovely flowers, but no one on the outside could look in. Hyde realized that he was probably blocking someone's private view. Too bad – I'm beautiful in my own way.

With that comforting thought, he stepped to the front entrance and pushed through the revolving doors. The bar was to the right. Hyde stepped down onto plush carpeting and stopped for a moment. He studied the occupants. No one seemed to give him a second look except the white-jacketed bartender, who wrinkled his forehead curiously.

Then Hyde saw the woman seated in the far corner beyond the window staring back at him. She hadn't looked up at first, but when she did there was a troubled expression on her face. And when she saw Hyde, she tilted her head to study him.

He nodded.

She nodded back.

So this was how you picked up a broad at the Ritz. He walked over to her table. "I'm Hyde."

Her eyes covered him quickly, his face, the clothes that didn't really make it at the Ritz Bar, the unshined, high-top shoes that had been ankle deep in so many basements of burnt-out buildings. She inclined her head toward the chair across the table from her.

She said nothing but her eyes narrowed as she studied his face carefully.

That irritated him. "So you're husband is a miserable son of a bitch."

"Yes." She pursed her lips and looked down into her glass of white wine. "Yes, he is. Tell me about yourself, Mr. Hyde, other than you work for the Boston Fire Department."

A cocktail waitress in an ankle-length gown appeared beside the table and looked down at Hyde. Her forehead was wrinkled like the bartender's. "May I take your order?"

"Bottle of beer."

"We have..."

"Anything Irish."

"We have Beck's, Heineken…"

"Either one. Your choice." He turned back to the woman across from him. "Like I told you on the phone. I'm an arson investigator. Right now, I have very little time. None in fact. If there's a next time, I'll give you all the details. Right now, you have a husband who is a son of a bitch and I'm on a case that is a real bitch. Too many people have died because I can't solve it."

Her eyes were shiny. "I'm sorry." She licked her lips. "I really am sorry."

He leaned forward and said as softly as possible, "Lady, the next one they kill may be my girl, a lady I think I may love very much. Now, does that tell you who I am?"

Carolina sipped her wine. "More than I wanted to know, Mr. Hyde. I'm not sure if it wasn't an accident that your phone number was in my husband's pocket. He's a lot of things, but I can't imagine him being a killer."

The waitress appeared beside the table with a bottle of Beck's on her tray and was about to pour it into a frosted pilsner glass when Hyde said, "Don't bother. Just the bottle."

The waitress placed both the bottle and the glass in front of him and left without a word.

"Let's cut to the heart of the matter. You know my name, what I do. All I know is you live on the North Shore. Am I asking too much for a name?"

"Carolina Fairchild."

Hyde reached across the table. "Henry Hyde." He shook her hand. "See. We're on even ground now. I'm not a bad guy even if I look funny here."

She managed a slight smile.

"Mrs. Fairchild, I heard a little gasp on the phone when I said I was an arson investigator. Tell me why. Was your husband ever involved in something like that?"

"Not in years. He told me once that when he was a boy, his father had punished him because he'd gotten caught starting some fires where he was brought up. But I don't think that was anything serious."

"What does he do now?"

"He says commercial real estate. But I don't think that's what brings in the real money. I don't ask too many questions because he gives me answers he thinks I want to hear."

"He operates in Boston though?"

"Yes. He has an office in one of those refurbished warehouses on a wharf."

"I'll bet some of his properties have had fire losses."

She looked up quickly, then took a sip of her wine. "Not recently. Not for a long time. I think when he was first starting out there were some losses. But I don't know much about them. I don't think it's relevant to what you do."

Hyde took a long pull from the bottle. "I'm going to tell you some things about a man we're looking for." He paused for a moment to organize his thoughts. There was so much. He needed to keep everything in order and he had to express himself so that his emotions didn't show. When he was ready, he spoke quietly, even indifferently, and found it was even tougher when you were describing a psychopath.

When he was finished, Hyde drank again from the bottle. "Does that sound like we're talking about the same son of a bitch, Mrs. Fairchild?"

She rolled the stem of her wine glass in her fingers and didn't look up.

"Speak to me," he said softly.

She raised her head and opened her mouth. But there were no words. Then she swallowed and gazed back into the glass.

"Alright," Hyde said. "let's get into the real son of a bitch. The man I described is a psychopath. He needs to have power over people one way or another. Women? Can't get enough of them. The more he has, the more he wants. Does your husband mess around with other women?"

She shook her head. "Not that I know of."

"Is that why you called my number? Because you just wanted to talk? You didn't think he was screwing around with someone?"

"I thought he might be."

"Why? Did he make a mistake. Some evidence that convinced you? You see, usually these guys are so bright they cover their tracks. But sooner or later, everyone makes a mistake. Did your husband make a mistake?"

She nodded again.

"The men I'm talking about – these psychopaths – aren't nice people. They're bright and charming, but kinky doesn't really describe how they operate with women. Unless a woman keeps them in control, they get more demanding, real ugly sometimes. That ever happen to you?"

She was weeping silently now.

"He got rough, didn't he?"

When she looked up, Hyde saw a pain beyond the tears in her eyes. That answered everything for him.

"Do you have a photograph of your husband?"

She removed a wallet from her purse and fumbled through the credit card section until she found what she was looking for. She handed Hyde a photo of a handsome family – herself, a proud, smiling husband with his arm around her shoulders, two teenagers, a boy beside his father, a girl next to her mother. He studied the photo more closely. They looked happy, but...the man's lips were smiling but the face wasn't. Hyde remembered the words he'd read about a psychopath – "...knows the words, but not the music." The smile wasn't really a smile.

"May I keep this photo for a while?"

"You're sure my husband" – she pointed at the man – "is the one?"

"I don't have a description. Never did. Look, Mrs. Fairchild, before I came over here, I went over the profile we developed for this guy. There were a dozen names on the final list. That got broken down to three. Your husband was one of those three. Why did he have my phone number in his pocket? The guy has been calling me day and night. Everything we got fits. And he hurt you."

Carolina Fairchild didn't respond.

"I don't think you want to stay here any longer, Mrs. Fairchild. And you don't want to go home either, just in case he's there. Will you let me take you some place where you'll be safe until this is over?"

She stared at this stranger for a moment before responding. He was tough, maybe hardened was more apt, but she could see he wanted her to be safe. "Alright."

"You can tell me all about him on the way."

18

Hyde desperately wanted to check his messages, and that required the services of a bellman discreetly pointing to a recessed area at the far end of the lobby. Boston's Ritz-Carlton would never consider pay phones part of its elegant decor.

There were two messages.

"I'm getting conflicting signals, Hyde. One minute I'm told that all that's left are the arrangements to transfer the money. Then I'm told that the famed arson investigator is close to getting his man. The sands of time are running out on your ass. Believe me, Hyde, this city has never seen fires like it's going to have in..." There was a pause. "...in about three quarters of an hour. You and Jordan are going to be begging for my instructions. And if you try to get near me...well Miss Cram's corpse won't be pretty if she dies in a fire."

That was from Carolina Fairchild's husband – whom Hyde now knew was Charles Jordan's closest confidant. He thought about his old high school buddies and wondered briefly if he could do to one of them what Fairchild was doing to Jordan. Hyde shook his head – not a chance – not when you lived under the code of the streets where you were brought up.

And the other message in Mayor Jordan's voice: "The commissioner told me this was the best way to get you,

Hyde. I've scheduled a meeting for six o'clock this evening in my office. Since you're the so-called bagman, be there."

And would Raymond Fairchild be there?

Hyde hung up the phone and leaned against the tiled wall. The tiles were cool, not comforting, but he needed a moment to think. *Bagman!* That asshole.

He looked at his watch. Almost 5:30PM. How the hell do you go from the Ritz to Southie to deliver Carolina Fairchild and then to City Hall in thirty minutes through rush hour traffic? You don't – unless you use the blue bubble machine and the siren, and there was still no way he was going to cover all that territory in thirty minutes. Forty maybe? Wouldn't some rookie cop just love to nail a suspended firefighter violating every rule in the book?

Considering how excited the mayor was going to be when he showed up late anyway, what the hell! It was worth a shot.

Hyde's index finger punched the doorbell irritably. "Come on, Leo. Open up. I'm running out..." – the door opened – "...of time."

Carmichael never spoke. He glanced briefly at the woman behind Hyde before walking back into his kitchen. Bobbie Scott was sitting at the kitchen table with Leo's wife, Marty.

Hyde followed them into the kitchen. "This is Mrs. Fairchild," he said. "Carolina Fairchild. She happens to be the wife of our main suspect. She needs to hang low until this shit is over. I told her she could stay here."

"Main suspect! I thought we still had it down to three names," Bobbie Scott said. "What makes you so sure?"

"He set fires as a kid. He's had aggression problems that have gotten more pronounced as he grew older. He had some commercial properties that were fire losses. He's done some increasingly strange things over the years with his wife. She didn't get into any detail but I could tell he's kinky, more than the average guy. He took it out on his wife and I'll put down money he likes to beat up on women. The more she told me about him, the more I recognized our man. And he had my phone number in his pocket, which frosts the fucking cake as far as I'm concerned. He fits the ideal psychopathic personality, which makes him a piece of shit."

"We called their offices. Fairchild's secretary hasn't a clue where he went or when he's coming back," Bobbie said. "So how do we grab him?"

"I don't know." It took the silence that followed for Hyde to realize that Leo's thoughts were elsewhere. "Leo, you look like it's the end of the world. We're getting close to our guy. What is it?"

Bobbie pointed at the two-way Motorola radio lying on the table. "Fire Alarm sounded ten-fifteen a few minutes ago." Ten-fifteen was the signal that a firefighter had died.

"Who?"

"A good friend of Leo's, Joey O'Bannion, from Engine Ten. At the Old South Meeting House. Wall collapsed. Died on the way to the hospital."

Hyde's gaze fell on Leo. He nodded. "I remember Joey. We were in Nam at the same time. The last time I saw him was down at Florian Hall at a Gaelic Fire Brigade meeting." He closed his eyes. "Firemen are dying to make a wacko rich."

Leo spoke for the first time, looking up at Carolina. "You got a photo of him?" He blinked his eyes rapidly, wiping away a tear.

Hyde extracted the photo from his pocket and handed it to Carmichael.

"Nice looking family. Joey had one, too." Leo, his eyes shiny, handed the photo to Bobbie and turned away. He seemed to be staring at his wife's framed picture of Jesus on the cross that hung by her kitchen sink, but he never saw it. "I'm going to kill this fucker."

"A lot of us want to."

Leo looked Carolina up and down. "So, Henry, you want this guy's wife to stay here...in my house...with my wife." His eyes turned to his wife. "Okay with you if Henry manages our lives?"

Marty Carmichael grew up on the top floor of a three-decker on East 5th Street behind Gate of Heaven Church, just two blocks from where her future husband lived. They knew each other in grade school, dated in high school, and she waited faithfully for Leo when he went to Vietnam. She never dreamed of dating anyone else. They were married a few months after he came back. Leo could do no wrong in her eyes.

"Whatever you think is right, hon," Marty answered. "Sounds to me like she needs help."

"Why here?" Leo wasn't happy. "What if her husband…"

Hyde interrupted. "He probably figures she's still home."

"Yeah, if her husband doesn't already know she's with you."

"Meaning?"

Leo's palms came down hard on the table. "Meaning they got a fuckin' tail on you, Henry. For Chrissakes, they know every move you make. They musta seen you meet her and they probably followed you here." He waved his arms in exaggeration. "They see you come out of here without her, they're gonna figure she stays here. Then what?"

"A tail?" Hyde faced Scott angrily. "You didn't say anything about a tail."

"That was the last time you called," Bobbie said. "Since then, Leo found out they been following you everywhere."

Hyde's eyes fell on Marty Carmichael. "If someone's seen me bring her here, I guess I can't leave her with you. You don't need that shit, Marty."

Marty looked at Leo. "Like I said, someone's gotta help her."

Leo turned to Carolina. "Did your husband do something to you, too?"

Carolina nodded.

"Whatever he did," Hyde said, "it wasn't nice. He's a sick son of a bitch."

Marty Carmichael watched the other woman blinking, struggling to hold back tears. "That's it," she said. She went over to the closet, reached up on the shelf, and brought down a pistol. From another corner of the shelf, she pulled out a full ammunition clip and inserted it into the grip, banging it into place with the heel of her hand. "Leo taught me how to use this thing if I ever had to."

"You're sure?" Leo said to her.

She pulled back the slide to insert a bullet into place, then set the safety. "I'm sure." She laid the gun on the kitchen table, then patted the wooden kitchen chair beside her. "Come on and sit down. You and me, we'll be alright, hon. I know how to handle that thing as good as Leo."

Raymond Fairchild let himself into the apartment with his own key.

Kai had just taken a shower. She came out of the bathroom with only a towel wrapped around her wet head. He was sitting in a chair he'd pushed into the hallway.

"Raymond!" Kai yelped.

Until this moment, the man had been nothing but generous and loving. She found the arrangement satisfactory. But now, now the expression on his face was frightening. His stare was so intense that she could feel it boring into her very being. When he looked into her eyes, there seemed to be no recognition. It was sheer instinct when she attempted to cover herself with arms and hands.

"Don't do that," he snapped. "I'm paying for this place and I came here to see every last inch of you."

This wasn't the Raymond she knew.

"Hands at your sides." His voice was a lash.

She dropped her hands.

"Now face me."

Kai did as she was told.

"Get that towel off your head."

She dropped the single towel at her feet.

She submitted to each order that followed.

She raised and lowered her arms on command.

She spread her legs.

Kai couldn't believe this was happening. Yet here she was obeying him.

She turned and bent over and stretched from a variety of positions.

When she was able to look into his eyes again, she experienced an even deeper fear. They were empty, devoid of emotion.

Quite suddenly, he was on his feet, hurling the chair back down the hallway.

Kai froze. Overcome with fear, all she could do was scream.

Fairchild lunged forward, grabbing a handful of wet hair. He yanked her backwards into the bedroom. Pain – fear and pain – shocked her back to reality. She found her voice, begging him to stop.

Her pleading was the ultimate thrill. Without removing his own clothes, he forced her to the floor on her knees, bending her backward until she screamed for mercy. Only then was he ready to rape her.

When it was over, she managed to speak through her pain. "Please, Raymond, I'll do anything you say...but please don't hurt me like that."

Pain! "I love pain!" Pain was intoxicating. "Get your ass up."

She turned her head and looked up at him. Raymond was on his knees, hands on hips, still erect, his lips curled back in an expression she couldn't have imagined. So cruel. He'd become an animal.

"Please, Raymond, why...?"

Then he was on top of her, behind her, smothering her with his weight. Kai knew he was raping her again but she no longer had the strength or will to resist.

Finally, mercifully, she felt unconsciousness roll over her in a wave that she now welcomed.

Raymond Fairchild rose to his feet. He sensed a renewal. His mind and body had been strengthened. Kai had given him power.

The night of Paul Revere's famous ride, a light was hung in the steeple of Old North Church to signify that the British were coming. Two hundred years later, on July 4, 1976, the President of the United States spoke to the nation from the pulpit of that venerable church. And a little less than a quarter century after that, the very same pulpit was turned to splinters by an explosion that sent a fireball into that very same steeple.

Flames engulfed the altar and spread to the offices in the rear. Intense heat quickly kindled the nearest pews as the fire began its inexorable march toward the choir loft.

In another section of the city on historic Beacon Street, flames in five separate locations in the basement of a Boston University dormitory licked hungrily at dried beams. They shorted out the main switchboard for the building. They climbed inside dusty, dry airspaces licking upwards from one floor to the next in mere seconds.

The flames searched for fuel and oxygen. They came through ventilating shafts into lavatories and hallways. They came through false ceilings and window frames and walls hollowed out by half a dozen remodelings.

Students who ate their dinners early were the lucky ones. The less fortunate were trapped in showers and rooms and stairwells and narrow hallways with thick coatings of wax that fed the hungry flames.

When the first companies arrived, firefighters had no time to fight the flames. Time and again, they placed their own lives in jeopardy to save people trapped inside. Desperately needed rescue equipment and emergency vehicles were recalled from the conflagration at Old North Church.

The doors to the Museum of Fine Arts had been closed for more than an hour and most of the staff had departed for the night when fires erupted in three separate locations. One housed the MFA's files and the valuable records of one of America's premier museums. A second occurred in a storage area where a collection of eighteenth century French artists' greatest works were being assembled. The third was a smoky blaze that originated in the central ventilation system. Dense, black smoke was pumped into every room of the museum.

Each of these fires, two of them in the same district, began at approximately the same time. Boston Fire Department companies responded within minutes of each alarm. In every instance, the on-scene commander requested second and third alarms within moments of arrival.

The incidents were radically different from each other. Within twenty five minutes, every company in BFD Division Two had been called. Equipment from Division One moved into Division Two firehouses to cover. Mutual Aid was called from cities and towns outside of Boston.

Fire Commissioner Duggan declared a state of fire emergency thirty three minutes after the first alarm sounded. Every Boston firefighter was recalled to duty.

Charles Jordan stretched his left arm out over the shiny mahogany table in one corner of his office and pulled back his sleeve. It was a dramatic gesture, perhaps the tenth time in the past five minutes, to show his guests that time was as critical to him as it was to them. He studied his watch as if an answer to his problems would materialize on its face. He then looked up at the others who were more patient than he. "I'll give him another five minutes."

His guests were Boston power brokers, two with old money, but most with the new. They had come to their city's aide because Charles Jordan had insisted Boston-as-they-knew-it would not survive without their help. They could be trusted to be discreet. They had agreed to coordinate the necessary financial arrangments on a strictly confidential basis.

The distant wail of sirens rose and sank as Mayor Jordan and his power brokers waited anxiously for the man who could never hope to be a part of their inner circle yet meant more to them than any citizen of the city at this moment. An uneasy conversation about the banal aspects of Boston social life was mercifully interrupted by the intercom from the outer office. "Mr. Hyde..."

The door burst open and Henry Hyde entered the room in the same clothes he'd worn at the Ritz. But he'd forgotten both to button his collar and pull up the tie. His jacket and slacks were wrinkled.

He was there no more than a minute, just enough time to shake hands around the table and accept a cup of coffee when they were interrupted by Jordan's secretary at the door.

"Commissioner Duggan has just declared a state of fire emergency, sir. All off-duty firefighters are being recalled."

Hyde was out the door before anyone could respond.

Nomi eyed the mug of hot tea sitting on the old, badly scratched table beside her chair. When she picked up the mug, there was a round spot in the dust that covered every flat surface in the dingy apartment. Did he clean anything? She placed the mug back on the table without drinking from it.

"What the matter, little lady? You scared of Jean-Paul's cooking?" His laugh was as deep as his voice. "There's nothing wrong with that tea." He had a steaming mug of his own. "See, same tea. Good." He blew on the tea in his own mug before sipping. "Very good."

Reluctantly, Nomi picked up her own mug. She was damned if she'd accept anything to eat. She was certain you gave a kidnapper the upper hand if you gave in to their offers, but she was tired and thirsty and tea sounded wonderful when he offered it. Accepting tea wasn't lessening your chances of survival.

The tea was hot and it was strong. She could feel herself reviving. Maybe she was getting the upper hand. She was more determined than ever now to continue to resist him.

"You see," he said. "My tea be good. My cooking even better. You should eat."

"No thank you."

Jean-Paul's phone rang. He looked over at it but didn't move until it continued to ring more than three times. Then he got up and went over to wait for the answering machine to pick up. Jean-Paul's message for callers was short.

"Hey, Jean-Paul. Pick me up if you there. It's important."

He recognized the voice of one of his own men who trailed Henry Hyde and reported his every move. "Go ahead," he said in his deep voice.

"Hyde meet a lady at hotel."

Jean-Paul listened as Hyde's moves were described, interrupting only once to ask for a description of the woman. He knew in an instant that it was Raymond Fairchild's wife but he asked a few more questions to be certain.

"Where she be now?" Jean-Paul's accent was now deep in his own island as he spoke rapidly.

The caller explained how he and one of the others had tracked Hyde to Leo Carmichael's house in South Boston.

"Is Hyde there now?"

"No. He and his two men left. Artur and Tres follow them."

"The lady still there?"

"Yes."

"Anybody else?"

"Don't know."

"If she come out, you follow." Wouldn't Fairchild be angry to know his wife had met with Hyde? Jean-Paul's man, like all the others, used a cell phone. "I call you when I know what to do."

There was an amused look on Jean-Paul's face when he turned to Nomi. His eyes sparkled. "Your man, Hyde, he know more than one lovely lady. I think he just made things even easier for Jean-Paul." He smiled broadly and winked at her. "This lady very pretty, very pretty indeed. You should be jealous."

Nomi put the mug down on the table with shaking hands. It suddenly tasted bitter.

19

Hyde called for Al Horgan on his radio as he ran down the granite steps of City Hall Plaza two at a time. "K-Five…K-Five, if you read me, switch to channel six." He repeated himself twice before Fire Alarm warned this unidentified voice off channel one. But Horgan would know who was calling.

His car was parked on Congress Street in a NO PARKING zone compliments of a BFD "Official Business" card on the dash. Hyde switched the selector on his radio to channel six, unlocked the door, started the engine, then waited impatiently by the curb for Horgan's call. There was no point in driving through the mayhem of Boston until he was certain which fireground Al was covering.

"This is K-Five, go ahead."

Al's voice! Al knew who was calling him.

"I'm outside City Hall," Hyde said. "What is your position?"

"Beacon and Charlesgate West."

"I'll be there in five." Al would wait for him.

Hyde's tires squealed as he gunned the car up Court Street in the direction of Beacon, blue light rotating on the dash, siren whooping. Cars pulled grudgingly out of his path – after all it was Boston – as he rocketed up the hill toward Tremont.

Downtown traffic had been cut off there – emergency vehicles only. He rounded the corner unto Beacon, raced past the golden dome of the state capital building and down Beacon Hill by the Common. As he neared the corner of Arlington, he saw that the police had cordoned off the intersection. Ambulances were streaming down Beacon in the wrong direction heading toward Mass. General Hospital. Hyde cut left, crossed the sidewalk onto Arlington, and was waved down Commonwealth by a policeman.

Duggan had declared a fire emergency and as far as Hyde was concerned, he was back on duty. But he was also on a mission – find Nomi, find Nomi at all costs. Somehow, he would find Nomi. He couldn't stop the fires from being set without locating her. But if he could find her, he'd find the black guy and the terror would end.

It was now up to Bobbie and Leo to intercept Fairchild's cell phone and pinpoint Jean-Paul's location.

As Kai lay on the floor of the bedroom, still unconscious, her blood congealing on the white rug, Raymond Fairchild sat down in a comfortable chair in the living room and dialed Jean-Paul's number on his cell phone. He allowed it to ring the usual three times, then disconnected.

He was freshly showered, wearing a new suit that had never been out of Kai's closet before, a freshly starched white shirt, and a silk Armani tie. The clothes had been kept at Kai's for a special purpose, which now seemed apt – travelling clothes!

Fairchild pressed redial.

His view across to the Gardens from the apartment window was spectacular. But even more impressive to Fairchild was the stream of emergency vehicles and the constant wail of sirens. Jean-Paul deserved every cent he would gain from this magnificent effort. If Fairchild had known that just moments ago a frantic Henry Hyde had passed nearby, he would have been overjoyed.

"Yes," was the only response Fairchild heard when Jean-Paul answered the phone. The deep, rich voice was reassuring.

"I don't have access to the fire department channels right now," Fairchild said. "However, I've been serenaded by sirens for over an hour. It sounds as if your people have done their jobs well."

"The fire commissioner declared a state of emergency." For the moment, his accent was barely perceptible. Jean-Paul was obviously in a business mood.

Fairchild also sensed that something was bothering Jean-Paul. He'd come to understand the nuances of the island accent and how he used it to convey a message. "Well I guess that about wraps it up. I'd say we're in a position to give Hyde the routing number for the money transfer."

His words were greeted by silence.

Fairchild paused for a second. Jean-Paul was a difficult man to please. Why did he pick a time like this, when every minute was so precious, to display his temperament? The man was playing a mind game. First Hyde, now Jean-Paul. *Choose your words carefully.*

"I think it's wise, Jean-Paul, that you're returning to your island, and I'm glad I don't know where it is because…"

"No one leave for anywhere. Not quite yet. We, both of us, have to talk again. I need to know exactly how my share come to me if we doan know where each udder be."

Okay, Fairchild noted, he's laying on the accent to make his point. Had there ever been a time dealing with lower level individuals when it wasn't money?

"As I have said before, you are taken care of. As soon as I know the money is in my account, then I transfer your share electronically to the financial institution using the routing number you have already provided to me."

"I been thinking about that, and perhaps I never hear from you again. I've already paid my people with my own money, and paid them very well. If you don't make the transfer, I lose everything."

"Of course I'll make the transfer. My word is…"

"I have Hyde's lady. As long as she be with Jean-Paul, you can use Hyde. If you don't meet me and pay me now, the lady may go free. Maybe you never see your money."

Fairchild struggled for control. *I don't need this shit now.* Mind games – Hyde and Jean-Paul weren't smart enough to compete with him. "Jean-Paul, this doesn't make sense. We worked everything out. The method I've set up is foolproof. It's the way to do it. We both get our money. We both disappear."

Jean-Paul grew more adamant. "The lady be right here. The lady look very happy because maybe Jean-Paul might let her go. And there's something else. Where your lady now?"

"What lady?"

"You know. Your lady. Your wife. Where she be?"

Fairchild gritted his teeth. Carolina was history. She no longer mattered. But why the hell was he asking about Carolina? Jean-Paul wasn't supposed to know about his personal life. "At home. Why?"

"Maybe you think so. You try to call the lady in the last few hours?"

Yeah, after Hyde's bullshit, but there was no answer. What the hell was Jean-Paul talking about? He wasn't about to give him the satisfaction. "No. Why?"

"Ahhh. Then you doan know who she been with?"

"Cut the shit," Fairchild snapped. "Why should you know or care where my wife is?"

"Because, Mr. Fairchild," Jean-Paul said in his deepest voice, "the lady, she been with Hyde. I bet she tell Hyde all about you."

Raymond Fairchild felt his throat constrict as if a large hand was wrapped around his neck, slowly squeezing his life away. It was impossible. How could…?

"The lady not go home. The lady with them now. My guess is she told them everything she know." Jean-Paul waited.

There was no response from Fairchild.

"I think the only choice is to take care of the lady before she say anymore. Like you say, time running out."

Fairchild closed his eyes. *That bitch...that no-good bitch.* Jean-Paul was right. He didn't care where Carolina was, but he did care what happened to her if she'd been in touch with Hyde. "Yes, you do that, Jean-Paul. You take care of her yourself."

"No. We meet just like I say, and you pay me half my money now. Jean-Paul have someone take care of the lady good."

Fairchild saw no other choice. Time was everything now. He'd been planning a stop at his office anyway to pick up the cash that he put aside to cover costs until he had access to the big money. At this time of the evening, most everyone would be gone.

"Alright, we're running out of time. You go ahead and have someone else take care of her. Where do you want to meet?"

"Near the final fire." Jean-Paul told Fairchild where his car would be waiting.

"I'll be there," Fairchild said. "And when I see you, I want to know that bitch of mine is dead."

He disconnected without waiting for an answer. Imagine Carolina pulling something like that on him – after all he'd done for her.

The final fire. South Boston. This was the one to stuff it up Jordan's ass. If there were ever last minute thoughts on Jordan's part, any grandstand stunts – this one would change his mind. The fire would be started on a street corner near Charles Jordan's home. His house was old and dry and would burn quickly with the entire block. It was to be the last straw if there was any hesitation on Jordan's part.

And Hyde's girlfriend would be watching it from inside one of those buildings.

Bobbie Scott sat at his desk in the Arson Squad's office and listened to the tape while Leo was in the bathroom. He knew the voices now – Raymond Fairchild and the guy with the island accent. The crazy bastards! He rewound the tape part way. When Leo returned, Bobbie said, "Listen to this shit. These fuckin' wack jobs are going to kill Mrs. Fairchild." He played the last part of the conversation.

Leo exploded. "The miserable pricks." He grabbed the phone and punched in his own number.

When his wife answered, he shouted, "Marty, get out of there. Now. Get down to Gate of Heaven. I'm on my way!" He tossed the phone on the table.

"Not just you – us!" Bobbie grabbed the back of Leo's belt. "Both of us are on the way. But don't go fucking crazy on me now."

Leo's eyes narrowed. "Let go, you son of a bitch!" His elbows flailed at Scott.

"Okay. Okay. Listen." Bobbie picked up the portable machine with his free hand. "There's more on here. There's gonna be another fire, a big sucker. I'll play the whole thing on the way." He let go of the belt and put an arm around Leo's shoulders. "Just don't go crazy, man. You lose your head, we might lose Marty, too. Together – okay?"

"Together."

They were out the door and running down the stairs.

Hyde didn't blame the cops for stopping him. He was still wearing the same wrinkled jacket and slacks. Probably looked like a stock broker coming home after a hard day of making a couple of mil. After being stopped twice, Hyde hung his badge on his jacket pocket.

He scanned the crowd. Arsonists loved to watch their work. Maybe Fairchild was wacky enough at this stage to show his face.

The fire was no longer devouring fresh fuel. The smoke that rose skyward was white now, mostly hot, smoldering ruins. The flames had been knocked down floor by floor the way Boston firefighters always fought a blaze – from the inside. That's how they were taught from the first day they entered the Academy at Moon Island. You take on the fire face to face, drive it back, knock it down, then overhaul, search for any sign that an ember might still exist before you take up your equipment and head back to wait for the next alarm.

If Al Horgan was waiting where he'd told Hyde, he couldn't be seen in the milling crowd. The ambulances had gone, leaving behind hysterical students who had no idea who'd survived and who'd been unfortunate. The crowd surged by police vehicles blocking every street leading up to the scene. Yellow tape established police lines but it required tremendous effort to hold them. EMTs aiding the police gently led dazed students back behind the yellow tape two and three times until they were able to recognize the same ones stumbling back over hose lines.

"Al," Hyde called over channel six, "where are you?"

"With the commissioner. I see you. Stay right there."

Commissioner Duggan in his white coat and helmet looked every inch the man in command until they were almost beside Hyde. Then he saw Duggan's face. He'd aged five years in a day. The darting black eyes were still there but they were puffy. The beard might have become a little greyer, the lines in his face a little deeper, and his shoulders seemed a little more rounded.

"The son of a bitch is mad," Duggan said. "Killing kids." He shook his head sadly. "Kids. The same age as my own." His eyes searched Hyde's. "Find his ass, Henry. Bring it to me. We'll take care of the fucker together."

Hyde turned to Al. "How many?"

"Hard to say. We've taken out seven bodies. That may be it. Our guys did a superhuman effort. The first engine company on the scene never missed a beat. Pulled on their Scott's gear and charged right into the smoke, crawled into room after room to drag 'em out. We had ladders on each floor. Got a lot that way, too. Over a dozen of our guys left by ambulance. Ladder Fifteen still has a guy missing."

"Seven kids," Duggan said. "Seven. I want his ass bad, Henry...more than ever."

"Maybe he's not too far away. Could be watching us right now. I finally know who the son of a bitch is. His name's Raymond Fairchild." Hyde showed them the photo.

Duggan's eyes narrowed.

"And our mayor's best buddy. He probably got everything fed to him from City Hall on a silver fucking platter by Jordan." Hyde looked at Horgan. "That's why he was so far ahead of us. Knew when we were awake and when we slept and when we were on the pot, and he laughed his ass off at us."

"The fucker was one jump ahead of us all the time."

"Right. And now he's disappeared, too," Hyde said. "Not a trace. It's his game now. Somehow, he's supposed to tell me how Jordan's gotta transfer that money, but I haven't a clue how he's going to contact me or when. What I know now is he's had me shadowed all the damn time, always knew where I was. And if he gets his hands on the big payoff, he disappears for good."

Duggan was wild. "How could Jordan transfer that money once he finds out about Fairchild?" But he knew the reason as soon as he spoke.

"What choice does he have?" Hyde looked hard at Duggan. "What choice do I have?" There was only one way to make his point. "How many more need to die before we give in? What's more important – lives or money that we might be lucky enough to get back some day?"

Al Horgan had been studying Hyde's face as he spoke to Duggan. "There's something else bugging you, too. What is it, Henry?"

"What do you mean?"

"Come on. Don't bullshit me. I can see it in your eyes. There's something else eating at you." He inclined his head toward the smoke. "Seven dead kids, maybe a firefighter, too. Henry Hyde's usually ready to tear their nuts off. Now you're ready to give in."

Hyde looked down at his shoes for a moment, then scratched the tip of his nose self consciously. When he spoke, his eyes went first to Horgan. "He's got Nomi." Then to Duggan. "The black guy grabbed her."

"That was to get your attention," Duggan said softly. "I'm sorry."

Hyde nodded. "And it's working, too."

Horgan heard the desperate call on channel six before the others. He handed his radio to Hyde. "Go ahead. It's your name someone's calling."

"Hyde here."

"We're in South Boston, heading for Leo's." It was Bobbie Scott. "They found out about you and Mrs. Fairchild. We're trying to get to Leo's before someone else does. And Fairchild's supposed to meet Jean-Paul in South Boston."

"Where?"

Scott gave him the location. "Picked it up off Fairchild's cell phone. They were arguing about money."

"They're supposed to settle up somehow," Leo shouted in the background.

"We need you here, Henry," Leo said.

"Corner of Broadway and Dorchester," Hyde answered. "Fifteen minutes."

Nomi shuddered as she took in every word of Jean-Paul's end of the phone conversation with Fairchild. There was no doubt in her mind that Jean-Paul had won. And she was also certain that if she went out that door with him, she was probably signing her own death warrant.

Jean-Paul pressed the off button on the phone and turned to Nomi. His face, always a mirror of his moods, was triumphant now. "Little lady, I got to put some things together. Nowhere you can go, so you be patient."

Jean-Paul went into his bedroom and was gone for perhaps ten minutes. During that time Nomi searched the small apartment for anything that might help her. But there was nothing, not even a knife in the kitchen. Nothing. She took a deep breath. *Don't cry. Don't be an asshole. Don't make it easy for him.*

When Jean-Paul reappeared, he was carrying a battered old suitcase with a rope around the middle. That was the convincer for Nomi. How many times had she seen islanders at Logan Airport waiting in line for the San Juan flights, their possessions in ancient suitcases and cardboard boxes, always with rope securing them? It was a way for a man like him to try to blend into the crowd.

"Where are you heading?" she asked.

"Oh, little lady, you would love my island." He gave her a sad look. "But you don't like Jean-Paul, so you can't go with me."

"I don't plan to go anywhere with you."

The keys were in his hand. "Yes, there be one last trip we have to make. Then I let you be free." He beckoned her to come with him. "Time to go, little lady."

Nomi sat down in a worn easy chair, her arms folded, hands tucked in her armpits to keep from shaking. She wasn't going to make it easy for him.

Jean-Paul put down the suitcase and returned the keys to his pocket. "Okay, so you want to make trouble for Jean-Paul. I make you come with me then." He covered the space between them in a few strides and reached out for one of her arms.

Nomi rolled sideways out of the chair, ducking under his hand. She rose to her feet, unsure of her next move, but out of his range. Jean-Paul advanced patiently, arms spread like wings to envelop her. Her eyes darted about the room, searching for something, anything at all, to fend him off. It didn't matter as long as it bought her more time.

She focused on a lamp, an old one with a pottery base, on a table ten feet away. She darted for it. But Jean-Paul was right behind her, quicker than she, a large hand grasping her shoulder, digging painfully into the muscle. Nomi's fingers wrapped around the neck of the lamp. She whirled, allowing him to pull her, and swung at the same time. Jean-Paul released her and turned his body away as quickly as he could. The heavy base of the lamp glanced off his shoulder. Then he came at her with both hands.

There was no chance to get away. One step back and she was against the wall. Jean-Paul reached for the lamp. In a last desperate attempt, Nomi lurched to one side, drew the lamp back, and swung wildly.

This time, Jean-Paul had underestimated her. The lamp caught him in the side of the head. He staggered backwards, stunned and surprised.

Maybe...

But he moved with amazing speed as she raised the lamp above her head again. Suddenly her arm was pinned against the wall. He squeezed until her hand seemed to go numb, then slammed her arm hard against the wall. The lamp crashed to the floor.

Nomi reached out, searching for his eyes with her fingernails. But he swung down with his free arm, knocking her hand away. And just as quickly, his own hand came up and around and hit her hard in the side of the face, then came back and snapped her head in the other direction. The room blurred and seemed to darken. Nomi could feel her body sliding down the wall. She shook her head. She didn't want to lose consciousness, but even before she could think what to do, Jean-Paul had pushed her roughly onto the floor, rolling her over face down. Her hands were jerked behind her back and she felt something wrapped around her wrists. She couldn't move her arms at all.

Jean-Paul yanked Nomi roughly to her feet, spun her around, and pushed her against the wall. "Little lady, you waste me time, make me mad."

When she lifted her head, she could see a trace of blood on the side of his face where she'd hit him with the lamp. At least it was something.

He unlocked the door, picked up the suitcase, and pushed her out into a dingy hallway. "You make all the noise you want," he said angrily. "No one care around here what hoppen to white lady with Jean-Paul. No one! We go now."

20

Carolina heard Leo's angry shout as if he was standing in front of her – "Get out of there!" She twisted in her chair toward Marty Carmichael, who clutched the telephone in an iron grip. The mug of coffee slipped from Carolina's fingers. An angry, dark stain ran down the front of her dress. The mug bounced off her knee and splintered on the floor.

The pretty, Irish blush drained from Marty's face. She stared, unseeing, as her arm dropped to her side. Leo was no longer there but she still held the phone. Her mouth opened but seconds passed before she finally said, "We have to get out of here. Leo said Gate of Heaven. We have to go there...right now."

"Gate of Heaven?" Carolina repeated the name without hearing her own voice. "What's that?"

Marty clapped her hands once, twice, three times. Leo had told her – how many times had he said it? – that the people who get hurt are the ones who are afraid. He said that if you're properly trained, you react to a situation and worry about what might have gone wrong later. Leo also said don't let anyone push you around or they'll push you around all the time. Leo taught his wife a lot of things.

Marty's jaw was set. "It's our church. Two blocks from here, maybe a little more," she said. She put the phone down on the table and picked up the pistol. Then she held out the gun nestled in the palm of her hand. "Look at this

Carolina. The clip I put in this gun carries fifteen bullets. Each one is a flat head. Leo bought them for me because he said they're stoppers. You hit someone with one of these, it knocks them backwards, spreads out, leaves a damn big hole. You follow me?"

Carolina nodded.

"I told you I knew how to use this and I do. If anyone gives us trouble, I'll shoot." She nodded her head and offered a weak smile. "Fifteen bullets. We're going to be okay, but it's going to be tough if you're too scared to do what I tell you. Do you understand?"

Carolina recognized the determination in the other woman's eyes. "I'm with you." She took a deep breath and drew back her shoulders. "And I do understand. We're going to get through this together."

"Good. Let's get it in gear, lady. Gate of Heaven Church."

Marty grabbed one of Leo's jackets off a hook in the hallway and slipped it on. When she pulled open the front door, the gun was out of sight in her jacket pocket, but her hand was wrapped firmly around the grip and her index finger clutched the trigger guard. A flat head bullet was in the chamber and the safety was off.

The sun had set half an hour before but the evening was still bright and the monument on Dorchester Heights was outlined against the sky. The two women turned left onto the sidewalk toward the spires of Gate of Heaven when Marty saw two black men coming from that direction. She put out an arm to stop Carolina.

"What...?"

"Too late!" Black males didn't walk the streets of this neighborhood at this time of night, not in Southie.

The men saw Marty grab Carolina's shoulder and started running toward them. The women turned together and sprinted back to the house.

Marty snapped the deadbolt as she shut the front door behind them. Then she ran to the door at the rear of the kitchen and did the same thing. She also slid the curtain across the half window that looked down on her backyard flower garden.

"Get upstairs," Marty told Carolina.

Carolina was on the first step when she stopped. "What about you?"

Marty held up the pistol in her hand. "You promised to do what I told you, now go on. If you stay with me, I got to worry about you, too. Let's hope Leo and Bobbie get here first." She waved Carolina away. "Now go on. Beat it."

Carolina ran upstairs.

Marty Carmichael pushed an old easy chair back into the far corner of the kitchen and crouched down behind it. From there she had the rear door well covered. Anyone who came through the front door would have to come down the hall and face her as they entered the kitchen because the stairs to the second floor were just to her right.

Marty was on her knees behind the chair, head and shoulders above it, arms resting on its back, gun aimed at the rear door. She closed her eyes, drew a deep breath, and forced herself to breathe normally when she opened them.

Then she waited, waited for a telltale sound that would mean she would have to protect her house. But she also waited for Leo's voice to call from outside that everything was okay.

The first sound she heard was someone jiggling the door knob out front. Then there was a solid thump against the door. It would take more than someone's shoulder to get through that big, heavy door.

She turned to another sound – at the rear of the house. Running feet came down the side alley, then thumped up the wooden back stoop. A shadow appeared behind the curtain over the window. The doorknob twisted. A hand jiggled it, then yanked a few times.

Out front, the other man was hurling himself against that door.

A shoulder smashed once against the lighter kitchen door. A man's voice, angry, uttered a string of profanity.

The window shattered. A hand ripped away the curtain. A black face peered through the broken window, then a hand reached in to turn the deadbolt.

Marty ducked down in fear. *No! Not now. You can do it.*

Cautiously, she peered around the chair and aimed her gun toward the door with one hand. Her first shot slammed into the wall to one side of the door. Her second was closer. The blast each time she pulled the trigger was deafening, terrifying – she was certain her heart stopped each time.

The hand disappeared. But just as quickly, a shiny, short-barreled revolver appeared in its place. As Marty pulled her trigger for a third time, an explosion louder than her own gun echoed through the kitchen. A bullet slammed into the plaster above her head. A second thudded into the chair near her left shoulder.

Marty grasped the pistol in both hands, just as Leo had taught her, moved to the right of the chair and raised the gun level with the middle of the door. She pulled the trigger five times. The barrel rose slightly with each shot.

When she stopped and peered through the smoke, there was no shiny revolver, no face looking back through the shattered window. There was a splintered door with four bullet holes. The fifth bullet probably went through the space where the window had been. She was certain she had at least scared away the bastard shooting at her.

Marty let her arms drop, the pistol still tightly in her grasp. Her entire body shook uncontrollably.

Then half a dozen shots shattered the lock and the deadbolt on the front door. The door crashed inward, slamming back against the wall.

Marty crawled across the kitchen floor and peered around the corner. A shadow filled the doorway. She saw a muzzle blast, heard an explosion. Instinctively she flattened herself on the floor.

Her pistol came up in both hands. She squeezed the trigger once, then again, and again. The gun bounced each time. She wasn't sure if she was shooting properly, but she kept pulling the trigger.

There were so many gun shots over the next second or two that she couldn't tell her own from the other.

She remembered seeing the form outlined by the doorway pitching back, then forward, but she kept pulling the trigger anyway – fifteen, twenty, thirty times. She was unaware that there were no more gunshots. Even the click of the hammer went unheard.

And when she finally opened her eyes and looked over the top of the gun, Leo stepped over a form in the hallway. Then he was kneeling, cradling her in his arms.

There were tears in Leo's eyes. Marty reached up and wiped them away. "I'm okay, hon."

Jean-Paul pulled his car into a space that had been painted red that day. "Remember what I say, little lady. You scream, you die now. Jean-Paul doan care. Do what I say, your chances may be bettah."

The sign hanging on the door of the tailor shop indicated that it was closed. Curtains were drawn across the windows. But that didn't stop Jean-Paul. Dragging Nomi behind him, he simply twisted the knob and pushed the door open.

Nomi saw the body of an older white man lying face down on the floor.

"Hey, Jean-Paul." The speaker was as black as Jean-Paul, and his accent was much the same.

After a short conversation, the man nodded towards Nomi. "She the one want to live up top?" His finger pointed skyward.

"She is," Jean-Paul answered. "Anyone else up there?"

"Nope. Both floors empty. They be remodel. All the workers gone home."

Jean-Paul dragged Nomi through a side door that opened to stairs leading to the second and third floors.

When three deckers were built, entrances to the apartments on each level were off an inside stairway. There were often two apartments on each level, the front one looking out on the street, the rear onto an alleyway. The structures were cheaply built to accommodate poor families who couldn't afford anything fancier. Boston's ethnic neighborhoods were full of three deckers by the turn of the century.

The hallways were full of tools and sawdust. The doors of the apartments had been removed. The owner of the building was remodeling each unit, converting the apartments to condos. Jean-Paul dragged an unwilling Nomi up the stairs to the third floor and pushed her down the hallway toward the rear. They went into the end apartment where the walls had been stripped down to the lath.

Jean-Paul's deep voice echoed off the walls of the empty apartment. "Well, little lady, you have your choice. Which room do you want?"

"What do you mean?"

"This be your new home. You stay here. Jean-Paul always want to keep the ladies happy. I don't want you mad when I leave. Which room do you want me to leave you in?" There was little trace of accent now. Jean-Paul was all business. "Tell me quick cause I got to meet a man."

Nomi remained silent. The bastard planned to leave her right here, alone in this empty building. She remembered his words on the telephone before leaving his place – "final fire." And this building would be part of that fire.

Her hands were still secured behind her back, but at least she could move. She walked over to a rear wall by a doorway and, with her back against the door frame, slid down until she was in a sitting position on the floor. It was uncomfortable with her hands still tied in back, but she could move after he left. "If I have to stay, I'll stay right here."

Jean-Paul smiled sadly. "You brave, little lady. Jean-Paul is almost sad he have to leave you. You need one more thing." He pulled a second length of rope from his back pocket. "This."

Dropping to his knees, he moved so quickly that it took a moment for Nomi to understand what he intended. She tried to kick, but Jean-Paul was too fast and too strong. Her ankles were secured together by the rope, leaving her completely immobile in a building that she knew would be part of the fire.

The dry, ancient structure would literally explode.

Bobbie Scott came through the front entrance of Leo Carmichael's house, revolver clutched in his hands, unsure of what he'd find. Gunshots from inside were echoing through the neighborhood as they'd pulled up. Leo vaulted from the still-moving car as Bobbie aimed it toward the curb.

Stepping cautiously over the corpse in the front hallway, Bobbie searched the front rooms to either side. Nothing.

Then he saw Marty and Leo inside the kitchen, holding each other tightly.

Bobbie edged past them, gun still ready, and moved over to one side of the splintered rear door. There were no sounds outside. He peered through the smashed window. In the dim evening light, he saw another body. This one had been knocked backwards by Marty's shots. It lay halfway down the rear stoop, shoe soles facing up toward Bobbie. The head was buried in Marty's flower garden.

Bobbie holstered his gun and turned back to Leo. "Second one out back. She blew 'em both away."

Marty's head was cradled on Leo's shoulder and she was crying silently. With Bobbie's words, the sobs rose from deep inside.

The stairs to the second floor creaked ominously. Bobbie waved them aside as he moved rapidly to one side of the stairway and brought his revolver back to the ready position.

"Mrs. Fairchild?" Leo whispered in Marty's ear.

"Upstairs."

Leo called out softly, "It's okay, Mrs. Fairchild. It's all over. You can come down now."

Bobbie holstered his gun and moved to the base of the stairs so she could see him. "You don't need to be frightened anymore, Mrs. Fairchild. Come on down."

Carolina took the final steps slowly. When she came into the light, fear and strain and tears had etched lines in her once youthful face. She went straight to Marty and buried her face in the other woman's neck.

Marty held Carolina tightly. "We're safe. We did it together," she murmured.

"Leo," Bobbie said. "Henry needs us."

"Yeah, and right now." He hated to leave Marty, but there was no choice. "We'll be back. Stay right here in the kitchen." He found another clip of bullets in the closet and slipped it into the pistol. "This is just in case. I don't think you'll be needing this anymore. We won't be gone long. We'll be back as fast as we can," he said reassuringly. "Call 911 and they'll send a car right away."

He followed Bobbie, stepping around the corpse in his front hall.

Hyde slowed as he came to the lights where Dorchester Avenue intersected Broadway. There was no ancient, black arson squad car in sight.

South Boston was peaceful as twilight dimmed and the streetlights began to come on. Most of the retail establishments were closed. Only the multi-colored lights of bars and restaurants stood out. But it was still early enough that families were taking their after-dinner stroll.

Where the hell were Leo and Bobbie? He didn't want to use the radio unless he was forced to because the bastards were probably monitoring that, too. The traffic light changed and Hyde turned right up Broadway. A car pulled out of a parking spot up the block and Hyde pulled into the space. He glanced down at the radio and cell phone lying on the car seat. *Do something, damn it!*

No instructions yet from Fairchild. The son of a bitch should have made contact by now. Mayor Jordan would be shitting in his pants sitting in his office, waiting. Hyde could imagine the money people, each one looking more superior than the next, each one making Charles Jordan feel smaller and smaller as the minutes ticked away. That was the one bright point he could picture, and that made him smile for a moment.

Hyde punched Jordan's office number into his phone.

Jordan answered on the first ring. "Hyde?"

"Yeah. Have you heard from him?"

"What do you mean? He's supposed to be giving you the routing data."

Hyde could hear the exasperation in Jordan's voice. "Yeah, but he hasn't. He's supposed to be meeting his main operative in South Boston right now. That may be holding him up. I just wanted to make sure he hadn't changed the rules." Hyde pushed the disconnect before Jordan could say anything more.

Fairchild drove up West Broadway and stopped his Mercedes for the red light. A small briefcase crammed with cash lay on the seat beside him. A larger one with even more cash was in the trunk. The slip of paper with all the phone numbers and routing numbers was burning a hole in the breast pocket of his white shirt.

He pulled back his sleeve and checked the time. Shit! Already off schedule – way off. That's how things got screwed up. Why the fuck couldn't the son of a bitch follow the original plans? He'd never thought about screwing Jean-Paul, not as long as he kept delivering.

Fairchild had a tremendous urge to jump the light. There was plenty of space before the vehicles approaching on Dorchester and Broadway. Then the WALK light flashed. Perfect. Everyone had to stop. The way was clear.

Hit it!

His right foot switched to the gas pedal. Just as he was about to dart ahead, a woman holding the hands of two small children stepped into the crosswalk. As Fairchild hit the brake, he noticed a Boston cop leaning against a light pole on the far side of the street. Hadn't even noticed the son of a bitch the way he blended with the pole.

Fairchild's fingers drummed a nervous cadence on the steering wheel until the light changed. He never noticed when he went by an old, dented, black car parked a block up Broadway, nor did the driver of that car see Fairchild pass by.

Jean-Paul stepped out the door of the tailor shop and waited on the sidewalk for the other man to lock the door. He had placed a timer in the cleaning fluids storage closet that would detonate in twenty minutes. If for some reason they ran into an unforeseen problem, or firefighters checked the spread of the fire they were about to ignite at the rear of the block, the benzene in the tailor shop would give them more than enough to play with.

They walked quickly down to the corner building on the block, hurried down the side street, and entered the alley at the rear. The basement door of the end building had already been jimmied open.

The process was quick and extremely efficient. Jean-Paul's men had already placed flammable materials throughout the structure. Copper wiring would conduct the heat.

Jean-Paul pulled the switch on the main electrical box. His partner made the final connection and nodded. The switch was pushed back on and the entire building once again had full electrical service.

They exited the basement rapidly and retraced their steps to the street corner. It was as odd a sight to see two black men in this South Boston neighborhood at this time of night as it had been in the Carmichaels'. But these men were decently dressed, they weren't running, and no one out for an evening walk felt threatened on the well-lighted street.

They got in their car and waited patiently. They were rewarded with a muffled thump, then a second, and a few seconds later a third. Once they recognized the familiar orange glow reflected on a third story window, Jean-Paul started the car.

Leona Blake's head snapped around at the sound of the telephone. Every call seemed to say fire.

Vartanian, at console number one, had it on the first ring. "Boston Fire Alarm." The caller's phone number and address on the screen was in South Boston. "Right." He was scribbling down the information. "Thank you." He pushed the button for the closest station house in District Six. "Engine Two and Ladder Nineteen, fire showing." He gave the address. "Fireground channel will be channel two."

Leona Blake took control at console number two where she would monitor the progress as Engine Two and Ladder Nineteen pulled out of the station house.

Jordan!

The name hit Hyde between the eyes – Jordan! Why hadn't he figured that out the moment Bobbie had called? Fairchild's last fire would hit Charles Jordan's home.

He snatched up the radio on his front seat. "Mayor Jordan's house," he shouted. It was down Broadway beyond Independence Park where South Boston's Vietnam Memorial was located.

Bobbie Scott whipped the car around in a U-turn, tires screeching, narrowly missing Engine Two, which had just turned onto Broadway.

21

Air...

     water...

          fire...

               earth.

The ancient Greeks believed four substances composed the physical universe. It was original, scientific thought in that era, but the Greeks never could have imagined how terrifying man would make fire a few centuries in the future. Combined with the oxygen in the air, fire brought to a critical temperature could turn almost any element into a fuel that would consume everything it touched.

Fire was an enigma that had transfixed man even before he learned to use it for himself. With the right combination of fuels, fire could scorch the earth itself. Man learned that the only way to quench fire was to remove air, or the fuel, or drown it with water.

But the Ancients never realized that man would use fire as a weapon.

Jean-Paul shifted into reverse, easing the car back until he was touching the bumper of the car behind. Then he cramped the wheel in the opposite direction to pull out into the street. He looked back at the building as he gently stepped on the gas pedal and that was when he placed his foot back on the brake. The sight was beautiful. The speed of a fire in the early stages could be hypnotizing.

Smoke, the byproduct of incomplete combustion, increases dramatically as the flames spread. The color of the flames changes as the fire grows depending on intensity, fuel supply, and heat. Sound magnifies as combustibles literally explode from the intense heat consuming them. Hungry flame sucks in oxygen creating miniature fire storms of energy. The fire becomes another living thing, a monster feeding on everything in its path.

Jean-Paul was captivated. The ancient, wooden structures in the block seemed to dance as his fire became that living thing. Individual rooms turned into exploding fireballs of heat as flashover occurred, their windows bursting out onto Broadway.

"What the fuck you waitin' for?"

That question brought Jean-Paul back to reality. He could hear the sirens screaming down Broadway, the never-ending race to the fireground between police cars and fire trucks.

Jean-Paul was half way into the street when he jammed his foot down on the brake. A speeding black car, rotating blue light on its dashboard larger than the fire itself, was suddenly on top of him – and then it was past. But the black car came to a screeching stop twenty yards away, sideways in the middle of the street. An interior switch popped open the trunk before the occupants emerged. As they appeared, one was speaking into a radio, the other went to pull fire gear from the trunk.

Jean-Paul looked to his rear. Fire apparatus already blocked the street from that direction. The black car had them trapped.

"We have to take them," Jean-Paul said, pointing at the black car. "Be lookin' for us pretty quick." He reached beneath his left arm and extracted a pistol. His partner took a revolver from his jacket pocket as they got out of their car.

Jean-Paul leveled his sights on Leo Carmichael's back.

Fairchild was still ahead of the fire engines, but the ominous wail of sirens was drawing closer. He searched frantically for a side street. Jesus – the flashing red lights seemed to fill his rear view mirror.

There! Just ahead! Between two old buildings. He yanked the wheel hard right.

Dead end!

South Boston was home to a variety of alleys that actually subdivided blocks. These alleys often opened into cul-de-sacs that created mini-neighborhoods. They rarely had exits and the residents preferred it that way. Strangers stayed away.

Fairchild stopped and shifted into reverse. The Mercedes reared backwards onto Broadway. He slammed it into drive as the flashing lights of a chief's red car seemed to vault over the rise behind him.

The Mercedes shot forward. Fairchild was frantically searching for a side street when he saw flames licking out of a building directly ahead.

He turned right at that corner and was again forced to jam on his brakes. He slid to a stop inches from a police car blocking his way. The light on top was flashing. The driver had already left his car to direct traffic.

Fairchild jumped out of the Mercedes. He ran over to the police car, yanked open the door, and slid in behind the wheel. He reached down to start the car. No keys!

Fuck Jean-Paul. Fuck everything. The fire was already burning. When Jordan heard about this one, he probably couldn't wire the money fast enough – then again, he couldn't wire the money without the routing numbers!

Oh, shit! Jean-Paul and his crazy last-minute ideas. This wouldn't have happened if...

Fairchild dashed back to the Mercedes for his cell phone.

•

The aroma of a fire varies with the fuel. Each element has a distinctive odor. The smell of an unseen fire creates a moment of fear, a moment when one wonders, *Am I going to burn?*

Though she couldn't see smoke or flame, or hear the fire crackling, Nomi Cram smelled it.

Fire is alive. It creates its own climate. Heat and a demand for oxygen move the air until it swirls. It carries the elements that haven't burned as the flames advance. The heat rises. The aroma of the fire expands – invisible gases creep under doors, through minute openings that the eye can't see, rising through hollow walls, a precursor to the coming terror.

Nomi shuddered. She was afraid and she knew there was good reason to be afraid.

She rolled away from the wall onto her stomach. From there, she forced herself up to her knees. With her hands behind her back and her ankles securely tied, she couldn't crawl. But she could inch her way across the floor to a window by swinging her shoulders.

Nomi fell three times and her face hit hard each time, but she felt little pain. When one is propelled by fear, there is no time for pain. She didn't know, nor would she have cared, that her sweating face was covered with another layer of sawdust and dirt each time she struggled back to her knees.

As she got closer to a window that faced Broadway, she could finally see the reflection of yellow flame in the windows of the building across the street. It seemed that the entire world was burning. The chaotic sounds of the fireground were what made her get to her knees each time. If she could get to the window, get to her feet, be seen by someone...

The district chief called in on channel two. "Fire Alarm, this is Car Six."

—226—

"Go ahead, Six."

"On the orders of Car Six, strike a third alarm." The heavy fire conditions and radiated heat kept his men outside and threatened to touch off parked vehicles on Broadway.

"Roger third alarm," Leona Blake said calmly.

Hyde experienced a brief moment of satisfaction. He'd been right. This was the block where Jordan lived and it was burning. Served the mayor right. His asshole buddy was getting even with him.

But being right was also being afraid. Not for himself, not for Jordan. For Nomi. She was here...somewhere. Where to start?

Hyde had to abandon his car. Broadway was blocked.

Ladder 19 and Engine 2 were the first on scene, their firehouse just a couple of blocks away on Broadway. Ladder 18 and Engine 39 were there moments after the second alarm was sounded. Rescue 1 was already on the scene. Two EMS ambulances and crews were there. The District Six chief's car had been first on scene because he'd been eating dinner at the Broadway firehouse. The communications van and the Division One chief's car were just ahead of Hyde's car. With the third alarm, the Tower was enroute along with the Collapse Unit and equipment from District Four.

Every fire scene appears to be chaos. Flame. The gagging stink of smoke. Hoses snaking in every direction as if there was no purpose, no rationale, no objective. But two and a half inch hose lines had already been hooked up to engines and were operating in a flanking position. The crew of another engine company dropped a five inch feeder line from a hydrant and hooked up the hydrant assist valve for deck gun operation. Ladders reached through thick smoke to roof tops. Firefighters, faceless and nameless behind the masks of their Scott's gear, climbed ladders, broke windows, and chopped holes to vent smoke so others preparing to haul heavy hose lines into the buildings could fight the flames from inside.

Command at a major fire is complex and fascinating. The senior officer now was the District Six chief who would relinquish overall command to the Division One chief when he arrived. But each ladder truck team venting the structures and each engine company team advancing into the heart of the blaze with hose lines were under the direction of their own officers.

The noise was overwhelming, deafening. Orders were issued by megaphone and radio. There was purpose in every command, every movement. It was a battle. Fire had attacked and had the upper hand. But the firefighters were establishing a line of defense. If they could hold until reinforcements arrived, then the counterattack would begin.

The thrill of the fire scene animated Hyde as it had from the day he faced his first blaze as a probationary firefighter. He could see at least four separate fires were consuming the block. Nomi had to be in one of the buildings and he had to figure out how he was going to find her. There were just minutes left...

And then, above the chaos surrounding him, he heard the sharp, unmistakable report of a gunshot.

Leo was leaning on the hood of the car, the radio to his ear when the first bullet shattered the windshield less than a foot from his head. For a split second his eyes were glued to the glass spiderweb emanating out from the bullet hole.

He was reaching back to his hip for his revolver and shouting to Bobbie when the impact of a bullet in the fleshy part of his upper arm spun him sideways. Leo fell to his knees. He pulled his gun from the holster and a third slug ripped into the fender by his shoulder. Leo fell face forward and started rolling. He could see two men standing on either side of a car about twenty five yards away. The crack of shots and the muzzle flashes seemed to blend with the waves of pain in his arm as he rolled. Then he was twisting his body, bending himself like a pretzel around the car wheel as he tried desperately to place something between himself and the two men who seemed to be concentrating on him alone.

Bobbie Scott whirled at the first shot and in the same motion dived behind the rear fender. He came to his knees with his revolver in his right hand and peered cautiously over the trunk of the car to see the two men coming toward him.

Everything Bobbie had been taught at the range came back as he looked down the sights of his gun at one of the men and pulled the trigger. The weapon jumped, then came back to the chest of the man he'd shot at. Nothing. He was still there, gun still aimed toward him, and there were bullets slamming into the car near his head. He couldn't see or hear Leo and there was no time to wonder about him. Just stop those fuckers who were trying to kill him.

Bobbie rose slightly, the revolver outstretched in both hands, and squeezed the trigger – once, twice, three...

The man jerked sideways, gun flying through the air toward Bobbie. He took one step, both hands grasping his middle, then crumpled forward onto the street.

Leo bellowed as a bullet richocheted off the pavement and dug a furrow across the top of his head. He had no idea what had happened. His head throbbed. He could feel himself losing consciousness. "Shit, shit, shit..."

Bobbie dropped to his knees and crawled toward the front of the car. Leo lay on his back, eyes closed. Bobbie saw blood flowing from Leo's head and arm.

"Shit...shit...shit..."

Leo's gun lay a few feet away and he kept repeating the word over and over. "Shit...shit...shit..."

Bobbie peered beneath the car. A pair of feet were heading toward them – purposefully, determined. He scrambled back for protection. But...Leo would be first!

With both hands wrapped around the grip, Bobbie rose to his knees and looked directly down his gun's sights into a pair of deadly eyes.

Jean-Paul was fast, darting to one side, darting to the other, still closing, then he stopped, brought his gun up with one hand and began to shoot.

One-two-three – each shot was off the mark.

Bobbie brought his gun around and...

Bobbie Scott didn't know he'd been hit until he was lying on his side. It had been like a fist slamming into his shoulder. One side of his body was numb but there was no pain. He could still move.

Jean-Paul came around the side of the car, his gun pointing down at Leo's head.

Rolling onto his stomach, Bobbie brought his gun up and pulled the trigger. The big man stopped and took an involuntary step back. A look of surprise came over his face. His free hand reached up to his chest and came away covered with blood.

Staring in surprise at Bobbie, Jean-Paul's hand began to rise. His gun wobbled unsteadily.

Bobbie saw the bright, red blood staining the man's shirt. He saw the gun wavering, swinging in his direction...wavering.

Bobbie pointed his own gun at Jean-Paul and squeezed the trigger.

Dry fire! No bullets.

He tossed the gun aside and rolled for Leo's.

When he came up with it and brought it around, he was looking into the muzzle of Jean-Paul's gun. The big man's hand shook wildly as he pulled the trigger. A bullet slammed into the pavement inches from Bobbie's face.

Without thinking, Bobbie kept squeezing the trigger until he realized he was dry firing again.

Jean-Paul slumped to his knees, hands empty. He stared at Bobbie with a strange, distant look in his eyes. His lips were moving but Bobbie couldn't make out any words above the chaos around them.

Another sound came to Raymond Fairchild above the surrounding noise. He heard the crack of gunfire. A single shot, followed by many. A pause. Then there were more shots – many more. Then they ceased and the din of the fireground again overwhelmed everything else.

He reached in the glove compartment and removed the pistol he'd bought a few years back for home protection. When he'd taken it from his closet shelf a few days before, he wondered why a man like himself bothered with a gun when he could pay people to use them. Now, as he stared at the weapon in the palm of his hand, he knew he would do anything to anyone who got in his way.

Jean-Paul lay on his back. Bobbie crawled across the space between them until they were facing each other. Blood was flowing from three separate wounds in Jean-Paul's chest. His eyes were open, watching, but he wasn't moving. Bobbie touched his own left shoulder where Jean-Paul's bullet had hit him. Pain came in waves now. His world was spinning.

"Where's the girl?" Bobbie asked. "Where's Nomi?"

Jean-Paul's eyes were cloudy. "What girl?" he whispered.

Bobbie whipped the barrel of his gun across Jean-Paul's face, ripping the man's nose open. "You know who I mean." He rammed the pistol into Jean-Paul's crotch. "I swear I'll blow your dick off and feed it to the dogs. Where is she?"

"What you care?" Jean-Paul coughed. Blood dribbled from the corner of his mouth

"Where is she?" Bobbie screamed. Christ, the pain was getting bad.

Jean-Paul frowned. *Feed it to the dogs?* No way. But what did things matter when you were dying? That little lady was a fighter. Maybe this man who dared to stand up to him could help her. "Above the shop...on top there..." His eyes closed. His face was resting in a puddle of blood.

Bobbie felt his head spinning. He couldn't let go, not when he had to tell someone about Nomi. But his world was growing dark. He was falling and even though he was already sprawled on the hot pavement it seemed so far down.

When he was sure that he'd landed, he looked up. Someone was close by. He tried to focus his eyes. That...that someone was standing over Leo. Bobbie blinked his eyes.

The man in the photo! Fairchild!

There was a gun in his hand and he was aiming it at Leo's head.

Bobbie tried to move. He had to help Leo. That was his last thought as he slipped into unconsciousness.

Hyde was running full tilt when he pulled the trigger. He knew he wouldn't hit Fairchild with the damn .38, but it didn't matter. The son of a bitch had a goddamn gun pointed right at Leo's head.

Fairchild's head whipped around.

Hyde fired three more shots.

Fairchild turned and ran. He wasn't going to let Hyde screw things up for him – not now!

Henry saw Bobbie Scott move, raise his arm.

"Henry..." Bobbie's arm fell to his side.

Hyde dropped to his knees and lifted Bobbie in his arms. He looked down at the silent Leo, bathed in blood. Bobbie's blood was drenching Hyde's shirt.

Hyde closed his eyes but blood seemed to paint his eyelids. He was back in the jungle. Thundering noise. Flames. Men dying. Screaming. Helicopters. Pandemonium. More blood. That's what a firefight was like in the jungle, and this was...

"Medic!" Hyde screamed. "Medic!"

He was still screaming at the fire gods when an EMT lifted Bobbie from his arms.

Hyde rose to his feet and turned in the direction Fairchild had gone. He reloaded his revolver – then he began to run.

Nomi could hear the crackling as she reached the window. With a final effort, she reared back and came to her feet. When she looked down toward the street, she could see flames reaching up toward her.

Would anyone see her at the window? Maybe if she broke it. She drew back and hurled herself, shoulder first. She hit the center strip of wood. The window seemed to bow, but it didn't break.

Nomi pulled back and took a deep breath. Smoke was beginning to fill the room. Once more, with her last reserve of strength, she threw herself at the window and it crashed outward. Sound flowed in. Sirens, more fire equipment, more police, ambulances arriving and departing, hydraulics lifting and moving ladders, diesel engines, pumpers, bullhorns, firefighters in battle. A live fire consuming everything in its path.

But she was still alive.

Frank Duggan looked up as the glass burst out of a third floor window. "Christ, I'm sure I saw someone at that window." The District Six chief had told him the building was being renovated and no one lived there. "This was supposed to be a deserted building."

As he spoke, the division chief called for a ladder to that window, but flames and roiling smoke from the benzene in the tailor shop were too thick. No one could make it up a ladder through that. They'd have to search for another way, or else try going in the front under a wall of water.

22

Raymond Fairchild was desperate. He had no idea which street to take. He'd put South Boston so far behind him that he couldn't remember how the streets ran. He had to get out somehow. He had to get hold of Jordan to transfer...

His mind stopped dead. Glancing over his shoulder, he saw a man darting between cars coming toward him – *with a gun in his hand!* And he was covered with blood. Then the man was in the street, running toward him, a nightmare in motion.

Maybe...Fairchild blinked. The figure was still there – even closer – when he opened his eyes.

Hyde!

The gun was heavy and awkward in his hand when he turned to shoot. He heard the sharp crack as he fired each bullet, but they had no effect on his target. The bloody apparition was bearing down on him.

He turned and dashed down a street between two buildings and...oh Christ!

Fairchild found himself in an alley that was ended abruptly by an ancient, windowless building.

Hyde advanced down the alley certain that he was impervious to Fairchild's bullets. He held his gun at his side. There was no need to waste any of his five shots. If

Fairchild hit him firing like that, it would be pure luck. And Henry Hyde didn't particularly care. The murdering son of a bitch was his now.

Hyde looked directly into Fairchild's eyes as he closed in. When he raised his gun, he wanted to see the pure animal fear that comes when a human being knows that the end has come. He wanted Fairchild to grovel, to beg for his life.

A bullet ricocheted harmlessly off the pavement at Hyde's feet. Then there was silence. Fairchild's face took on a new look as he realized that nothing was happening when he pulled the trigger. His gun was empty.

Fairchild backed up until he could go no farther, his shoulders against a wall – cornered.

Hyde stopped about eight feet away. "End of the road?" He wanted the other man to see his eyes, to understand what hate really meant. And he especially wanted the man to know how it felt to be trapped. "Do you want me to let you live?"

Fairchild's eyes glistened and he opened his mouth, but there was no response.

Hyde raised his revolver slowly and aimed with one hand at Fairchild's forehead. The result was more than he could ever have hoped for. *Look out for the cornered rat, Henry.*

"So you'd like another chance?"

Fairchild nodded once.

"Like you gave all the people who died in your fires?"

Fairchild blinked.

Time for the prick to squirm.

The muzzle of the gun slowly descended from Fairchild's head to his chest to his stomach to his crotch, then back up to his chest, a little to the right, below the shoulder, the heart – *Squirm, you prick* – right about...

Fairchild lunged before Hyde could speak.

Hyde pulled the trigger.

Fairchild was knocked backwards as the bullet shattered his left shoulder. His head smashed against the wall behind him. He howled in pain, grasped his arm with his right hand for a split second, then hurled himself toward the gun.

The crazy bastard! Hyde took a step back as he fired.

Fairchild's body jerked with the impact and he bellowed in anger. Blood pumped from a hole on the right side of his chest. When he looked up at Hyde, his eyes were full of helpless rage. The wall he leaned against for support was bright with his blood.

Hyde could feel a grin forming at the corners of his mouth. "Does it hurt?"

Fairchild closed his eyes and nodded. "It hurts."

"Open your eyes." There was no reaction. "I said open your fucking eyes."

Fairchild opened them. "You're a lousy shot, Hyde. It takes a better man than you to stop me."

"Surprise, asshole!" Hyde could feel himself losing control. His gun moved from Fairchild's head to his heart to his groin in increasingly larger circles.

Don't do it, Henry. You're still a lawman. Don't get down on his level.

His free hand felt for the handcuffs above his back pocket. "You're going to have your picture on the front page of the *Globe*." He moved a step closer. "Turn around."

Fairchild's right foot lashed out at the gun.

Hyde pulled the trigger again. "You crazy shit!"

Fairchild screamed in agony as his knee exploded into a bloody pulp of flesh and cartilage and bone. He teetered, then his leg gave way and he fell, landing hard because he was unable to put out his arm.

Hyde had the cuffs in his other hand. "Look at me!"

Fairchild's head twisted slowly until he was staring up at Henry Hyde, covered with blood, standing over him with a sardonic grin, swinging the handcuffs above his head.

Fairchild closed his eyes and shook his head from side to side very slowly. "Go fuck yourself, Hyde."

Hyde kneeled down. "Open your eyes!" His voice was shrill. "Open your fucking eyes, asshole!"

Fairchild opened his eyes and glared back.

Hyde saw pain. He saw anger. He also recognized a cornered animal.

Fairchild heaved himself painfully to one knee.

"Stick out your right arm." Hyde held an open handcuff forward.

Fairchild slowly raised his arm. His eyes never left Hyde's.

"Palm down."

Fairchild turned his palm down.

Hyde reached forward slowly with the open cuff, his eyes darting from Fairchild's face to his hands, back and forth. The cuff touched Fairchild's hand.

"Don't move, asshole. Not a muscle." His gun remained pointed at Fairchild's chest. He moved the cuff slowly, turning it until it came in contact with Fairchild's wrist.

When Raymond Fairchild made his move, it wasn't for the handcuffs, nor for Hyde. His hand was a bloody flash, snaking out at the gun. His fingers closed around Hyde's hand and the gun. He squeezed with all his strength.

Hyde dropped the cuffs and reached for Fairchild's wrist with his free hand, but he was an instant too late.

The gun fired once, the bullet glancing off the wall by Fairchild's head. Then Hyde felt his hand pulled by a force much stronger than him. With a desperate burst of strength, Raymond Fairchild yanked the gun, with Hyde's hand still holding it, into his open mouth. His teeth shattered as the gun bucked and his head slammed back against the wall. The mess that was Fairchild's head splattered over Hyde.

Henry Hyde would never be sure which one of them pulled the trigger.

The EMT was strapping Bobbie Scott to a stretcher when he recognized the same man who'd been holding Bobbie in his arms and shouting for a medic just minutes before. The man's shirt was soaked with blood and his face was spattered with it. His expression was unfathomable.

"Are you...injured, sir?"

"Never been better," Hyde said with a twisted grin. "How about my guys?" He indicated Bobbie and Leo. "They gonna be okay?"

"Looks like it. The guy with the mustache has a hell of a headache. That one," he indicated Bobbie, "he's been asking for someone when he's conscious. Slips in and out. Your name Henry?"

"Yeah, that's me."

"Henry!" Leo raised himself on an elbow. His voice was soft so only Hyde could hear him, but it was also sharp. "Your holster's empty."

"You worried about my gun at a time like this?" he asked. Then he said, "I got the fucker, Leo. He's history."

"Who?" This wasn't the Henry Hyde he knew, not with this wild, glazed look. Henry always had control of himself. "What are you talking about?"

"Fairchild. I got the son of a bitch. Blew his fucking head off." He turned away.

"Henry! Give me a second." What had the crazy bastard done?

Hyde bent over him.

Leo placed his mouth close to Hyde's ear. "Now, tell me, where is your gun?"

"In his fuckin' mouth."

"Are you shitting me? Or did you really do that? Tell me again where the goddamn gun is."

"Like I said, in his fucking mouth."

"I believe you." He saw it in Hyde's eyes. "Henry, tell me where Fairchild is."

"In an alley back there." His eyes turned briefly down the street.

"Hey, mister," the EMT called to Henry, "your buddy wants to talk to you before we load him."

Bobbie was strapped to a stretcher that they were about to slide into the back of an ambulance.

"Henry..." Bobbie's voice was a hoarse whisper.

Hyde went over to him and placed a hand on his shoulder. "You did good. You blew that prick away before I had my chance."

"Nomi..." Bobbie's voice was growing softer. "He left her in one of the buildings...the one with some kind of a shop on the street. On the top floor."

Bobbie Scott was unconscious when the stretcher slid into the back of the ambulance and the doors closed.

Al Horgan's ruddy Irish face paled when he recognized Hyde running toward him. Henry looked like the devil they used to imagine back in parochial school days when they smoked cigarettes under the Tobin Bridge. He was covered with blood. The expression on his face was wilder than when he made his tough-guy reputation beating up punks down by the Charlestown docks.

Horgan intercepted him before he could be seen by the command group. "Henry, what the..."

Hyde gripped Al's arm. "Nomi...she's in there. A shop of some kind, Al. A shop. Bobbie said the building's got a shop."

Horgan nodded toward the fully engulfed tailor shop. "Right there. Blew out a few minutes ago. Frank and I figure it was benzene."

Hyde's eyes ran up the front of the building. The second floor was fully involved. The top floor was vaguely visible through smoke and flames. "That broken window." He pointed at the third floor window. "Our guys do that?"

"Nope. Frank said he thought he saw someone at that window. But we couldn't send anyone up a ladder. The heat. They're using a deck gun to drive back the flames now, and some guys went around to the back. We're also gonna try to send some guys in with a hose over 'em."

"Then that's where Nomi is. I know it. I need your gear, Al."

"You can't go in that building yet, Henry."

"Nomi's up there. Give me your fuckin' gear or I'll get some from someone else."

Horgan handed over his helmet. "You're a crazy bastard," he said as he took off his bunker coat. "But you're not going in there without a mask." He held the coat for Hyde.

"Boots and gloves, too," Hyde said as he kicked off his shoes.

Horgan called to a nearby firefighter. "Larry, Henry needs your Scott's gear real bad."

Larry slipped the straps for the breathing equipment off his shoulders. "No more than ten or fifteen minutes left in the tank," he said to Hyde. "Put this on while I get another tank from the air supply truck."

Horgan was already unscrewing the tank valve. "Super quick, Larry. I can't keep him here much longer." Horgan had a hand through the belt at Hyde's waist. His mouth was close to Hyde's ear. "Where'd all the blood come from?"

"Dead animal."

Larry returned with a new air tank and slipped it into position.

"Lemme go, Al."

"The tank's not tight yet," Horgan said. "Where's the dead animal?"

"Just plain dead." Hyde slapped down on Horgan's arm and jerked away, sprinting toward the building.

Frank Duggan had seen Horgan and Hyde. He saw Hyde putting on bunker gear and thought nothing more of it until Hyde broke away and ran for the entrance to the triple decker. "Get a line up there," Duggan bellowed, pointing toward Hyde, who was disappearing into the smoke. "Soak him down. Follow him."

Phil Mezey, the engine company lieutenant who'd seen his old friend coming out of the Sports Depot fire just days before, had water on Hyde before Duggan finished. Then he ordered his men to move their hose in behind Hyde

Leo looked down at his hands. They were covered with the blood from Hyde's clothing. *I got the son of a bitch...blew his fucking head off...in his fucking mouth.* He rose to a sitting position on the stretcher and sat there for a moment with his feet dangling over the edge. Christ, his head hurt. He wiggled his toes, stretched out his arms and wiggled his fingers. He sure did hurt but all the necessary parts still seemed to be operating.

"Hey," said the EMT, "you're on your way to the hospital."

"Sorry, guy." Leo hopped off the stretcher. His head throbbed, his blood-soaked arm ached, but he knew he could make it. "Got a job to do. Thanks for the help."

Leo headed down Broadway, looking down each alley until he came to one where he saw something huddled against the back wall.

He moved cautiously toward the pile, more tentative when he saw blood. It was spattered everywhere, smeared down the wall, blackening against the pavement, congealing in puddles. Only when he reached the object could he tell it was once a human being. The back of its head was gone. He saw the bone and gristle and blood on the arms and knees.

"Jesus Christ, Henry!"

Leo reached out his right foot and pushed the body over. He saw blood still oozing from the groin. And just as Henry had said, there was the grip of his gun sticking out of Raymond Fairchild's mouth.

You got the son of a bitch good, Henry.

Leo Carmichael knew there was only one thing he could do for Hyde. He had a tiny address book in his wallet that he rarely used. He went directly to the O-P section. Being Boston, the listings were almost entirely *O'.* The number for Sean O'Connor was in pencil and blurred by the years. It had been a long time since Carmichael had talked with Sean. Anyone related to law enforcement knew better. He snapped open his cell phone, hoping it was still the right number, and punched the buttons.

"O'Connor here."

"Hi, Sean. This is Leo Carmichael."

"Long time between hi's, Leo."

"Matter of necessity. It's not that I don't love you, Sean, but dancing with you attracts attention."

"My friends say the same about you, so we're even. I'll bet you need something."

"I need a favor – not for me, for Henry."

"Henry! Anything for Henry."

"I need a mess cleaned up. The faster your guys can do it, the better chance Henry has of staying out of the joint."

Sean remembered the joint. He also remembered how Henry Hyde had saved his teenage life on the streets of Charlestown. "Like I said, anything for Henry."

Leo explained about the fire, about the police lines, how to find the alley, and what Sean would find when he got there. No names were ever mentioned. "I know you can handle it. I don't want anyone to ever find our friend. I don't want that gun to ever turn up again anywhere in the world. You still with me, Sean?"

"Like I said, Leo, anything for Henry."

Leo snapped the phone shut and slipped it back into his pocket. Sean would make sure nothing was left.

He headed up the alley without a backward look and turned right down Broadway until he found what he needed. There was a roll of yellow police tape lying where a cop had wrapped it around a light pole. He picked up the roll, cut the tape with his pocket knife, and went back to the head of the alley. He stretched the tape across the entrance.

The yellow tape should keep the curious out of the alley for a while and, of course, Sean had never seen a police line he didn't want to cross. Everything in that alley would be taken care of before anyone knew what had happened there.

Now, where the hell was Henry?

23

Heat – instantly more dangerous than anything cold. Ice was slow and calming; fire was quick and painful.

Hyde could feel the heat increasing around the edges of his mask as he pushed forward into the smoky cauldron. Flames licked out and up at the top of the entrance as he ducked low and moved inside. Behind, the man on the nozzle doused him with cooling water.

Entering a burning building against blinding smoke and searing flames demands experience and courage.

Hyde dropped to his hands and knees, inching forward, gloved hands reaching out to touch, to judge what was before him. At the point where the hypnotizing glare of fire made him hesitate, a sheet of cooling water flowed overhead, clearing the air momentarily. He saw a flight of stairs ahead to his right. The sheet of curling flames running up the charred wall disappeared with another blast of water. The guys hauling the hose line were doing a great job.

He came to his feet and started up the stairs. The feel of each step under his boots was like walking on popcorn. The flames had charred and weakened them.

Hyde dropped down again, reaching out with his hands to spread his weight. Christ! The wood was still so hot he could feel it through the gloves. If these stairs were still burning underneath, he could be heading for the basement any second.

Once again, cooling water cascaded over him as the team on the hose line concentrated their flow on the flames devouring the landing above. Moving like an animal on all fours, Henry came to the top of the stairs.

Fire danced over his head as he went flat on the second floor landing. The sounds of destruction were overwhelming – the crackle of dry wood being consumed, the eerie wail of flame and heat surging upward in a never-ending search for more oxygen, the crash of falling ceilings.

He felt something career off his shoulder. Then a much heavier weight crashed down on his helmet. A piece slipped down his neck, scalding his back. Boiling plaster! It would be falling faster with this heat.

His ears began to tingle, the first indication that they would soon burn. After that, his protective outer gear would begin to fray and char. A firefighter's outfit was so heat resistant that by the time you realized temperatures were getting too high, your time was already running out.

Another blast of water. It was a direct hit and knocked him to one side and he had to struggle against the water pressure to roll and cool himself. He could picture the steam rising off him like a swamp monster as he got to his knees.

The water also neutralized the fire momentarily and he could see the foot of the stairs to the third floor. He rose to his feet and was moving cautiously down the steamy, smoking hallway when he heard frantic shouts from the men on the hose line. The staircase behind him collapsed with a roar in a shower of sparks and soot.

A black hole existed where four men had been hauling hose seconds before. He was alone now and he could no longer get out the way he'd come in.

A howling, eerie, engulfing sound, all too familiar to a firefighter, came from the room facing the street to his right. Hyde flattened himself. The entire space exploded into the hallway with an orange flame – flashover! Fire had a way of searching out each tiny crevice and air space as it climbed. The floor above would ignite any minute now.

Frank Duggan witnessed the flashover, too. He saw the terrible glow as the entire room reached flash point, then the explosion of flame as two windows burst into the street. He could also make out a human form outlined in the front hall window, the fire helmet silhouetted for just an instant by the orange glare. Then it disappeared. But Duggan knew Hyde had at least made it to the third floor stairway.

While firefighters scrambled to rescue the team that had fallen into the basement, Duggan ordered the Tower Company to direct their stream into the second level. Firefighters from Ladder 17 climbed to the roof of an adjacent building and bridged their way across to a position where they could begin to ventilate the third floor of the burning structure. Ladder 4 had just arrived and Duggan ordered Lt. O'Brien to get a ladder to the third floor in the rear.

When Duggan saw flames begin to dance behind the third floor windows, seconds began to tick off like minutes.

Time, Henry, time...

Hyde's mouth was bone dry, sand dry, desert dry. His outer gear protected his skin and the mask saved his lungs, but they were both false confidence as precious body fluids were drained by the heat. Firefighters could lapse into unconsciousness without realizing they were in danger – and too often it could happen when they had already placed themselves in a position where rescue was impossible.

Hyde knew he was running out of time.

Flame followed him up the stairs to the third level, licking at his heels. He flattened himself on the landing to regain his bearings through the smoke. Tools and equipment were scattered about. Most of the walls had been removed, leaving the structural beams to support the ceiling. Dense smoke hovered two feet above the floor as he crawled across the landing.

Bobbie had only been able to tell him – top floor, above the shop.

Duggan thought he might have seen someone at the front window as it broke out. *Try the front first.*

As he crawled, he saw that the floorboards were turning dark. Tendrils of smoke oozed up between them, followed by tiny darting flames seeking more fuel, more air. Sawdust nourished them and they scurried across the floor…climbed the dry beams…danced across the ceiling.

Time…

Hyde's instinct told him that the temperature was already so high that the entire third floor would reach flashover shortly.

He crawled toward the front of the building, then turned to his right into what had been the front apartment. Sawdust turned to black ash and smoke as colorful threads of flame gamboled across the floor. The density of the smoke varied with the movement of the air. Soon it would reach the floor and once again Henry would be searching blind.

Then he caught sight of a shadowy form across the floor against the far wall. As he crawled in that direction, a sheet of flame came through the broken front window and raced across the ceiling, lighting the area in an awesome combination of colors. But a stream of water followed through the same window, turning to steam as it washed over flat surfaces.

Time…

Nomi was barely conscious when he got to her. Her nose was buried in her blouse. Her soot-blackened face streamed with perspiration. She opened her eyes slightly when she felt his hand, but they were red and swollen almost shut from the smoke. She tried to speak but could only cough up blackened saliva.

Air! She needed air. Flipping off his helmet, Hyde yanked the mask off his face and clapped it over hers. Her hands came up instantly and grasped the mask, sucking deeply on the fresh air.

The intense heat on his newly exposed skin made his face tingle. It wouldn't be long before his features bubbled into blisters and his hair began to burn. The sharp pain of smoke ripped at his lungs as he was forced to breathe. He wouldn't be able to get either of them out if...

He found a small carpenter's saw lying on the floor and cut through the rope on her wrists. Then he cut the hem of her skirt in two places.

Time...

Another breath...hot, searing pain.

He yanked up on the skirt, ripping until he had a ragged strip of cloth, then tore across until a piece came off in his hands. He folded it in half, covered his nose and mouth, and drew his next desperate breath.

The cloth helped, the pain wasn't as intense, but it was still there. He was buying time but the lack of oxygen in the air was weakening him quickly.

Hyde shook Nomi until she opened her eyes. He put his face next to hers and shouted. "We've got to share the air. Do you understand me?"

Nomi nodded weakly.

He pulled the mask from her hands, held it in place and took a few deep breaths, then clapped it back over her face again.

"You have to hold it on. I need both hands."

She held the mask tightly.

Time...

Then he covered his nose and mouth with the strip of skirt and tied it around his head. He got to his feet in a low crouch so the mask wouldn't pull away from her. With his eyes shut tightly against the smoke, he began to drag her back toward the rear of the building where the heat would be less intense for a few moments.

Seconds later, firefighters on the roof broke through and the ceiling came crashing down near the spot they'd just left. Smoke and flame surged toward the opening.

The air that he sucked in through the skirt was hot. It was mostly smoke. He choked and gagged. His head was spinning. He staggered another few steps, then fell heavily to the floor, rolling on top of her.

There was a crash nearby as a second hole was cut through the ceiling. For a fleeting moment, the smoke around them lifted and surged upwards, but the flames also followed and Hyde felt them licking just feet above their heads. Blisters raised on his neck and cheeks. His hair crackled.

"Air," he gasped into Nomi's ear. Then he took the mask and pulled deeply on the precious air, held his breath, then covered her face with the mask. "Hold on tight!"

Time...

From somewhere deep within, Hyde drew upon a final source of strength and got them to the rear of the building. When his rump hit the rear wall, he lay Nomi on the floor. He shrugged out of the harness that held the air tank and dropped it beside her.

He felt his way along the flat surface until he came to a window. He fumbled with his hands, but there wasn't enough sensation to feel the frame. His head spun. Smoke blinded him. His knees were turning to rubber.

There was only one chance left.

Hyde hurled his entire weight against the window. The glass shattered. The frame splintered. And he felt himself falling forward. Jagged shards of glass in the bottom of the frame dug into his bunker coat and kept him from plunging three stories.

He fell back into the room across Nomi's still form.

When Lt. O'Brien from Ladder 4 came through the window, Nomi Cram was pressing the mask to Hyde's face and screaming for him to take a breath.

•

Nomi was on a stretcher and two men were working Hyde down the ladder when the roof collapsed in a thunderous roar that sent sparks into the dark Boston sky.

When they laid Hyde down on the hard surface of Broadway, it was Frank Duggan who lifted Henry's head and pressed an oxygen mask to his face.

Time, Henry...time...

"Goddammit, suck it in, you son of a bitch," Duggan bellowed, his eyes staring up at a smoke-filled Boston sky.

Hyde's chest rose as he took a deep breath.

Epilogue

Three days after the fire in South Boston, Channel 7 telecast a special program in place of its six o'clock news. Boston newspapers carried announcements for the event that day and radio stations noted the unusual programming during their newscasts. Local Channels 2, 4, and 5 offered to purchase and carry the special half hour segment. Seven provided the program gratis. There were no commercial breaks.

At exactly six o'clock that evening, Boston's television screens were darkened as the eerie wail of bagpipes echoed across the city. Screens slowly brightened. Viewers were brought into a large empty room to the strains of "Amazing Grace". There was a small podium in front of faded red curtains that shaded the windows behind. Three flags – American, City of Boston, Boston Fire Department – were gracefully displayed to one side of the podium. "MEMORIAL HALL, BOSTON FIRE HEADQUARTERS" scrolled across the screen. The camera rose to the upper border of the hall and settled briefly on an ancient photograph of a mustached firefighter in uniform. Then it slowly swept down a long row of photographs that covered three walls, while the words "155 Boston firefighters who have answered the last alarm" appeared at the bottom of the screen. The camera drew back and settled on the most recent photos – eight men in their Boston Fire Department dress uniforms.

Bagpipe music softened as a background voice spoke. "This is Herman Neubauer, Channel Seven News Director. The music you are hearing was provided today by the Boston Gaelic Fire Brigade's Bagpipe Band at the funerals for the two Boston firefighters who died in the line of duty three days ago in South Boston." The picture faded to a procession of firefighters, more than two thousand of them in dress uniform, marching behind two shining fire trucks – the ladder truck from the company of one of the fallen men, the pumper from the engine company of the other. The trucks bore the flag-draped caskets of their comrades. Each dead firefighter's wife and children followed directly behind his company truck.

Then Herman Neubauer appeared behind a simple desk with no station markings. "There have been too many fire department funerals in our city over the past few weeks. Eight firefighters have died in the line of duty. We are assured these sad events have reached an end. There is closure for the City of Boston, for the Boston Fire Department, and for the families who suffered these losses. These firefighters died fighting blazes that were deliberately set. It appears that this wave of arson has come to an end, the perpetrators neutralized through the efforts of the Boston Fire Department's little-known Arson Squad. The facts behind this crime wave are not fully available and sources indicate there are months of investigation before the details will be released.

"The purpose of this broadcast is not to expose crime, but to honor the public service of an institution and the individuals who are part of that service. No single media organization need take credit for this presentation; all sources have contributed. This television station coordinated the report because one of our own was directly involved in the investigation and came close to losing her life as a result."

Herman Neubauer's voice analyzed the assault on Boston as a series of dramatic film clips beginning with the Boston Harbor Hotel and ending with the South

Boston conflagration filled the screen. The tremendous cost in life and dollars was detailed following each event. Interviews with Commissioner Duggan were interspersed with those of division and district chiefs, captains and lieutenants, and firefighters as each blaze was covered.

Nomi Cram appeared at the desk beside Neubauer. What remained of her hair was covered by a bright scarf. Her missing eyebrows were emphasized by dark pencilled lines that stood out against the medicated salve on her shiny, red face. The bandage on her left ear appeared below the scarf.

"Boston's reign of terror is over," she said with a sad smile. "Our city has experienced tremendous loss but in the end Boston won. The bad guys lost. As Herman Neubauer has explained, it has not been without sacrifice and sadness. While Mayor Jordan has explained that the investigative process precludes any detailed explanation of the reasons behind the fires, we can honor those who brought the crime wave to a halt."

Nomi outlined the makeup and history of the Arson Squad, the special training of each individual, and their law enforcement authority. She explained the processes employed to investigate the early fires and how they had concluded that the same individuals were involved in each incident. Nothing was said about extortion, nor was Raymond Fairchild's name ever mentioned.

The next picture showed official vehicles arriving outside Boston Medical Center, and focused on Mayor Jordan waving to the prepared entourage who greeted him outside. Commissioner Duggan, in dress uniform, remained back in the crowd.

"Two members of the Arson Squad were honored today by Mayor Charles Jordan and Fire Commissioner Frank Duggan during bedside ceremonies at Boston Medical Center. Fire Investigators Leo Carmichael and Robert Scott were awarded the city's highest honors. Both men were injured near the scene of the South Boston fire during a confrontation that ended the arson wave.

"As they approached the arson suspects at the height of the blaze for questioning, the suspects opened fire on them at close range. Although both Carmichael and Scott were wounded, they were able to return fire. Their attackers were mortally wounded before they could escape.

"At a separate ceremony in the Boston Fire Department's Memorial Hall, Commissioner Duggan presented Lieutenant Henry Hyde with the department's highest award for his part in the investigation, and for his rescue of a civilian at the height of the fire."

Nomi reappeared on television screens in a close-up shot. Her smile was broad as she said, "I was that civilian and I'm alive today because of the efforts of a firefighter. But we are not asking for your attention now for those of us who are living. Instead we close with this segment honoring all of those who answered their last alarm."

The final scene was the same one that opened the half-hour segment – the photos surrounding Memorial Hall at Fire Headquarters.

There was the haunting echo of bagpipes in the background.

Henry Hyde reached for the remote and turned off the television. But the sound of the bagpipes remained. He closed his eyes. But he saw the polished fire engines – a flag-draped ladder truck and a flag-draped pumper – followed by firefighters...hundreds of them...thousands of them...tens of thosands of them. They were marching, their heads held high, their eyes shiny, and he could hear their hearts beating proudly over the wail of the pipes.

Henry went into the bedroom and turned down the sheets. Nomi would be coming up the stairs soon and maybe he could grab a nap before she wore out an old guy. Then he smiled. Nomi was going to make a great firefighter's wife. And she understood why he'd be up early the next morning to report for his regular shift.